ACCLAIM FOR ASKOLD MELNYCZUK

For *Ambassador of the Dead*

A *Los Angeles Times* Book of the Year

"Melnyczuk's writing aches with realism, but is also imbued with a hazy sense of wonder. The result: a novel so precise and understated, it's stunning."—*Esquire*

"A triumph of style and storytelling. . . . [Melnyczuk] has brought the great tradition of Russian literature to American soil in a transplant that is a work of art."—*The Los Angeles Times*

"Melnyczuk is an able analyst of character and a superb storyteller. That he is also a stylist who bids English speak with a bold new accent makes his readers all the more grateful."—*Newsday*

"[Melnyczuk] skillfully demonstrates how the violence and mysticism of the Old World re-enact themselves as psychological disease and self-destruction."—Jeffrey Eugenides, *The New York Times Book Review*

"Melnyczuk . . . explores profound questions related to violence, the weight of the past, and the kind of pain from which it is impossible to recover. A very powerful and disturbing novel."—*Library Journal*

"One of the rare qualities of the Askold Melnyczuk's intelligent, beauti- fully written second novel is his ability to naturally and fluidly combine thematic seriousness with narrative immediacy."—Tova Reich, *The New Leader*

"*Ambassador of the Dead* is an extraordinary novel, passionately and intelli- gently written . . . Askold Melnyczuk has brought to light the flip side of the American dream shaded by the dark loneliness of the human heart."—Ha Jin

For *What Is Told*

A *New York Times* Notable Book

"A great novel of unresentful sorrow and half-requited loss."—Seamus Heaney

"*What Is Told* is Myth and History and Lust. . . . Melnyczuk's writing sings pictures. They are extraordinary adventures in themselves."—Leonard Michaels

"To fall in love with [Melnyczuk's] voice is no trouble at all. . . . Clearly, he was carefully listening to his own ghosts when he concocted this inventive, enormously assured novel."—*The New York Times Book Review*

"This novel, brimming with ideas so lucidly writ, is simultaneously witty, serious, fantastic, accurate, unsparing, and moving. How he achieves all this is, fortunately, not the reader's job to figure out."—Yuri Andrukhovych, *Süddeutsche Zeitung* (Munich)

"Magnificent in scope . . . Brilliantly Melnyczuk skips across decades and continents, from lyric passage to coarse account, from domestic scene to philosophical musing. His blend of myth and realism—punctuated with violence and comedy—recalls García Márquez."—*The Boston Globe*

THE HOUSE OF WIDOWS

OTHER BOOKS BY ASKOLD MELNYCZUK

Blind Angel

Ambassador of the Dead

What Is Told

The House of Widows

AN ORAL HISTORY

Askold Melnyczuk

Graywolf Press

SAINT PAUL, MINNESOTA

Publication of this volume is made possible in part by a grant provided by the Minnesota State Arts Board, through an appropriation by the Minnesota State Legislature; a grant from the Wells Fargo Foundation Minnesota; and a grant from the National Endowment for the Arts, which believes that a great nation deserves great art. Significant support has also been provided by the Bush Foundation; Target; the McKnight Foundation; and other generous contributions from foundations, corporations, and individuals. To these organizations and individuals we offer our heartfelt thanks.

Several chapters have appeared in different form in the *Harvard Review, Ploughshares,* and the *Southwest Review.*

Published by Graywolf Press
2402 University Avenue, Suite 203
Saint Paul, Minnesota 55114
All rights reserved.

www.graywolfpress.org

Published in the United States of America

ISBN 978-1-55597-491-6

2 4 6 8 9 7 5 3 1
First Graywolf Printing, 2008

Library of Congress Control Number: 2007925193

Cover design: Kyle G. Hunter
Cover photos: (c) Getty Images / (c) Veer

More from than to Alex

Contents

History is the lies we agree upon.
VOLTAIRE

Does the imagination dwell the most
Upon a woman or woman lost?
If on the lost, admit you turned aside
From a great labyrinth out of pride . . .
W. B. YEATS

We must not be sentimental.
SIR ANTHONY EDEN

ONE

A Theory of the Turn

Vienna, 1 May 2006: Morning

The most common grammatical error is the lie.

This came to me as I hurried down the stairs of my apartment building near the opera house and stepped, slightly winded, into the bristling air of the year's first brilliant day. We live and breathe it, I thought, squinting. The lie. At the edge of the curb, I bent to tie a lace. I was late. I imagined Silvia's brow arching as she glanced to the clock over the door behind which the ambassador sat in her meeting. I glared at the light—trapped, like so many, in the weather of the past—when a dark-haired girl in a yellow scarf across the street caused a catch in the breath. A prick at the heart. Unlikely as it seemed, I was sure it was Selena. She'd been on my mind. I raised my hand and was about to shout her name—on the off chance, since life is full of implausible turns—when a flatbed truck heaped with skinned hares heading for the Naschmarkt roared by, splashing my shoes with yesterday's rain.

A second truck, glistening with imported tomatoes, obstructed my view. I stared at the season's unnatural fruits, then back at my shoes.

Yes, all around us the syntax of deceit rises up as the public realm of newspapers, television, the Web. Don't expect it to change, either. If it did, so would we.

Unfortunately, the private sphere is no haven.

My father taught me this. Not in so many words. He preferred to lead by example.

Before killing himself—sixteen years ago this very week—he gave me a letter in a language he knew I couldn't read. I was his only son. His patrimony consisted of the contents of a dusty studio apartment he'd rented after abandoning Sheila Donovan, his wife of thirty years. My mother's bitterness was compounded by her self-imposed isolation. She was a proud woman. Her cardamom-colored hair and high cheeks deserved better. The hopes her own widowed mother planted were worth more than this. After he left, she refused to ask her family for help. Every one of them (except Uncle Bill) had warned her against the lanky Slav with the cold lapis eyes of a Husky who one night lingered late at the bar where she worked. Had I been around, I'd have warned her too.

By the time the trucks passed, the girl was history.

Walking across from the park, I felt the pulse of the new Vienna. Trees itching to blossom. The sweet ache of spring. No longer the city of pensioners, it's now a cultural mecca. UNESCO sites everywhere. Blond whippets from Prague giggle by, followed by tarts from Japan. Sushi in skirts. Bursts of tulips circle the chestnuts. The breast of earth's going green again. The young from Central and Eastern Europe flock to it. The art market's booming.

That's not why I feel at home here. Until a decade ago, I had family living in the city: my grandmother Vera, and my uncle Kij. Both dead. Not gone are the scabs of war, for which I'm grateful. Only among the guilty do I ever breathe free.

At the Frauenhuber, I downed an espresso and gorged on a Dobos torte. Too rich for the hour, but weight's the least of my worries.

"Zahlen, bitte," I signaled to Franz, who smiled and hustled over for this latest installment of his son's college fees. Higher education cost almost nothing until Socialist Europe bought the American plan: each tub on Dad's bottom. Tips must adjust for inflation if I'm to stay on terms with the natives.

———•◦•———

Who knows why some lies surface while others sink down the black hole of an administrator's file cabinet or get crunched in the trash of a battered laptop with a missing "n"? Who ever told the truth about Braunschweig, that human cattle-yard where daylight itself turned sentence? Among my Viennese friends, could any imagine the story of Selena, Vera, or Father?

On my way in I passed Freud's house again. 19 Berggasse. The sun winked off a window. For years I've felt the pull, but resisted—yet every few weeks I detour. Why not enter? Afraid of being disappointed? Maybe. The shrink's couch is in London. I've heard they play loops of Freud's home movies, but at forty I need the aura of lacquered cabinets, onyx gods, African masks. Cigar smoke. Hacking coughs. People. No doubt my reasons lie deeper. It's myself I'm disappointed by. The conjugations of betrayal always begin with the first person, present tense.

Perhaps that can change.

Silvia, tall, dark skinned, and crescent eyed, swoops into my office and drops files on my desk without looking my way. They fall like a slap. I stare. Today she's wearing black pin-striped pants over boots, but I recall the curve of her calves by heart. Such discoveries aren't soon forgotten, or forgiven—something I learned at considerable cost years ago with Selena. My first S.

"Hawelka at noon," she murmurs.

I nod in silence, forcing her to look over.

The ambassador knows how to pick them.

Beyond the door I hear the click of computer keys under voices weaving German and English into a web of nervous patter. I already know the drift of this day's whispers: the British report on climate change, a cry of fire in a crowded theater with no exits. Suddenly they're worried: we're killing the planet. Surprise.

The bulky manila mailer under Silvia's files is stamped *Do Not Circulate*. The fact that it's addressed to me is troubling. *James Pak* is scrawled on the TO: line—it's one of those reusable, interoffice envelopes—but the FROM: remains blank. Whoever sent this is either looking for help or trying to trap me. By the time any word reaches here it's usually cold news. This is different: there's no expiration date.

Below it lie pages from a manuscript in your narrator's scrawl. His *Oral History*. Every day he promises himself tomorrow, for sure, he'll return to it. Feckless flirt. Then Silvia reappears with a fresh stack of folders.

She doesn't need to. She knows I'd get them myself. Or she could e-mail. We both like to taunt me.

"Einen Kaffee? Schwartz?" she asks, with a wave of her dark, long-fingered hand. A theater minor at the university, she likes to steal every scene. She's impatient, can't wait, first he's late, now what's up? Her eyes avoid mine. It's because of last night. She pretends to count the tassels on the oriental rug.

I play my game. When Silvia finally raises her head, she thrusts forward her chin and pulls back her shoulders like a cat. You can't tell if she's set to flee or to pounce—the same uncertainty I felt near Selena, who sometimes stared just like Silvia before expelling a storm cloud of smoke. Afterward, she'd smile, a simulacrum of desire.

Silvia doesn't smoke; Selena never stopped.

All is layers: stacks on stacks, facts covering fictions resting on facts, sediments of a century hardly begun yet already sagging, waiting for the inevitable tectonic shifts to shake things up.

"*Bitte,*" I say.

She turns away. Maybe she's admiring my computer-enhanced portrait of Sir Anthony Eden with Cuttlefish, spawned by my new hobby: Photoshop.

The door shuts. Silvia leaves in her wake a trace of scorn I find bracing and just. But, as the silence crowds in, I unfold yesterday's *Trib*. Unlike my colleagues, whose thirst for the daily lie knows no bounds, I prefer to let my news steep for a day.

Starting from the back, I fact-check the weather. It's the best way to gauge their forecasting skills. So often wrong when the odds are even, how right can they be with affairs far more complex?

Exile is bitter even when self-imposed. I chose Vienna. A decade had elapsed since my earlier visit. With my father's family gone, I thought the city might inspire me to finish my "oral history" of that time. The stories and people from then stumble through my dreams like refugees denied at the border. But, since the divorce, things haven't gone my way. When the new administration bought Pennsylvania Avenue, I was sure I was out. They already owned the Utilities, Boardwalk, and Jail. Anxious years. My title, Assistant to the U.S. Counsel of Public Affairs, commands a certain prestige on paper. In practice, I suspect they see me as a fugitive from another era who slipped through the cracks so long ago it would be embarrassing now to axe him. Nobody asked how I got here, and I walked fast to keep it that way. I was, after all, merely an ashtray, a vase crying out for a new end table, or worst case, a quiet burial in the basement. Yet I'm not without value. I've published, not perished: two highly unpopular books of popular history. One on Byron, Blunt, and the British Imperial Dream. Another about *das Wiener Schnitzel,* as my ex liked to joke: Arthur Schnitzler's Vienna. Worse, I speak multiple tongues, including German, which I didn't have when I visited earlier. Trading the security of academic life (Georgetown, tenure track) for the drama of public service, I was sure my path aimed straight for the Olympus of Cultural Attaché. Naïve little prof. The party saves that post for prettier people with fund-raising skills.

Still, at forty I'm not exactly ready to bag it—it's only the pace that's picked up.

These days I feel the need to remind my colleagues of the birthplace listed on my passport: Boston. As in Samuel Adams, the Tea Party, Harvard, the Red Sox, Thoreau. I'm one of you. Really.

No condolences, thanks.

I have a choice to make, maybe my last, is all.

Sorry, that's cheap.

In yesterday's newspaper, I spot a story about an explosion in Hanover, Germany. A bomb we left there in 1945 waited sixty years for two children, a boy and a girl, to find it. (At once I think of little Mustafa the Bean curled in his crib at the Children's Hospital and make a mental note to remember to bring him a gift.) I imagine my counterpart from the American Embassy in Berlin calling the parents to mumble regrets. No apologies, ever. Not even flowers. In Europe, six decades out, hundreds of bombs still await triggers—amateurs, mostly; often kids.

That's why I love it here. This is the city at the heart of all betrayals.

The resealed envelope waits between Silvia's folders and my manuscript. Transcripts; depositions; declarations of intent to desert. The documentary evidence of unspeakable crimes. Torture, beheadings, rape—the catalogue raisonné of all wars. What kind of noise would this make were the wrong person to stumble on *it*? Who might that be?

I just may know him.

Finally I switch on my computer. When my home page opens, it's like a mirror in reverse: I become what I behold.

Al Jazeera. As always, there's news.

In a minute I'll check e-mail for messages from my anonymous informant. The last was eloquent: *The whole world is watching*.

No pressure. Thanks.

From the drawer I pluck my first cigarette of the day. I'm trying to quit by smoking only at work, where it's not legal anyway.

Silvia forgot my *Kaffee*. I rise with a sigh.

~ 2 ~

Late one night, a week after Father's death, I finished sweeping the bulk of my inheritance into four giant trash bags and heaved them into the Dumpster at the construction site around the corner from his apartment. Then I sat down at the two-person coffee table in the middle of his kitchen, the fluorescent light loud as cicadas, and examined the three things I'd kept. My trove consisted of his British military ID from the forties—a ragged card of stiff, creased paper stained with what looked like blood but was probably mud—and a heavy, cracked glass jar I'd found wrapped in blankets under some old clothes in his closet. The ID I understood. But why keep a jar?

The third item was the letter.

I remember the afternoon he gave it to me: spring on the Atlantic, waves of warmth lapping the bolts of forsythia. A day not unlike this.

I was twenty-five.

His studio, above the used furniture store in downtown Devon on the Massachusetts North Shore, felt crowded by the two wooden chairs, the table, the cot. On the slope-shouldered refrigerator, branded with yellowed pieces of tape, was a photograph of the three of us at the Topsfield County Fair twenty years back, grouped around giant pumpkins, smiling.

I'd arrived to find him cleaning his rifle. He'd broken it down. Stock and barrel lay side by side. The long opal stem of the Remington gleamed like a gemstone. A spray bottle of Hoppe's Elite Gun Cleaner stood alongside a jar of Choke Shine Elixir.

"This is news," he said when I told him I'd received the traveling scholarship I'd been nominated for and would be leaving for England soon.

Dressed neatly in a T-shirt and khakis, he looked handsomer than ever, as though burnished by his inexplicable and solitary grief. Like many ex-military types, he had a love-hate affair with order. The dishes piled in the sink and along the counter suggested a flagging of ardor.

He put down the cleaning fluid he'd been shaking like a martini.

"Is this why she left you?" he asked, harpooning me with his gaze.

We'd never spoken about my ex-girlfriend, Charlotte, before.

You're why she left me, I thought to myself—which was true only in part.

Who knew she would one day make a brief but consequential return in the role of First Wife?

"Anyway, your business is your business. Don't dwell on it. Congratulations," he extended his hand for a temperate squeeze.

Pressing this lifeless flesh of my flesh, I tried imagining the wildness that once electrified Mother.

My mother's older brother hadn't held their separation against him—maybe because Uncle Bill's own marital scorecard was marred by more than one mark—and that weekend Father was heading to Uncle Bill's cabin in New Hampshire.

"How's your mother?"

"She's fine," I answered, just as I'd promised her I would. Don't you ever talk about me to him, she'd insisted. Never. Don't you dare say even my name. I'm dead to him. You understand?

"That's good," he nodded, eyes on his rifle. "That's good."

He didn't care, really. In his heart, we were history.

On the other hand, I kept reminding myself, I was the one who had driven him to this dead end—or so I feared. If not for me, he might still be living at home.

We let the silence soak up the rest of the questions.

Smells of the beach at low tide drifted in and the air fogged, as though from a storm of fine dust.

"What will you do on this trip?" he asked.

I told him I planned to study British involvement in various liberation movements sweeping Europe and the Middle East in the nineteenth century. I would focus on men like Byron, who died—by a misapplication of leeches—fighting for Greek independence from the Ottomans, and Wilfred Scawen Blunt, who backed both the Irish and the Egyptians in their bids for freedom and who also imported the first Arabian stallions to England. He was married to Byron's granddaughter. The idealism of individuals confident they knew what was right for others intrigued me: the noble impulse in the ignoble man. The project meant visiting Rome, Vienna, Moscow, Istanbul, and of course England. Imperial command centers all.

He gazed out the window, beyond the waters we'd once walked on together.

"So you'll be in Europe before classes begin?"

I nodded.

Then he asked if I'd visit Vera. His request forced a wince. It had been our fights over Vera that led to his leaving.

Vera was his mother, who for decades he claimed was dead. The line worked when I was younger; but as I began taking my interest in history more seriously, I made the mistake of bringing my questions home. A box of letters from Vienna gathering years in a closet started me down this road I'm still on.

"Of course I'll see her."

"That's good." His voice was soft as the pelt of the seal he'd once carried into the house. "There's something I'd like you to give her."

He rose and marched to the cot in the corner, below the plain wooden cross, returning with a large envelope.

Either he'd been expecting me or he'd planned to visit Mother.

"What is it?"

"She's poor," he said. "They're poor as worms."

"Anything more you want to tell me?"

"Money, and a letter." He nodded. "Before you go, call this lady."

He handed me a slip of paper with a name and a number.

"Marian Gordon? Who's she?"

"You're the historian. Find out yourself. See the good job you've done already? She lives in Oxford."

Even now he wasn't giving anything away.

I asked if he planned on returning to the fish-packing plant where he sometimes worked. He assured me he would. In the meantime, did I want to join him at Uncle Bill's?

"You go ahead," I said. Suddenly I was flooded with contempt—for his weakness, his fumbling silence, for the failure hunching before me. I'd just won a traveling scholarship to Oxford. What had he ever done but make a mess of our lives?

Ever since that Thursday I've wondered what might have happened had I said yes, turned away from my own plans, and gone with him. I had a theory about it then: my theory of the turn. It was nothing very profound, this idea that amid the world's variety you could find anything you imagined—indeed, your imagining brought the thing, life itself, into being: at any given moment the world contained all you'd ever dreamed of—you only had to turn to it and it would come alive, as if it had been waiting for you. Turning to one thing, though, you had of course to turn away from another. Everything gripped you because its very life depended on you. Without you, it would disappear into some other dimension.

I turned from Father and look what happened to him.

What if is every historian's favorite game.

———·•·———

What if I send these files out right now? Either way, someone took a risk getting them to me. They're the open secret no one talks about—which, I suppose, makes them neither open, nor secret. What if I call my friend at *Der Standard?* What if I don't? What if I bury them in a drawer, or shred them, or make paper boats to float down the sluggish green Danube dividing old Vienna from new? I guessed their contents even before untying the flap: testimonials; letters; pages from diaries; unofficial depositions. All from my countrymen, who chose to serve a nation at war and have seen things no humans should. Done them, too. On orders, or alone. And now they're deserting—or trying to—by the thousands. Eight hundred in Stuttgart alone. Nearly six hundred more outside Hamburg.

The question is: Why pass such ugly truths on to the public, whose delicate sensibilities might short-circuit? Why spread the poison? Still, we might have warned the kids before they signed. Every generation is born ignorant as the first—yet no school dare teach what people really should know.

———·•·———

Silvia pops in to remind me about the Hawelka—as though I had so much on my mind I'd forget. She doesn't wait for my thanks. She knows how expansive I grow after lunch, and cognac.

It's what I live for, to dock in the harbor of long afternoons inside the walnut and smoke-stained café with friends: Italians, Israelis, Norwegians, and Turks. Of course Austrians; some Americans, too. Unlikely bedfellows anywhere else but Vienna. They're minor diplomats, UN employees, foreign doctors, journalists. We began gathering in the wake of September 11th, when part of my job was delivering information—or, more accurately, party lines. In those days there was plenty of work even for the Assistant Counsel because all our affairs seemed public. Without planning it, we gelled into a group I count on for venting and chat. The proprietor's wife, Frau Hawelka, recently died, and it's a sadder, lonelier Herr who still fusses amid the tightly packed tables, the sticky smell of espresso and Gauloises Lights. I thrive in such places just as I wither in the cozy slickness of Starbucks.

Since I've missed our informal talks these past several weeks, my friends will ask what I've been up to. What to show for my time?

A mouthful of air. Two fists of dust. Four trips to Stuttgart. A file of letters that may, or may not, self-destruct. A new DVD.

Let not false modesty bury completely my few achievements. My job at the embassy doesn't define me. I write stories—others call them history, but I know better: they're nothing more than tales peopled by characters with familiar names. None lived happily, that I promise.

I have cause to be skeptical of my avocation. The most cherished personal memories are dubious. Freud doubted we could even recall childhood. All we had, he proposed, were images relating to it. No surprise Herodotus was dubbed father of history, father of lies. I say this because I'm old enough to place my faith in uncertainty and my trust in the piety of the skeptic. And if what follows feels like a fever dream, believe me, it was. Less than two weeks after scattering his ashes into his beloved Atlantic, I found myself flying above it on my way to England to stay with a friend I never knew Father had until just before he died.

TWO

Among the Anglos

The tongueless man gets his land took.
TONY HARRISON

~ 1 ~

The day I arrived at my "digs" in the gray-stone Georgian townhouse, Oxford was wet. It was the last decade of the last century, definitely *fin de siècle.* I was twenty-five, on my first trip abroad. During the hour-long train ride from Heathrow I pressed my face to the window, my senses strained with excitement at seeing the place whose literature I'd steeped in so long, its damp countryside mossy and glistening. When the cityscape changed to hills the color of snow peas and church spires like chanterelles or wizard's hats poked through the web of wires, I felt myself falling into a book. What kind of book I wasn't sure. Rain strafed the glass, blurring the names of the towns—Reading, Abingdon—through which we rolled. Beyond Oxford lay Burnt Norton, Kenilworth, Stratford-upon-Avon, the Thames threading among them—maybe I'm confusing my geography, so many years gone, but at the time each echoed with the deep brass of legend.

My father had traveled around here, I thought. He may have taken this very train. At the ticket booth, I counted the change, fingering the strange currency, each coin a talisman.

Drops from my Tilley splattered my shoes as I stood on the stoop, imagining what my landlady, Marian Gordon, would be like. I rubbed my right temple—a headache set a vein pulsing. A wave of nausea shivered through me. I tried shrugging it off and wiped my nose with the back of my hand.

How much did she already know about Father or Vera? Be cautious. Say nothing.

She'd been his friend when he lived in England, long before he met

Mother. Although he was born in Ukraine, my father served in the British army. The demobilization uniform in his closet had been an object of fascination throughout my childhood. It hung there until the day before he died in it. Like a lot of veterans, he never talked about his old life. He'd turned his back on it completely. But what your father rejects becomes you. Eyes he hated you love. What he was not you must be. I know this now. Knew it then, instinctively. When my father walked away from his past, whole decades went missing; what could I do but try tracking them down?

The door was opened by a tall, thin man dressed in black, looking as if he'd pranced out of a Gorey cartoon. His long nose seemed to tug his head down, emphasizing his tonsure—a bald spot with patches of gray erupting from the sides like shrubs on a ledge. His wet blue eyes stared at me for a minute before he cried out in a high voice:

"Christianity is a terrible thing. Terrible for unbelievers since they're forced to endure the scorn or the mercy of believers. Still worse for believers struggling to make sense of a pack of lies, nonsense, and half-truths and a bloody history that God on Judgment Day will not forgive. He will not."

My mouth must have dropped because Bulwer chuckled to himself. His feet pumped the air a few times as though he were rehearsing a march. It was something he did when especially amused.

Then he looked up at me and said:

"So sorry. Good morning. You're the American." He thrust his neck forward to study: "Don't look a thing like your father."

He held out his hand, clucking. His fingers were chicken bones sheathed in slub silk.

"Your arrival has been much anticipated, but we kept forgetting your name. My sister has an excellent memory for everything except names. Ever since her husband passed, it's gotten much worse."

He chuckled again.

This is nuts, I thought: What's so tough about James?

When I coughed, he said:

"You have a cold? Don't look well."

He leaned forward on his toes and pressed his hand to my forehead.

"Sizzling like a rasher."

A claw seized my shoulder, dragging me over the threshold. I barely kept a grip on my pack.

"Marian! Marian!" he cried. "Your American is ill. Hope he's not dying! Come quickly. Bring the gin!"

He winked. "The gin is for me."

It was probably the fever, but crossing the threshold, I felt my foot had roiled muddy waters. All kinds of creatures came sniffing. Locks turned, doors slammed up and down halls, followed by the slap of countless feet. Before I could refocus, my landlady's brother had disappeared and in his place rose a figure equally tall, also in black, though with a less angular jaw and a softer, more measured voice. I'd have put her in her late forties, but I knew she was at least twenty years older.

"He's right," she said, "you don't look at all well. Normally I discount Bulwer's reads. Hysteric. Years of missionary work in the tropics. Let's get you to your room. Look at that blister."

"Missionary work?"

"I'm teasing. We tease a lot around here. Only way to survive this nasty world." Her thin lips pulled back in a smile. "Bully," she shouted up the stairwell, "Ring Dr. Sheridan, would you?"

"Thanks," I said, "I'll be fine."

She was abrasively thin, with the exaggerated posture of a military man's daughter. Her brows, nose, and lips were as pressed and straight as the rest of her. She wore no makeup and needed none. Her face had that wholesome, slightly formidable look of a Victorian daguerreotype.

We walked up the stairs and along a hallway papered in reddish trompe l'oeil showing baskets of roses that might have come from William Morris's workshop. The sconces on the wall shed a bright light on the long Turkish runners. I'd never seen such high ceilings.

I put my hand to my lips. I had not until then paid much attention to how I was feeling. The weeks after Father's death, stressful on all fronts, finally caught up with me. On the plane I hardly closed my eyes—it was my first flight, and I'd been too excited to eat or sleep, pitying those bored by the majesty of our passage through grandstanding clouds. I was young—and I was anxious over my mission.

When I confronted him about Vera, Father broke down. Yes, she was his mother. No, she was not dead. She lived in poverty in Vienna with her two bachelor sons. His brothers.

Unfortunately, we were in no position to bring anyone over from the old country. While I was born and grew up on the coast north of Boston, we might as well have been living in the third world ourselves. Both my parents were what I call "job-disabled." This had nothing to do with their physical health. No, it was the rudeness, the vulgarity, the sheer violation of working they couldn't fathom and wouldn't submit to. Their attitude had something to do with the fact that they were both exceptionally good-looking people, maybe the handsomest couple I've ever seen, and knew it, and took every advantage of it, as the beautiful so often do. The material demands of life were an insult. They had been born for better things. Along with their fellow citizens, they *aspired*—though it was never clear to what. I knew only that it was something rarer, grander, and brighter than to what we had or were. It glowed inside them, their aspiration. I could almost see it, the shimmering future, an embryo of hope that they nourished with beer, wine, or whiskey, depending on the occasion. Their pooled but intermittent salaries barely kept us afloat. Besides, there was Mother's mother to tend to, addled cousin Moira down the street, and then the liquor store on the corner stopped offering credit. The only disposable assets they stockpiled were charm, humor, and warmth. By the time I turned ten, they'd squandered even these.

Still, we weren't poor as worms, and that was the difference.

Now I was dizzy, and the urgency of my hosts unnerved me. I staggered to my room and sank onto the bed while Marian urged me to take advantage of the University Health Services—or at least allow her to summon her doctor friend. But the prospect of more strange faces, medical offices, fluorescent lights, probing hands, and insurance forms in a foreign land put me off the idea. "No, thank you very much," I said.

I preferred to sweat and shiver in silence. The body, I believed then and still do, follows its own logic and knows what it needs. Best simply to listen and attend. Gen-X science, my ex-girlfriend Charlotte dubbed it—no doubt she joked about it with her new boyfriend.

The image of the two of them huddling on a bus, laughing and pawing each other—which was how I first saw them together—was a scab I didn't care to reopen.

And so my landlady drew the curtains against the gray ruling that summer and left me lying there in a perpetual twilight while faces peered over me like the rotating zodiac: Marian and Bulwer and another, both brighter and darker than the rest.

My second day, staggering to the WC, I saw a young woman racing down the hall, pink-streaked hair in a tumult, as though she were wearing a breeze.

Seeing me, she froze for a second, dropped both arms, and cocked her head at an angle. Then, hinging her right wrist, she gave an abrupt, alarmingly charming wave:

"Hullo."

I tried cracking a smile, but before my lips curled into place, she was gone. Pretty thing. I'd see a lot more of her over the next weeks. By the time I left England, she'd become the measure, the hourglass, of my days. I'd no idea yet how quickly sand ran.

Several days passed before I could take in my surroundings. My room was damp and cold, and I kept drawing up the blankets, then throwing them off.

My fever plagiarized images from headlines splashed across papers Marian fed me—of assassinations, explosions, weddings. I'd brought my turmoil with me. After Charlotte and I parted, and even before my father's suicide, I'd taken an oath to chart in silence the progress of my own death. At twenty-five I felt it near. What is history but an evolving topography of death and dying? On this battlefield, in that kingdom, on such a day. . . . Death, somebody wrote, was the dark backing a mirror needs if we're to see anything. The most natural thing in the world. The ink in history's pen. The implications of birth explode around us. Beyond that lies what we can't see, to which, in war, we dispatch old and young, stranger and kinsman, without waiting for a report from the front before throwing up another wave. Then we ourselves break on its shore. In death, maybe we'll think about life.

And how can I forget that the children of suicides often inherit the gift?

These thoughts tumbled over one another like laundry, while shadows stirred all around.

My life had been on the verge of falling apart when word of the fellowship I'd all but given up on arrived. Suddenly, Europe beckoned. Reprieved, I longed to rinse my face in the fjords of Norway, get smashed in Oslo, see a sex show in Amsterdam—somehow make up for a decade lost to books by sinking into the mess of the world. Hadn't the mess itself sought me out in the form of Father's death and Charlotte's departure? I'd take in as much as I could. Then I'd sit tight for a year or two and write the Continent back into its own right mind. My humble dream.

———•·•———

Eventually I sat up. A silver-plated spittoon stood by the pigeonholed mahogany desk under the mullioned window, next to the four-foot-high African mask of a long face with painted red lips and eyes and, mounted over my bed, the head of a gnu—apparently my landlady's father had been a hunter. I ran my hand down its fur. The stillness of places loved and abandoned rose up around me. Watched by these trophies of empire, I listened to my heart keeping time with the clock on the sideboard.

A sepia photograph in an ebony frame hanging over the fireplace showed a woman dressed as Cleopatra. Looking closer, I saw that the model was none other than my landlady.

Most unsettling of all were a series of small watercolors on one of the walls in my room. The scenes depicted life in a village somewhere in Central or Eastern Europe—or maybe the Middle East—where mosques rubbed cornices with onion-domed churches: there were people carrying stones to the foundation of a house and veiled women walking up high golden hills. One picture was ominous, showing soldiers aiming rifles at a circle of women and men by a river.

"Very theatrical," I said to Marian.

Those first days, she tended to me as though I were family, the last survivor of a splintered clan. Her fingers tested my pulse, and her eyes offered a warmth and concern far beyond what her obligations as a landlady demanded.

The girl in the hall also reappeared, showing up with Marian to change my compress and thrust a thermometer between my lips. Her brows almost met above her nose and her wide eyes welled with light—some of which was also reflected off the studs piercing her sensory organs like rivets on a flower. The bead in her lip was tipped with tiny silver crossbones; the one on her tongue, which she poked out a bit when she was lost in thought, was crowned with a skull.

"What's your name?" I asked.

She stepped back as though I'd taken a swipe at her. Her lip stud trembled. Deer in headlights, with teeth.

Then she turned and hurried out.

The next time Marian stopped by, I asked about the mystery girl.

"I'm starting to feel like I'm in a Wilkie Collins novel," I said. "This is still John Major's England? Have I gone through a wormhole?"

Marian put her hand on her hip.

"Selena is a *long* story. She'll be starting University in the fall along with you."

"What college is she in?"

"St. Antony's. Undergraduate, of course."

"Why won't she answer me?"

"More tea?"

"No, why?"

"She's very shy."

"Where's she from?"

"You're not at all like your father."

"Sorry," I said. "Tell me about him."

"You tell me. I haven't seen him in forty years. Until you called . . ."

"Where's she from?" I turned my neck toward the hall.

"What? Outside Jerusalem," Marian cut me short. "When you're well, I'll tell you stories."

"Did you really have trouble remembering my name?"

"Silly," she giggled. "That's Bulwer."

Selena walked in with a cold compress curled in a bowl.

"Please tell her I'm one of those nonbiting Americans," I said.

"That's quite rare, isn't it?" Marian said.

I smiled at Selena, who hovered over Marian's shoulder. Hers was the face of a Spanish grandee, with Moorish blood, posing for Goya while Napoleon's armies rumbled in the distance, knowing the days of the monarchy, and her way of life, were numbered. To which she responded by getting a tat.

After she left, I prompted Marian: "Jerusalem . . ."

"There will be time," she said, shaking her head.

And I believed her. In those days, time spread before me like the sky over the Atlantic above my native Cape Ann on a clear morning in June— enough for every purpose under heaven, for sure.

Over the next week, my hosts abetted my recovery a thousand ways. Without their teas, oranges, soups, and, toward the end, when I could keep solid foods down, raisin scones with lemon butter, I'm sure I would have withered away, leaving behind only Mother to mourn. This saddened me, so I called home daily to say all was well in England; I was determined not to worry her any more than I already had simply by going away.

But I had to go, for more reasons than one. She never said so, yet I knew Mother blamed me for Father's suicide. And, while her feelings about him were necessarily complicated, that wasn't a charge I wanted hanging over me the rest of my life. I'd set something in motion that I had to see through to its end.

———•—•———

A few days later, I was sitting up in bed when Bulwer walked in bearing the tea tray and announced in his high voice:

"Marian has gone to London for the day."

"It's Bulwer the Brit!" I cried. I was feeling better at the moment—but the nausea had a way of striking just when I thought it had passed.

He smiled, bowing in acknowledgment.

Then he sat down on the red-velvet chair and, peering at me through thick lozenges, as though assuring himself I wasn't contagious, asked:

"Is there anything I can tell you about our town?"

I shook my head. About Oxford I knew everything. To me this was no mere heap of leaping spires, tilting chimneys, and storied bricks; it went beyond mullioned windows and pitched slate roofs linked by glassy archways above cobbled streets and common rooms five stories high; it was more, even, than a landscape of boyhood fantasies. Reading its history, I'd felt elated, as though I'd solved a mystery: here was continuity, wisdom. It entered the record books in the days of Edward the Elder in 912—there were older universities, far more ancient cities in the world, yet had any rooted a civilization half as powerful, with their language and values proposed as everyone's norms? What was the secret of their not unbloody success? How had so few come to dominate so many? Why had they wanted to? Had it been worth it? At what cost to them?

The Protestant spit learned to turn on this ground.

I gestured at Cleopatra on the wall.

"Was she an actress?"

"In the sixties and seventies. Gave it up when she and Hugh moved to Oxford. Still knows a lot of those awful people, I'm afraid."

"What was she in?"

"Shakespeare, mostly. A few films. Suzie Wong. Before your time. Something with that boring Italian. Antonini?"

He kept his eyes on the ground. He was clearly impatient with this line of questioning and preferred discussing ideas.

"You are writing about Blunt and Byron?"

What game was this Englishman playing? I was suspicious, fearing a trap, being shown up a rube. Brits scared me—it was their literature, their history I was studying: they owned the language I spoke and dreamed in. Would I ever feel completely at home inside it? But such moments of panic only strengthened my determination to make it my own—which, of course, it already was.

"You're wondering what drove them mad." His fingers flew at me like arrows.

"Were they mad?"

"Mad as Hölderlin."

The German poet Hölderlin was a contemporary of Byron and Shelley's. As a young man he'd been a revolutionary, thrilled like many of his generation by the toppling of the monarchy in France. Democracy was the light of that particular dawn. Then he began losing his mind. The light must have been blinding. He spent his last years in religious fever-dreams, cared for by a crippled violinist.

When Bulwer leaned forward and whispered, I could smell the decay.

"As to Christians," he said, returning to the theme with which he'd greeted me, "I studied in that school many years, darling."

His pale blue eyes burned.

"I even found a few people of faith here and there, true cousins of Christ. But I had to go hunting. All led anonymous lives, helping others, in hospitals and community centers and places you could never imagine. Each had light, passion, gentleness, and humility."

To keep from dozing, I parried off-topic:

"Was she a good actress?"

Bulwer looked pained by the question.

"You really care? You aren't one of those pitiable celebrity hounds? God save us. And the Queen. Queen first, then us."

"So you knew my father?"

"He was a sweet child. The war changed many people."

I sat up.

"Anyway, that's poor Marian's story," he said.

Then he added: "Byron, Blunt, Hölderlin—all adulterers. This issue is generally glossed over by liberal intellectuals unwilling to face the evidence when the facts aren't to their liking. But this seems to me the problem of Hölderlin, Byron, and Europe in general."

"Adultery?"

Bulwer rubbed the tip of his long nose as though it were a magic lamp. His eyes blinked twice.

"Hiding from uncomfortable facts, ignoring the evidence," he said. "It's clear you've understood nothing."

With that, he rose angrily and stalked out.

I fretted. I'd insulted my landlady's brother. If she were to turn me out, where would I go?

I imagined myself homeless, nestled in an alley behind Blackwell's, or below a stairway in the Radcliffe Camera.

Then I got angry. Who did he think he was, acting the kid?

But when I asked Marian about him later, she sighed, placing two fingers to her temple, and said Bulwer was a family heirloom she'd inherited. I should pay no mind to his rants.

"Why is he so angry with Christians?"

Marian, who'd been warding a fly off with a magazine, dropped her arm.

"Well, for one thing, on my mother's side we're Jews."

~ 2 ~

The first time I took lunch with Marian was in her garden off the conservatory.

I was a little embarrassed. Two days earlier I'd rocked the house by vomiting in the bathroom at three in the morning. A fresh impression was called for—for my own sake—so I'd put on my best dress slacks, a white shirt, a blue blazer I'd bought just for Oxford.

She was prostrating before the roses trellised against the gray stone when I came out. I shielded my eyes against the sun.

Moss covered the flagstones; even the birdbath sported a five o'clock shadow of green.

"Oh good," she said, looking over her shoulder. "You've emerged."

My American chrysalis burned clear away.

She wore black pants, long yellow gloves, and a straw hat. The hat was an impressive affair, with a wide brim set for safari.

Pineapple finials crowned the stone posts in the patio's corners alongside huge ceramic tubs sprouting lemon trees I assumed wintered indoors.

Roused by the warmth, flies and beetles spilled through the air.

"You'd think by now I'd know something about gardens," she said. "They remain a mystery I hope to spend my golden years unraveling. I never remember when to prune, tie, or add nutrients."

She threw up her hands.

"A miracle they survive."

Tumbling off the copper piping, the roses were dark hued—reds, purples, blues.

I didn't really understand flowers. They wanted you to slow down too much. You had to run on their time to see them. I wasn't ready for that. I was too busy, too poor and ambitious, with too many places to go. It was like talking—Charlotte had wanted me to discuss my feelings. You never talk about things, she'd say to me. I never know what you're thinking. *If I had, would you have stayed?*

The clippers in Marian's hand were steel blue, surgical looking. I watched her wipe them down with a checked cloth.

Selena appeared, carrying a tea tray she set down on the table.

After a burst of birdsong, I asked Marian:

"Was that a nightingale?"

"Wish I knew," Marian shrugged. "Daddy must have told me a thousand times. Never took. Join us, Lena," Marian asked.

Pale-skinned, hair streaked, eyes dark as space always down, Selena seemed a somnambulist, someone unwittingly wooed back from the borderlands of the dead.

At the same time, she was just a teenager whose fingers on my face helped cool my fever.

She half smiled, clutching her hands before her as though to wring them. Then she spun on her heels, clicked them twice, and left.

"What's it going to take? I've known squirrels more relaxed."

Marian shrugged.

"You're looking much better? I assume the headache has abated?" she probed, baiting her sentences with question marks. I appreciated the delicacy, but felt underneath it the presence of a mind whose assessments contained no rosy hues.

I fished an egg and tomato sandwich from a spread that included a pile of toast and several veined cheeses. A wren landed on the flagstones under the table, and Marian tossed it a scrap of bread.

I suspected we'd fence awhile—her British reserve outmaneuvering my self-doubt. But she was not who I thought she was. She moved right into things with buoying candor.

The tea released a mist that sparkled in the light, and the glossy ivy snaking up her chimney shuddered, exposing the leaves' flat green undersides. Everything has two faces. I remembered my advisor saying: history is that dog you saved from the pound. You think you've befriended it, but watch out, that's when it bites.

"Americans always want to know what people did," I said.

"Very little, besides play and go to school."

"I mean the Cleopatra photo."

She looked at me, blushing.

"I must take that down. Hugh liked poking fun at me. He knew it embarrassed me. My pathetic attempts at Shakespeare. Met some nice people, though."

She'd no more intention of talking about this than Bulwer.

"Have you called Vera yet?"

"Soon," I said. "What about those other trophies?"

"My father's."

"A hunter."

"In a way. Foreign service. Began as an officer back in the first war. Just before Palestine."

"Palestine. Now there's history." Which was what I'd come to Oxford to study. "That was in the twenties?"

"Before I was born, but I certainly heard about it."

Her eyes narrowed as though she'd set her sights on a bee.

Before I was born—catnip to a historian. I should clarify that in Boston I'd specialized in oral history. My skill was getting people to tell me their stories, while allowing me to keep mine to myself: the historian as vessel, a barroom pal to whom you opened your heart, betraying friends, co-workers, family, never knowing you were being led, slyly, deliberately, on a narrative trek. It's easy getting a lush to gush or a stranger on a plane to spill; it's another matter entirely to tempt someone more modest to soul-bearing. A pro leaves his subjects euphoric, feeling they'd saved the world with their news. Success in the field takes genius.

One I didn't possess.

Moreover, I'd come to England wanting to improve my craft with written texts. But my confidence had been shaken. History was a game played in library stacks until Father showed just how rough a sport it could be.

Marian had my attention, and I took care to show facial expressions—calibrated smiles, nods, Magoo-like squints—to keep her talking.

"In Palestine, my father worked for Sir Charles Tegart, the High Commissioner's counter-terrorism expert," she explained. "That's one subject our people know well."

"Counter-terrorism. The hyphen is older than I realized. This is about Selena?" I asked.

"In a way, I suppose," she said.

She folded her hands in her lap and looked down. Some strong feeling had taken hold. A thought moved over her face like a boat rowing slowly across a lake.

"In those days the word terrorist usually meant Jews, not Arabs," she said. "Wasn't their country yet. They were fighting block by block, pushing people out of homes and neighborhoods. And we were half helping and half hindering them. We were afraid of the Jews, and we didn't trust the

Arabs. Both sides were picking off our officers, blowing up cars, and generally making it inconvenient for us to stay as brokers of the peace. The term
must be understood in quotations. More tea?"

"Please. I thought you said you're Jewish."

"We are—on my mother's side. But we're English first. We believed in
Israel then and still do. But in a rational way."

"Isn't that sacrilegious or something?"

She shook her head.

"Americans. Of course Jews need Israel. As much as we need Great
Britain or you the United States. But who was it that forced us—now you
see you've got me confused—that kept Jews searching for home? Now the
Palestinians must pay. Why hide from the truth?"

Why indeed?

She poured from a pot with a blue floral design.

"To Father, Herbert Samuel seemed radical."

I recognized the name.

"First High Commissioner to Palestine."

"I'm impressed. Didn't think the Middle East was your field." Marian
smiled.

"Only as it relates to England," I explained.

"I heard so much about Palestine from Mother," she went on. "Tegart
was born in Ireland and honed his craft in India. Mother said he imported
Dobermans able to sniff out an Arab from a Jew or an Englishman on
command. Bred in South Africa. For the hunting of people."

But how much more intense Marian's father's job must have been I was
about to find out.

"Daddy's work could be awful, too. He never spoke about it—you
know how men are—but years later Mother told me stories. He spent
mornings observing executions, then making sure the autopsies were done
right. Gives you quite a perspective on the day, to see a few men dangle by
the neck before lunch."

She had stepped outside herself. I watched her pushing open rusty
black gates, walking through them into a world that lived only in memory.
History is a long corridor in a house of infinite extension. The house, of
course, is time, a maze of stairways and horizonless halls lined with mir-
rored doors from behind which drift moans, laughter, and occasionally,
shots.

"Tegart believed in torture, too. We'd used it quite a bit in India and Kenya, where I hear our boys roasted babies alive. Sounds like a bad joke, I know. But it's true. A student here is writing a paper about it. We forget the present is fodder for scholars. People like you. Horrible world. Don't mean you, of course. More sugar? I want some. Excuse me a moment."

When she left, I let my eye follow the line of the wall. The neighboring houses were all handsome cut stone with high, mullioned windows and heavy curtains.

As my strength returned, I began feeling restless. A little confined. Things seemed too peaceful, too self-contained. You'd never know that beyond these walls, cars clogged Oxford's streets at rush hour, or that computers, spies from the twenty-first century, were quietly worming their way under the sidewalks, through walls and sockets into our lives. This was a few years before the Internet forever reshaped time and space. Transformation was in the air. Things were about to change—just as they did for Adam, who absolutely had to get himself banished. What spirited boy would keep pruning his father's garden when he could have one of his own for just the sweat of his brow?

Marian returned with more sugar and a plate of petits fours.

"And Selena?"

"Try one. From around the corner. We're not known for our sweets, but we should be."

She pushed the plate forward.

"Sorry. Went off a bit there. You'd think I had no one to talk to. My brother—my *other* brother—worked at the British consulate in Belgrade. Lena was one of hundreds of orphans we brought here for adoption."

My eyes narrowed, and I looked more closely at Marian. Her gaze remained locked on the roses.

"I thought you said she was born in Jerusalem."

"Did I? Oh? Don't know why I bother lying. Why does anyone? But we do, all the time. Fine. All right. You're a historian. You want to know history. I'll tell you."

I leaned back in the heavy iron chair. She seemed to be worrying the matter intensely. Her eyes moved from my face to her lap, and her teeth gnawed at her lower lip.

At that moment Bulwer came out:

"Aidan on the line."

Marian appeared startled.

"Excuse me," she said, getting up again.

Clouds had swept in like piles of dust. The air cooled rapidly.

A robin dropped from the pear, piercing a beetle. Insatiable world. The death of a mouse by cancer, an Englishman wrote, is after all nothing less than the sack of Rome—for the mouse.

Marian returned looking suddenly anxious.

"My younger brother Aidan. Little brother, big trouble. Must go to London again," she said. "Leaving immediately, I'm afraid. Watch out for Bulwer. Don't think you'll need much tending from here on anyway."

She studied her garden.

Aidan. The name tripped a wire.

"Unlike the roses. Back soon. We'll finish then."

I nodded, rising to carry the pot.

I still hadn't said anything to Marian about Father partly because I didn't want to influence whatever she might tell me. If she knew, she might tailor her memories. That wasn't what I needed. I needed to know I wasn't the one who'd driven him to his death.

Marian, for her part, didn't seem in a hurry to ask about him.

I stared at the flickering ivy and wondered why Father insisted I visit her in the first place.

Selena the Magnificent

My real education in England began long before the official start of the term, toward the end of my convalescence, with informal "classes" held two or three afternoons a week in Marian's parlor, where people of all ages—dons, students, bohemians, and the occasional former MP—stopped for tea. Bulwer claimed they'd heard she had an American staying with her and extended themselves out of sympathy.

I'd have felt lost in that world had it not been for the companionability of the room itself, with its high windows embracing the light, the many tasseled lamps for corners the sun couldn't reach, the choice carpets under our feet; for the buttery yellow walls offering, with no whiff of pretense, a landscape by Millais, as well as fine pieces by Vanessa Bell and Burne-Jones, all presided over by a softly ticking yet assertive clock Bulwer said once dominated the hall of the country home of Mr. Benjamin Disraeli. Here everyone became part of the furniture, a little less historically significant than the rest.

One of my favorite visitors was Rajini Roy, a lively Indian woman in her early thirties who claimed to know Salman Rushdie (*have you ever actually finished one of his books?* she asked). Her grandfather had been one of Gandhi's subministers. She was doing a comparative study of postcolonial abuses by the British military in India and Kenya. I remembered Marian mentioning her. Dressed in tight pin-striped skirts and soft, touch-me sweaters, she always wore heels, a sartorial stab I've never grasped. She was tall, dark skinned, with long black hair covering large ears whose pendulous lobes she once unveiled, saying: "One of the eighty-four signs of the Buddha, my dears."

"Can a woman be a Buddha?"

"Baby, come on," she blinked her long-lashed eyes in my direction.

"Are you a Buddhist?" I asked, watching the midsummer light inching up the blue Persian rug, the air sweet with the smell of lilies Marian carried in before leaving.

"Hindu, man. And you know what I like about it?"

"What?"

She stirred her tea in the cool of the parlor while Bulwer fidgeted on the sofa, "Its sanity about sex."

"What do you mean?"

"Well, pardon me, I'm sure I understand nothing about your Judeo-Christian traditions, but from what I've read, your people have a gruesome relationship to sex. You're so scared of it! You structure your marriages around an idea that's unrealistic. As a result, my young friend, the legislators of desire have you by the balls."

"My old friend," I flirted. "Do tell."

"Teach a man his urge opposes God's will, set up a class of professional middlemen to pardon you when you sin—and you will, because, I don't have to tell you why—and you'll rule the world. In no time. Try it."

"Which part?"

"Now Rajini," Bulwer chided. "You're making a fool of this young man. You mustn't speak to him as though he were simple just because he's an American. He's also a *historian*." He drew the word out so it seemed to have a dozen syllables. "Are you really saying Hinduism has a good record with women?"

I glanced at Selena, who followed the banter intently. She sat in a corner, alone but listening. Her hands, sheathed in kinky black fishnet, gripped the armrests, and her studs glistened in the light cascading through the washed glass.

While Marian was away, I finally got to spend time with her. Just that morning we'd walked down Banbury, along the Cherwell, toward the center of town. She had a very clean smell, like a tumbler of sand. I liked standing near her. In her presence I felt myself changed, the way we're made new by a landscape we've never seen before. But it was complicated. There was something both accommodating and grating about her, like sandpaper. She showed no inclination to please, or even to connect. Although I'd tried my best gambits, she was as stubborn as prisoners I'd once worked with in Walpole. What piece of evidence was she withholding? Unlike most beautiful women, she wasn't dying to be interviewed about herself. Near her, my senses sharpened, and I felt myself absorbing more than I could see.

"Beautiful city."

"If you take out the Brits."

"What are you reading?"

"Japanese history."

Yet her lips contained a smile.

"Nothing like this back home," I said, gesturing toward a medieval arch.

"Take it with you when you go."

She kept her gaze straight. The raccoon-band of her sunglasses gave her a gloss of glamour.

At that moment I sensed something else passing between us. I realized I didn't care what we were talking about, or whether we spoke at all. A force moved unseen through the air, quickening the energy field without and within like a vial of simmering magnesium shot into the blood, careening down veins, swelling the skin, cold and burning. Desire's too thin a word.

I was in those days still something of a student, a novice in banter, but I remembered how much Charlotte loved talking about the games she played as a child. It relaxed her, made her feel comfortable and secure.

"What kind of games did you play when you were a kid?"

The glasses swiveled my way in an exaggerated gesture. What do you care, she seemed to say. But then she answered me.

"Underwater tea."

"What?"

"Our neighbors across the street had a villa. In the middle was a huge courtyard, the size of an entire city—or it seemed that way to a little girl. And in the center of that courtyard rose a fountain. The spray of water rose high as the house itself, covering all around in a soft mist. Three sisters lived in that house. They were Palestinian, but their father was more British than any Englishman I've met. He and my father were friends. We'd often go there for tea. While the grown-ups riddled their world, the four of us—they were a few years older than me, and when we stood together people said: *Look, someone's unpacked the Russian dolls*—the four of us got our own tiny tea service and took it to the fountain. Then, not minding our dresses, we threw our feet over the low wall and waded into the water where we sat down. The water was just waist high. Then we'd pour the tea underwater. That way, our cups were never empty. We entertained countless guests and never ran dry. Eventually one of the grown-ups—Mother most likely—noticed and began to scream and shout how I'd spoiled my dress and we came out, dripping, yet pleased nonetheless.

"All that's gone of course."

And she fell silent again.

Finally, I tried another approach. After swearing her to secrecy, I told her about Father.

"Horrible."

Yet for a moment, in her company, a tiny bit less so.

Her fingers squeezed my wrist, then let go.

"You think it's your fault?"

"He was drinking a lot. He'd moved out of the house. But when I started asking about Vera, he freaked."

"How did you find out about her?"

"He had all these letters from Vienna. I couldn't read them, but they gave me an address. I tried drawing him out. Then I got frontal about it. Once I had the fellowship, he asked me to see her. He was the one who gave me Marian's name. At that point I decided he wanted me to know—though I'd have to find out the details on my own."

"But why did he top himself?"

My question exactly.

"No, really," she insisted. The matter interested her.

Changing the subject—something I'm likely to do even now—I asked Selena what she remembered about Jerusalem.

For a second time, she stopped dead on the street and cocked her head at me.

"You don't know the story, do you?" she finally said, her eyes and half-smile unreadable. "Thank God one person on the planet doesn't see me as a case."

"Everyone is."

She ran her scarlet-tipped nails through a streak of hair the color of cotton candy.

We walked in silence a couple of blocks. We finally stopped before the Sheldonian and pretended to study the concert schedule. She turned to me and said: "It's so fucking boring being Palestinian. You have no idea.

You have a part, a script they hand you the minute you're born. I fucking hate it."

To cover my surprise, I blurted;

"Is that why you never talk?"

"You fucking bet. Soon as I can I'm moving somewhere where people have never heard of Israel or Jerusalem or Arafat. Otherwise I'll go nuts. Fuck everyone."

"Well, that's a position. Perfectly respectable, I'd say."

Watching her roll a cigarette with one hand in a calculated parlor trick, I noticed the tiny red tic-tac-toe board of seams on her wrist. And I understood her interest in Father.

Up to this moment, her restraint—and all it implied—embodied for me one of the most recognizable and intriguing elements of Englishness: that fabled tightness of lip, albeit pierced. No surprise it showed up in someone not exactly pure Brit. Extracting secrets was my trade, however— in addition to her other lures, she posed a professional challenge. The game, as Holmes might say, was afoot—though the stitches on her hand signaled: *proceed with caution.*

"Smoke?"

"Thanks."

"Offer a girl a light?" she asked.

I felt my pockets.

"Sorry."

She shook her head and pulled out a lighter.

"Do you want me to smoke it for you?" She said after lighting both our cigarettes, then watching me cough away.

Suddenly she plucked it from my lips. Before I could grab it back, she flicked it into a puddle where it hissed like something hurt.

"You don't smoke, do you?"

"Sometimes. Not so much," I confessed, strangely embarrassed. Mental note: *cultivate vices.* And, that summer, I did.

A couple punted on the river. In a moment of goofiness, I waved, successfully mortifying Selena. The cars, meanwhile, sounded loud and out of place amid the medieval buildings.

"You have no fucking idea the position I find myself in."

The fading light bounced off the water, casting waves over her lightly perspiring face, dabbed by a breeze.

Her head whiplashed side to side as if she were checking for spies.

"A life of special pleading. Eyeing people, second-guessing. Almost as much trouble as being black. Fuck, worse. You know what I mean. But how the hell avoid it? Specialize in Byzantine tesserae and hang out only with other Byzantinologists? Maybe I'll rap, shout crazy shit in pubs like that," she gestured toward a cellar with leaded windows.

I laughed and told her I knew how she felt.

"No. You don't," she assured me. "It's mostly because of you fucking Americans, and the Brits of course, mucking about with the Middle East, playing with your Jews and your Arabs as if life were a board game, a fucking three-dimensional version of *Risk*."

When I asked how she came to live with Marian, she said:

"Marian's a fucking saint, that's why I'm here. Didn't I just say how glad I was you weren't clued in to every detail of my ridiculous life? Ask Marian. She loves telling the story. I think maybe her maiden name's Scheherazade."

We stopped before a store window piled with cheeses. For a few minutes we paused to admire the Stiltons, the cheddars, the plump cushions of Brie.

—·—

Now, in Marian's drawing room, I worked my way over to Selena, but she refused to look at me.

"Hey," I whispered.

She stared straight ahead. Her moodiness *was* her charm.

So I returned to the lopsided circle where Rajini was instructing a coterie of skeptics.

"You know the Brits refused to bring Arabists to Arabia? Afraid they'd mingle with the natives." She glanced over at Selena, whose eyes stayed on her cigarette. "People might have connected, become human to each other. Point was to keep that from happening. Instead, they made the locals learn English. First step toward complete subjugation."

"This is after all a Christian country, and there's nothing to which Christians won't stoop. In my humble opinion," Bulwer added, lips quivering.

At that moment the clock struck five.

The late-afternoon sun played across the room. I'm not sure why I'd grown excited hearing Rajini's accusations—it was as though I'd under-stood something at last. I'd discovered a key—held it in my hand. Only I needed to find the right lock.

One of the regulars, a minor local politician whose Airedale sat alertly at his feet, sighed and said:

"It feels so passé, this postcolonial blather. Aren't you academics ready to move on to the next thing?"

"Dear Bannister, tell me again: In what year was that Second Temple destroyed? Are you over it yet? What we're talking about happened in our parents' lifetime—to our older sisters and brothers, man. The people involved are walking the earth. Death is also a cliché, until it's your turn."

– 2 –

A few days after she returned from London, Marian and I finally crossed paths again in the sitting room, where she was writing in a ledger.

"How's your brother?"

Her cheeks seemed to sag a bit, and her eyes through the new silver-rimmed glasses she was wearing, looked worried.

"With Aidan nothing is simple. You'll meet him soon."

In mid-afternoon the room had a gray, conspiratorial glow.

I reminded her I was leaving the next day.

"Pity. Couldn't stay the weekend?"

Had my tickets all ready, I explained. Two weeks of convalescence had thrown me off schedule. My flu, virus, stress reaction, or whatever it was, hadn't gone away. I still felt weaker and more tired than usual. But I hadn't come this far, hadn't lost my father, so I could nap.

"We're having a visitor Saturday. Mr. Ted Hughes. Aidan's bringing him up."

"The laureate?"

Two suicides for wives. Quite a record. And me just one dad.

"A friend of my late husband's from college. Well, at least you'll meet Aidan. He's stopping here first. How are you traveling to Vienna?"

"Train from Rome."

"Why Rome?"

Seat of empire. Model for all the rest, I explained, saying that I was flying to the Eternal City so that I could begin my journey from there. I added I hoped she'd finish her story about the elusive yet deliciously tart-mouthed Selena before I left.

"Tonight, after dinner? Or are you out?"

I'd already registered at the university, visited the library, booked my flight, picked up my Eurail Pass, packed, and was ready to go.

"I'll be here."

"Good," she sighed, and fingered her ledger.

"My diary," she replied to my unstated question and closed the book.

———·•·———

That evening, we sat down in the garden again. Bougainvillea that Bulwer dragged from the conservatory sweetened the air. A cricket declared itself from under a flower.

"Loud little bugger," she said. "Maybe I'll sic Bulwer on it. Has he shown you his collection?"

In fact, he'd invited me up to the attic where he'd brought out the test tubes full of insects—grasshoppers and crickets, mainly—and the microscope under which he examined their limbs. He was working on a design for an improved prosthetic leg and had already submitted a few patents.

Selena poked her head out:

"I'm off. Back in a bit."

I tried out my most memorable smile.

Earlier that day I'd come upon Selena in this very garden, painting and singing to herself in Arabic.

"Cézanne's a good model," I'd said.

She didn't look away from her canvas. "Well, I knew you weren't stupid. Or you wouldn't be here, would you?"

I bowed my head in mock humility.

"So very generous."

"Mind you don't prove me wrong."

"What were you singing?"

"A limit to your cleverness? The boundary already?"

"You're just trying to throw me off balance because you like me."

She snorted. "I hardly know you."

"Honeymoon period."

"Then the divorce?"

"Besides," I continued unfazed, "people make too much of knowing. It's like they think everyone has this little box inside them hiding a scroll scribbled with a tagline from a fortune cookie: *Young American male struggling to come to terms with his father's suicide is doomed to fail in his quest.* Or: *Strong chin, weak knees.*"

"What's that mean?"

"You figure it out."

She'd stepped back from her painting, giving me a better look at the landscape, a bluish green field of overlapping rectangles fastened down by tall palms.

"Is that home?"

"What's mine?"

"Your what? Home?"

"My sentence."

"Seething chick finds solace in arms of handsome American."

"Are there such beasts? Anyway, you'll excuse me if I ignore you? I'm just a Sunday painter, you know, and as it's Tuesday this is going to take some concentration."

Realizing there was no breaching the divide at this moment, I retreated back to the house.

Now I asked Marian about Selena's paintings.

"She showed her talent young," Marian replied. "We hired a tutor from the university, an Egyptian named Vanina. It was Vanina who discovered how much Lena had to say with a box of crayons. But she's very private about it. Several people have suggested she show them to a dealer. She won't hear of it. Raising her wasn't easy. She was in shock almost a year."

"Why?"

She seemed not to have heard me.

"Brandy?"

"You bet."

Marian brought out two heavy crystal glasses.

"Where did we leave off?"

"You were telling me about your brother."

"Yes, Sebastian went to Jerusalem after the war. Where Father had been decades before. My brother was one of the most radical people I'd ever met, though you'd never guess it, he was so soft spoken—except about Father. Because Father was a soldier, Sebastian became a pacifist. He'd been a pacifist well into the second war. In Israel he tried to restart Brit Shalom."

"Brit Shalom?"

"A peace movement. One of the people who began it was Edwin Samuel, Herbert's son."

I nodded, though my knowledge at this level grew sketchy.

"Sebastian was a compulsive letter writer. At least twice a month we received several pages of family chronicles. He went in 1948 and never came back.

"Occasionally he telephoned. He married a Palestinian woman— Selena's mother had been a doctor working with one of the international relief agencies. Sebastian became a strong supporter of the right of return, of course.

"Then one of his sons became a fundamentalist—I never met the boys, or his wife. They never came to England. Don't think they liked us much. Don't blame them. Well, apparently, what we figured out happened . . . I'm sorry, this is still hard for me . . . so many years later . . . the boy had joined a militant organization. He was preparing for a mission. One of those sad, horrible acts of rage. And the bomb went off before he even left the house. It destroyed everything. Killed everyone. His brothers, his sisters. It killed his parents—my brother. Only Selena, who'd been playing with a friend next door, survived. I was told she found several of the pieces—who knows what, a brother's hand, a sister's foot, a father's lips."

The underwater tea parties, I thought—did Marian know about them?

"She was five when she arrived here, a tiny, tiny thing. A lovely thing. My own daughter had died earlier that year in a car accident. She'd been thirty. Nineteen seventy-eight was not a good year for the Gordon-Brimsleys. Until Selena. Selena gave me another chance."

Marian stopped a minute. Her eyes shut. She took a deep breath.

"Selena's my daughter now. She was—still is—shy, and underneath all that she's angry. We educated her at home until we were sure she could stand up for herself. Sometimes I worry we kept her away from others too long."

I said nothing of what lay on the other side of that shyness.

"What about your husband?"

"Dead seven years. Heart attack. That's all right, I appreciate it," she said in response to my clumsy condolences.

The garden seemed to wrap itself around us as she spoke, growing very still. Even the crickets fell silent. The air was cool.

"Getting chilly," she said.

"It's nice."

"You don't want a fire?"

She stood up.

"Let's let it go then, shall we?"

On the threshold she turned and looked back out again.

"Strange how important it's become to me, this garden," she said.

"I remember Mother telling me about her friend Jane Lancaster back in Palestine. It was as the British were leaving, summoned home, just before Israel declared independence. Jane went to the head of the Jewish Agency's political department. By then the violence was terrible. They'd grown sick of us, both the Israelis and the Arabs. Both felt betrayed. Anyway, Jane asked the woman at the agency to take care of her garden. Many of the plants were very rare. Jane wanted to be sure they would be all right."

Marian paused.

"I doubt she ever saw it again."

Her shoulders had hunched. Now she straightened up, as though shrugging off the burden of history that had dropped on her with the mantle of evening.

"There's an incandescent quality to Selena," she suddenly added. "She likes you. I see that. But be careful. Don't know what she's told you. She's already tried to kill herself once."

I blushed and shuddered. I wondered if Marian had ever heard Selena speaking candidly ("Fucking Brits. Fucking Arabs. Fucking Jews. And what are you? A poor fucking Irish American Slav! Think they'll ever let you forget it?").

"She'll be at St. Antony's. But I told you that already. It's where they do Eastern Europe. Your father's part of the world. Rajini's husband teaches there. Don't think you've met him yet. It's late. There's more to tell, but it will have to keep."

"I'm leaving tomorrow," I reminded her.

"You'll be back," she said confidently.

"Tell me this. How well did you know my father?"

She leaned toward me. I could smell lavender soap. Then she took my hands between hers and squeezed them tight.

Her eyes dazzled a little.

"We grew up together," she said.

The look on my face must have touched her, and she said: "It's quite a story. You should go see Vera. I understand she's sick. Who knows how long she has?

"There will be time when you return."

I almost told her about Father then, but I held back. Candor is never sold cheap. Why should I give it away? There was a lot Marian wasn't telling me, either.

I stopped at the edge of the path and looked down at the slug inching up the side of the planter.

Then Marian stepped forward, took my wrist again, fixed her gaze on me and said:

"I wish you'd told me he was dead."

And then there was no holding me back.

I'd gone up to Uncle Bill's cabin in New Hampshire on a hunch.

Father's invitation to go hunting with him rang in my ears long after he left, and all weekend I regretted not going. But I'd driven to Woodsville once before, and that time I hadn't found him where he said he'd be. Pissed, I never went again.

All the way up I had a bad feeling. My insistence on knowing about Vera had triggered a set of reactions I feared hadn't ended yet. Had I been less aggressive in tracking his story, Father might never have left. I reached Franconia Notch as the sun burned through the fog. Around me, the White Mountains urged calm. Our manias were nothing to them. They'd abided our kind for millennia. But once off the highway, winding up and down the rougher back roads, which moved from pavement to gravel to dirt, through an ever-thickening canopy of trees, I began feeling nervous again.

After I found Vera's letters and figured out who she was, I went at him like a prosecuting attorney. How could I keep from becoming my father if I didn't know who he was? But, maybe, just maybe, I'd gone about it the wrong way.

What did I know about him, anyway? That he'd come to the United States via Canada from Britain. That he was born in Ukraine and raised in England, where he'd served in the army. In cursory, truncated answers to my barrage of questions, he let me know he'd worked countless anonymous jobs on his way to the erratic life he finally fell into on Boston's North Shore. The work had been beneath him. I got that. He was not only handsome, he was smart, and he was educated. He read a lot, mainly history. But there was something else, something in him that made him choose to fly under the radar, to suppress himself, to hide who he was, maybe even from himself. Booze was a symptom, not a cause.

The last stretch of road to the camp was a single lane rutted with roots and rocks I took at five miles an hour so as not to rupture the exhaust or bust the struts. Even Springsteen couldn't distract me. I turned him off. Gradually, I began tuning in to the very different frequency of the woods: the rattle of woodpeckers, screeching squirrels, the trill of myriad anonymous birds.

At last I reached the cabin. Father's Ford Galaxy nosed the porch stairs. The surroundings were landscaped in early trailer park. Two battered pickups had rusted into planters for stinkweed. An adding machine stood on an upside-down bathtub beside a tower of tires. Back from the cabin, a target pinned to a maple was riddled with holes far from the center.

I walked out and called toward the house:

"Hey, Dad, you there?" I added: "Don't shoot, it's me."

The door swung open, and he stepped out onto the porch.

Instead of the ratty green camouflage he'd inherited from Uncle Bill, he had on his British soldier's uniform. In place of the rifle I'd watched him clean time and again, he clutched a pistol.

The door behind remained open, and he turned slowly to close it, as though he hesitated to show me his back. When he turned again, he seemed lost in a thought that had started so long ago I didn't know if I would ever reach far enough to find its source.

"Hey, Dad. What's with the uniform?"

He didn't answer. He shifted from foot to foot. His large palm buffed the gun barrel. His thick brows arched up. He looked good, I thought. The uniform he'd worn as a young man still fit him.

He looked about to say something. The sun turned a bottle into a magnifying glass on a bale of leaves by the tub. Why, I wonder today, had I pushed him so hard? What, after all, did his past matter to me?

His face showed no surprise—he'd been expecting me. Birds beat the leaves in the trees as he turned the gun to his face and put his mouth around the tip.

Stop, I wanted to shout, but no words came. I brushed a mosquito away from my face.

Then he pulled the trigger.

His blue eyes kept staring at me long after the back of his head was gone.

For a minute it was as though my own brains had been dashed.

What had he done? Why?

No matter how difficult he had become in these last years, he was still my father. He had raised me, sent me to piano lessons, taught me to fish. But regret is a road that curves and turns so often it's impossible to see what lies up ahead till you're there.

Later I overheard cops on the scene debating why, if he'd planned to kill himself, he had put on that uniform.

One of them made it clear he doubted my story. He wasn't at all convinced things had happened as I said.

But I had seen it, and I was in Europe now to find out why he had given me the terrible gift of such a dramatic last act. Besides, what kind of historian doesn't even know his own story?

Marian's face paled.

When I was through, she put her arms around me, and we stood in the hall a few minutes while she wept.

The child may well be the father of the man, but I dare anyone to draw a straight line between them.

After telling Marian the story, my headache returned. I sat alone in my room, thinking about something Charlotte had said. She told me she had never trusted my father—his silences spooked her. I remember feeling frustrated that I couldn't convey to her the many things he'd been before becoming who he was by the time they met. Father was like an artist with several distinct periods. They say art requires perfecting one's skill at omission, and Father was a master of the unsaid. And at a critical moment in life, we'd been friends.

Once we drove to Plum Island in late August to see the monarch butterflies who paused there yearly on their way to Mexico. Walking around, I spotted one with its wing broken. Cupping it in my hands, I showed it to Father, who let me keep it. Home, we set about building a terrarium from a fish tank, pilfering my model railroad to create a miniature Devon. Several times daily I dipped my middle finger in sugar water, then watched my pet tap the bead with its probe. Soon it was more domesticated than a cat.

Seeing how well it had done in captivity, I persuaded Father to return to the island where we harvested a dozen more wounded comrades. We bought cracked fish tanks cheap and before long my room was transformed into a butterfly hospital. At feeding time, I dribbled sugar water from shoulder to wrist and liberated my charges, who zigzagged their way over until my arm looked alive under their clapping wings.

One evening, after doing my homework, I sprayed my arm and removed the tank tops when I heard the door slam, followed by Mother's loudest scream. I ran out.

In the living room stood Father, something huge and black in his arms looking like a mummy greased in glistening oil. The room smelled as though someone had uncorked the ocean. It took a minute to figure out that Father was holding a baby seal. Winters, hurt and lost seals frequently washed up onshore.

"Fill the tub," he barked. "Cold water."

Mother did but she accidentally turned on the hot tap, then left to grab some old towels from the laundry, and Father yelled: *"You trying to kill the pup?"* She emptied the tub and refilled it with cold while I jumped about like a marionette.

The month before I'd done a report for school about the life cycle of the harbor seal. *Phoca vitulina concolor.* While their ancestors, fifteen million years back, walked on land, these were strictly aquatic, capable of remaining underwater for half an hour, able to plunge down three hundred feet. You see them lounging on rocks alongside their buds in the harbor, but basically they're loners who socialize mainly to mate, then repose in safety.

Their courtship rituals, I told the class, included bubble-blowing and mouthing each other's necks.

Father deposited the creature gently into the tub. It was then I noticed its flipper bent in the wrong direction. The three of us watched its black eyes staring out.

"Where's its mother?" Mother asked.

"Who knows," Father said. "S-s-sometimes these little fellows get caught in a current and dragged away. If they can't find their way b-b-back before they're ready to be on their own, well, you ca-ca-can imagine," he said, wiping his face and hands on the towel.

Later, when I returned to my room the first thing I saw was the billowing curtain. I'd forgotten all about the butterflies. The tanks were empty—my pets had all fled, to their doom, out the window. All but one, which had tangled and died in the lace. I unwrapped the shroud and held the broken wind-hoverer in my palm, its frail body shuddering under my breath.

I leaned my forehead on the glass and looked to the harbor. Lights flickered over the water, riding the waves to the edges of the world, beyond which I would one day go.

That may have been the first time I saw the law of exchange in action. The seal entered; the butterflies fled. A trade had occurred. Unfortunately, I wanted both. Not being able to get both led in time to my theory of the turn.

The next morning Dr. Looby, the town vet, came by.

"You should bring it to the aquarium in Boston," he said after examining the seal and wrapping its flipper in adhesive.

"It's a she, by the way."

"Should," Father shook his head, "b-b-but . . ." He looked over at me ". . . won't. James here could stand another c-c-companion."

"You know how much they eat," Dr. Looby said softly.

"Ten to eighteen pounds a day," I rattled off. "Shrimp, salmon, squid, and mollusks."

"A tithe off your take," the doctor said.

Father shrugged.

My father owned a beat-up old boat, and when he was really hard up, after a layoff, when unemployment ran out, he did a little wild-cat fishing. Out at four, he returned as darkness smoked from the water. Like most of his colleagues, he drank, though its effect on him then still seemed reliably soothing. But he was away a lot. At night Mother and I worked on projects together: we built a Viking ship from peanut shells, painted what we thought the weather gods looked like, and made elaborate costumes for Halloween. Our preparations began in December. We hardly noticed Christmas. When I was a boy I asked why, while other kids decorated trees, we were installing grow lights and planting pumpkin seeds, and my mother told me about Jesus. Mother's sister, my aunt Joan, was a nun, which made Mother an authority on the subject. She said Jesus taught that you should love everything that lives, even people who don't like you. I said, I don't like Mr. Maynard, a neighbor who complained whenever we chased a ball into his yard. She said: You should try loving Mr. Maynard especially. Just try, she said.

Anyway, that was how I spent several weeks caretaking a seal. We bought a huge wading pool, which we set up on the porch in front of the house. I'd get right in with Sheba, who delighted in squirting me with water from her pursed lips. She put weight on fast. At feedings, she swallowed whole shrimp and clams.

I was beginning to dread returning her to the sea when, one morning, I woke and padded out, still sleepy, eyes gummed shut, to say *G'day* as Crocodile Dundee had blurted it the week before at the movies, only to find her lying on the porch floor. She'd worked her way out of the tub. She wasn't moving. Her skin, normally glistening, had already dried and begun to crack. A fly circled her nostril.

I shouted loud enough to bring Mother running from the kitchen. We threw ourselves at the creature, poking and probing, hoping to revive it, but it was too late.

Later that night, Father had to carry her out. I wanted to bury her in our yard, but Father insisted the right thing was to send her home to the sea, so we placed her, swaddled in tarp, in the backseat of his Ford Galaxy, and drove to the water. There, standing on the tip of the jetty, we heaved Sheba back to the source. A bitter wind sprayed our faces. Father put his hand on my shoulder, and we returned home in silence.

We said nothing more to each other—but that night, alone in my room, I sobbed.

Soon after, Father decided I needed to learn how to play the piano, so he signed me up for lessons with our neighbor downstairs. Once a week I descended to Ms. Johnson's apartment. The place smelled clean and inviting, as though she'd scrubbed her floors with cookie dough. Tall, big-haired, large-busted, full of jokes, she wore long, flowing, brightly colored dresses and earrings the size of basketball hoops. Romare Bearden prints hung on her walls, and an imposing African drum with a tight leather face rose in the corner of the living room.

Since we couldn't afford a piano, Father painted a keyboard for me on a two-by-four. I practiced an hour each night, running my fingers up and down the fake keys. Mother watched skeptically, asking: "Can you really practice like that?"

"Shostakovich did, when he had to," I snapped.

The difference was that I had no ear for music, though a lively imagination let me hear myself playing, no problem at all. The notes rose up in four dimensions. I raced through finger exercises, scales, and arpeggios. Before long, I preferred the chords I imagined to a real piano, which invariably sounded off key. I hammered away, window open, lace curtains swaying to my silent, pitch-perfect tune.

———•———

"You're leaving tomorrow," Selena said, draping the doorway. It was late.

While I *was* a bit older, Selena's edges gave her authority and a style both distancing and attractive. Yet we found common ground in rejecting the yoke of a past we could never reform.

I'd been kneeling on the floor above my suitcase, looking again at Father's British military ID card. I had not, of course, brought the heavy glass jar I'd found carefully wrapped in a shoe box in his closet after his death. It was old and cracked and the stamp on the bottom said it had been made in England. Why save a jar? I'd have to ask Marian.

"Don't just sit there, babe."

She seemed to glow in the door frame.

When I stood up, she shimmied into my arms. The unpredictable young. It was like embracing a stream.

The hair on her nape was clipped silk. In the cheek-peck of siblings our lips slipped, and my arms moved along her neck, down her back, then up into the vale between shoulder blades where the feathers had been. My dark angel, de-winged.

It's impossible to say anything fresh about a kiss. Paint me the taste of oysters swallowed by moonlight; teach Homer to pigeons; build Paris with a spoon. If you're lucky in love, the kisses you've won blur like a view of the infinite, fading tiers of the Himalayas. Yet, once, maybe twice, in a lifetime a kiss comes along that changes everything, and the clock of one's life is reset.

In its sweep nothing of the past mattered—not Charlotte, not my father, not even my work.

"How many tattoos do you have?" I stalled after pulling away.

"Seven."

"Show me."

She didn't hesitate, her eyes veiled like a dawn lake.

"All right," she smiled. "Here's one."

She turned and yanked the waist of her jeans down a few inches. A fist in a heart bloomed on her hip, to which I pressed a finger.

"Next?"

Turning again, she rolled her black T-shirt up above a belly button ringed by what looked like a loop of thorns or barbed wire. I traced the braille of her embroidered omphalos.

We might have gone further, but Marian's tread on the stairs pried us apart.

A knock on the door.

"Oh God, that's probably Boy."

"Who?"

"Marian's brother, Aidan," she whispered.

"What's wrong with Aidan?"

"Tell you later."

"Excuse me," Marian said, peering in. "I just wanted you to meet Aidan."

She lingered a moment, appraising the scene.

Then I recovered myself and stepped out into the hall where, below the Watteau, Marian introduced us.

The oblong fellow in the three-piece banker's suit and bow tie might have been her father. A sliver of graying mustache bristled like a silverfish above his lip.

"How . . . how . . . how'd you do?" he stuttered. Like my father, also a stutterer.

"Pleasure to meet you," I said.

"She's been tree-tree-treating you well, I expect."

"Better than I deserve."

"You we-we-weren't well?"

I shrugged.

"I know," he said inexplicably.

Marian hovered, ready to step in.

"We'll see mo-mo-more of each other," Aidan said, his sleepy-eyed oval face deadpan. It had been a long drive.

After they left, I looked around for Selena, who had of course disappeared.

When I knocked on her door, there was no answer.

I wasn't sure what I'd done wrong. Was it the kiss, or that I'd broken away? But she was only eighteen, I reminded myself—eighteen has reasons reason knows nothing of.

Our fleeting, unexpected embrace imprinted itself like a promise, however, and I lay in bed fantasizing about a life among the heather and lavender of the moors I hadn't yet seen. The past was metamorphic and took many shapes, but so did the future: it was a person, a gun, or a kiss. We had to go either through or around them since neither the past nor the future exist, except in the way they wall us off from the moment in which we actually live.

Fortunately, this was a time in the world when the walls were tumbling down everywhere.

Sometime after midnight, I'd barely nodded off when there was a knock on my door. I shot up, heart pounding, vaguely washed in a dream in which Father was stalking me with a bow and arrow.

"Can't sleep," Selena murmured.

Her Screaming Skulls T-shirt covered her knees.

I rubbed my eyes and tried smiling while she nested down on the other side of the bed. She seemed troubled.

"That your spout dripping?" she said.

"What?"

I'd fallen asleep in my underwear. I drew a blanket up to my hips.

"You a plumber?"

"A girl's got to have skills."

But her heart wasn't in it.

"What's up?" I asked, dazed.

"While you've been tracking your family, your president's drawn a line in the sand. You know he's about to use your country to fuck us over again?"

An American president from a family that consolidated its fortune doing business with the Nazis was earning his keep by defending British Petroleum's private protectorate, better known as Kuwait.

I hadn't paid much attention to the world these last weeks. Her passion was bracing.

"Fucking impossible place I'm in. Who helped me? Marian. Who fucked me over? Marian's father."

"I feel the same way. You wake up in a situation. They call it birth. They give you points for waking up. Then, one by one, they take them all away again."

She inched up the bed.

"You're an American. Can't compare."

"But I get it. White men. Brutal, selfish, white men. In other parts of the world, the men are colored. Let's say then: men."

"Please. Spare me the solidarity shit."

"Boy, you sure curse a lot! You want me to say fuck it, and leave?" I asked, rubbing my eye.

"How fucking long will this legacy of the cave go on?" Selena burst out in a hot voice. "If you cut me, do I not bleed? You expect me to forget the millions of my people living in camps for half a century just because you have? Because you and the rest of the world don't want to know?"

"I don't expect you to forget a thing. Not yet. That comes later. Maybe."

Two worlds ripen in an eye, but in Selena's I thought I'd glimpsed a third—the future. I leaned toward her and, at just the same moment, her center of gravity also shifted.

And so we kissed again. For hours we became our mouths and our fingers, and more. We were quiet, strangling our moans, in hushed joy. We knew the strangely derelict residents of this house might not have approved. They seemed to have grown past sex. Maybe it had been civilized out of them, turned into culture or dogma or doubt. Maybe we were primitive people, amoebic, anabolic, heretical, sinners, decadents, doomed. But doom is the destiny of all women and men, no matter what they may think. Having got nowhere describing a kiss, I won't try to translate how our bodies lit up the room, but I imagined it was as though a small nameless star had dropped from the sky and lay flailing on its back in the middle of Oxford.

Afterward, I said:

"Not your first time?"

"Polly. What century are you in?"

I don't remember when she first began calling me Pollyanna.

"I just thought . . ."

"Orientalism."

"Sorry."

Blunt eighteen.

"Why? Feeling guilty? You want to feel free to fuck other girls when you go?"

Shadows bannered the ceiling.

She giggled.

"Like I care? It's your body, do what you want."

"You too," I said, not sure I meant it.

"I intend to," she replied firmly. "I've been thinking. About this identity business. Big thing with you academics, isn't it?"

"Listen, jailbait. I'm not an academic. Remember, you're about to become a student yourself."

She drew the sheet above her breasts.

"I'm not. Jailbait, I mean. I'm eighteen. But all that's a crock, isn't it? It's not like I became a different person all of a sudden on April twentieth. It's that awful legalistic shit people pile on life so they can get the better of you. Tie you up in a billion little knots until you forget who you are."

"You've been hanging around Rajini."

Thank God for women, I thought. And still do.

But I added:

"Some of it's helpful. Human rights and all that."

She looked at me and smiled.

"I mean it. You have to remember these things forever. You're what, seven years older? Already you're trapped up in your head, Polly. A head is a terrible place in which to live."

"Maybe." I turned over and looked at her paintings on the wall.

"You are. It's thinking too much that's killing you. All that history. All that father."

Eighteen was glory. Free to walk away from the torment of mediating my parents' struggles, the daily battles, screams of recrimination—about money and time, and just about everything I imagined they had once loved in each other. Stepping away from it felt so good. But Father's death yanked me back into history. Away from *this*: the Eden of two alone in a bed. I would try never to forget it again. This was truth; all else, a fiction.

I turned back and sat up.

"Let me ask you," she continued, suddenly chatty. "While we were fucking, did you feel yourself American? Did you know I was Palestinian? And Jewish, a little?"

"My turn to laugh."

"But it's amazing how whatever space you're in changes you. Swimming, in the shower, eating, do you have a name? I don't."

Then she said:

"You never talk about your ex."

Footsteps echoed down the hall and I held my breath like a scared little boy.

"Did I even mention her to you?"

"When you told me about your father."

"Oh. Big mistake."

I watched her closely. Her face revealed nothing.

"You still love her? No kids?"

"Now who's calling who Polly?"

"Sex. Man. It makes people crazy as money."

She switched subjects.

"You know, Polly, I've got some hard stuff ahead. Only now starting to realize what I've been through. I saw them, you know. Pieces of my family. After the bomb. I'll never forget."

Her finger traced lines on the sheet.

"What do you think *I'm* doing here?" I said.

"Fucking the piss out of me, that's what."

And we laughed. We kissed. Then she pushed me away.

"I also saw something. It's what you choose to remember about it that counts," I offered, uncertainly.

"But I know what you mean," she added. "We have to walk out of this room eventually and meet people stuck in stories into which they want to drag us. It's bullshit. All concepts."

"You bet. We know it so long as we're here," I said. "Like you said, it's tougher once you step out."

"What do I do then?"

"You mentioned Byzantium?"

"Ha ha." She shook her candy-colored head.

"No, it's a good idea. Study Byzantine art. Give your mind something hard and beautiful not tied to all this stuff called self or identity or history."

"I see that. But Byzantine art is a little too close."

"You're the one who mentioned it. Doesn't matter what. The history of coal mining in Argentina. Anything. You'll grow. Otherwise the world will shove you back into your body with some dumb-fuck label you barely understand because you don't see yourself that way but they do because they have no imagination. They know only the fables their dads and moms laid on them while torturing them into adulthood. Black people know this better than anyone."

We had both stretched out, staring at the ceiling.

"I know."

I put my finger on the tip of her nipple.

"Hey."

"Getting kinda of heavy."

"One more question," she said softly.

"Okay."

"Who is your enemy?"

"My enemy?"

"Yeah. You have enemies, don't you?"

"Probably. Hope so. Maybe. Why?"

"Well, when I'm feeling especially Palestinian, I think: What about Jews?"

She turned to face me.

"What do you mean?"

"You know my situation. And I know the way Jews and Palestinians talk about each other."

"You have Palestinian friends here?" I asked.

"And Israeli. I hear both sides like you'd never believe."

"It's tricky. So much bad shit. To the Jews. Palestinians. By Jews. Brits. Americans. Other Arabs. Oh, and the rest—"

"Bulwer says it goes back to Cromwell," she interrupted. "The Puritan mission. Convert the Jews. Conquer Jerusalem. Then *Hullo, Loving Jesus!*"

"And Bulwer is a reliable guide. Still, why stop with Cromwell? Why not go back to his ancestors, the Wittelsbachs, in tenth-century Bavaria? But I think you said it yourself. Basically you have to remember the truth of this room."

"I already forgot. You know our papers call the Queen and her people 'the Germans'?"

She pressed closer. Her breath was moist and minty. But I was caught up in my own ideas.

"Everybody," I began optimistically, "no matter how poor, lies in a room with one other person, just like us, and wonders how to get out of the mess. Why build a whole city, when all you need is a room? In what space is identity formed? The classroom, the temple, the madrass? At the movies? In bed? The library stacks?

"That's why I'm doing history. It helps me remember: before this, came that. Once I was an infant with no name and no past. It's what I've done since that confuses me. And what I've done depended on how others saw me, how I fit into their view. Or how I fit myself in." Then I laughed. "Hell, I don't understand any of it."

"Who is your enemy, you asked a minute ago? Your own mind, love. Your mind."

The comic sage for a minute.

"But I've seen pictures of the refugee camps. And these are definitely not just in my mind." She moved back a bit, and suddenly I regretted the politics.

"I have too," I assured her. "Do all you can. Tell people. Let me help. It's tough. But don't act like you were there yourself—"

"My brother—"

"And look where it got him."

"He had a right—"

"A right? I don't know. When you found his foot in the bricks, did you think it was a Palestinian foot? A right foot? A right-to-return foot?"

"A right to live. A right to breathe. A right to return. Of course."

We were sitting up now.

"And nothing will change," I said more softly. "And things will lurch on. Anyway, it's my country that's the problem."

"Fucking right. That's why I think you should set an example: shoot your mother and invite a homeless man to take her place in your house. Then you'll have some street cred."

"Look, I know. It's geography. We think we've earned our perks. But we're destroying ourselves. Eating ourselves alive from within."

"I agree. But I have a confession."

"*Ego te absolvo!* In advance."

I put my index finger to the tip of her nose.

"Gee, I knew someone could. Didn't know it was you."

"Now you do."

"Okay. This isn't the only time I've been in a room with one other person in a bed."

"I'm shocked. What are you saying?"

"Did your mother ever sing to you, Polly?"

A direction I hadn't expected.

I looked at the face that until this moment had seemed so grown up and suddenly I saw the child.

"Did she ever sing you songs that, even before you knew the words, surrounded you with such piercing sweetness, you felt yourself in something like heaven?"

Her lips trembled. I reached over and caressed her cheek with the back of my hand.

"A sad heaven. No. My mother wasn't a singer. *Merrily merrily merrily merrily, life is but a dream* is about all I remember. And a neighbor who sang opera."

"They have funny names like *Ya Lel Ma Atwalak.*"

"What's it mean?"

"This Never Ending Night."

"Cheery. Sing it."

She thought for a moment. Then she lowered her head and sang.

I shut my eyes and watched a pair of geese flying across a burning red sun.

After a silence she said.

"They leave their mark. A mother's songs. You carry them into the world."

Then she added:

"Oprah."

"What?"

"When Oprah does a show about the Occupied Territories, then I'll know things have started to change."

"You're right. When Spielberg does the biopic on Arafat and the massacre in Qana."

"Yeah," she murmured, nuzzling her silky head against my shoulder. "You're sweet." She kissed me lightly on the neck. I took it as a cue and put my hand on her breast, but she brushed it away.

"Not now, Polly, I need sleep."

"Don't you think you should go back to your room?"

"Because of Marian? Polly, have some balls," she murmured.

I was about to say something back, but she put her finger to my lips.

"Shhh."

"But—"

"Shhhhhhhh. Balls, Polly. Hush."

———•–•———

The next day felt frantic. I woke late and unrested. The space where Selena had fallen asleep was empty. I rubbed my eyes and lurched out of bed. A tray of toast and coffee had gone cold outside my door. After a quick wash, I dressed and rechecked my bag. Racing down the stairs with my pack, I was sure I had forgotten a thousand things. But I had the letter.

In the foyer, I bumped into Aidan, who appeared to have been waiting for me.

He looked stern and resentful, as if he hadn't slept too well either. His puffy cheeks and the unlit cigar in his hand made me think of Churchill.

He stepped up very close and, after looking conspiratorially over his shoulder, huffed:

"How do-do-does it feel, young m-m-man? To think you've gotten a-a-away with it?"

"What?" I said, turning red. He pulled his head back. His lips curled up in contemptuous scrolls.

"Why, mu-mu-murder, of course. Mu-mu-murder."

There was a rough glee in his voice. I thought I smelled whiskey. He flashed a swift smile, turned, and walked away. I had no time to pursue him to ask what he meant. I was already late.

Marian, who'd been waiting outside, gave me a kiss and a warm hug. I wondered if she could read the bewilderment on my face.

Selena, who had offered to drive me to the airport, was in the car, waiting.

I sped down the stairs with Aidan's words ringing in my head.

We didn't say much along the way. A light drizzle teared up the glass.

"About yesterday," I probed the thickening silence, afraid that if I didn't start talking, my head would explode.

I tried inhaling that clear open smell I associated with Selena, but the air had grown thick, damp, and English.

"Listen, don't bother."

"We should talk."

"Now you're my mother? What are you going to do? Invade me?"

I looked out the window. A lone cow stared at us from behind a fence. My journey hadn't begun as I'd planned. What had Aidan meant? What did he think I had done? How would he know? It would be weeks before I could confront him.

Selena locked her eyes straight ahead and put pedal to metal. As we raced past lumbering trucks—wrong side of the road and all—my fingers dug into the armrest.

At the airport she parked and got out. She walked beside me in silence. Nearing the gate, we stopped. My head pounded. We turned to each other. Then she clamped both hands on my shoulders, guiding me to her as though to make sure our lips didn't repeat their mistake, and we kissed twice on the cheeks. I tried to flash a meaningful look into which I poured my pain and confusion—which were only partly about her—but her eyes fixed on the floor.

Before stepping into the chute, I glanced over my shoulder. I half expected to see her standing there teary eyed, waving.

Or maybe not. Wasn't that how Orpheus finally shook off Eurydice, though mythmakers bend over backward persuading us he'd made a mistake and was grief-stricken to lose her? But *Don't look back* was his only instruction. *Glance over your shoulder just once, and she's gone*—and what did he do?

I no longer know what I hoped for. What I found was a man with a canvas bag from Waterstones rolling back on the balls of his heels, watching planes. Selena had flown.

And in truth, I didn't feel half bad.

Maybe this was what my father had wanted, what most men desire at some point in their lives: to walk away from the past—from a child, a woman, a country—as though they didn't exist, hoping never to know the aftershock of their leaving.

"Something wrong, sir?" the steward asked after I'd taken my seat.

"No," I answered. "Not yet."

———·•·———

I didn't look back a second time.

My thoughts began turning to Vera. Knowing as little as I did, my image of her grew until she shadowed me like a spreading chestnut: eventually I'd have to face her. She was dying an agonizing death—so I imagined—with only her two sons for company, and they were *as poor as worms*.

And here I was, dallying, neglecting my mission, which included delivering the letter Father left for Vera written in that language—Ukrainian—I couldn't speak, never mind read.

The excitement I'd felt on landing in England returned. With Britain as my base, I planned to plunder the Continent for easy spoils before penetrating the newly breached Eastern borders. Shards of the Berlin Wall were already being sold in museums around the globe. The Iron Curtain was melting, and it was possible, aided by visas, to drive a tank or, in the spirit of the times, ride a bus, straight through to just about anywhere. I would finally see the places where Father began.

THREE

The Siege of Vienna

— 1 —

"Hurry or I will never see you in this world," Vera said when I called her from Rome.

Her voice was raspy and melancholic, evoking the mossy undersides of city fountains, fissured marble, a horse limping stoically before a cart heaped with sheaves of rotting wheat.

"I'll be there tomorrow," I promised.

That summer it rained almost every day, cutting into the tourist trade. The train was nearly empty, and I had no trouble upgrading myself from second class to first. Around Milan the conductor, mustached and in a uniform so neatly creased you could have used it to open letters, came in and, taking one look at me scowled, *Seconda classe,* tilting back his head so his cap threatened to slide off.

I grabbed my backpack and returned to my proper station. In the corridor stood an old man, bald and unshaven, in a dirty brown suit, wearing shredded walnut-colored work boots, shoelaces untied, staring at his fingernails. When I squeezed by him, he looked up, nodded, then returned to his brooding.

My three days in Rome clarified the meaning of Imperial scale: the Colosseum, the Forum, the Pantheon, the piazzas, their fountains full of kids splashing like innocent birds in the waters of time. I spent hardly a minute at the hostel. One night I found myself at dawn sprawled on the Spanish Steps in heated debate with a couple from Prague who insisted their president was neither a good politician nor a gifted writer.

Now I entered an empty compartment and slumped into a seat next to a window, which at that second flaunted an army of pines. I imagined the trees on a forced march, lashed by a wind that kept changing its course,

63

holding them mired in one spot forever. I thought about what Aidan had said, at what might have been behind it. Selena's unexpected coldness. Ted Hughes. My father. Stalin, two of whose wives had also killed themselves. His son: suicide. What if Dante were right, and suicides returned as trees? I imagined bodies dangling in the grove outside. In the nineteenth century, Vienna was known as the suicide capital of the world. Every empire has its price. Here lonely men leapt from rooftops and clowns set themselves aflame and lovers slit wrists in mutual pacts. Its most famous self-destroyer was none other than the emperor's son, Crown Prince Rudolf, in the late 1880s. He might have saved the empire, had anyone taken him seriously enough to listen to his warnings. He wanted to modernize, admired Edison, and everything new. But the new was not yet synonymous with the good and the true, and his father wasn't ready to cede his throne. So history turns, on familial whims.

At forty, the question of suicide is more interesting than ever. A recent survey reported that in the United States nearly half the people killed daily by handguns are white men doing themselves in.

I was lighting a cigarette when the door opened and a girl with a tanned bare midriff and tight reddish brown curls came in and settled diagonally across from me. Skinny, high-cheeked, faintly pre-legal, she smiled and fluffed her bangs. When she leaned forward, her wisp of a skirt disappeared almost entirely.

Looking into her face, I noticed what on first glance I'd missed: a bruised cheek, a cut lip, a fading shadow under one eye.

"*Haben Sie eine Zigarette?*"

"*Bitte, ich spreche nur Amerikanisch.*"

She smiled and said: "But you know what I mean."

I smiled back. To my crude, as yet untutored ear, the accent suggested Dietrich.

And it seemed that all the good-looking women in Europe were smokers.

I tapped out a Marlboro.

We talked about traveling. She'd seen Europe. Next year she would do India.

Where was she coming from now?

"I have been to Samos," she said.

"I hope to go to Greece eventually, too."

"You must avoid Samos."

"Why?"

"It is a bad island."

"How can an island be bad?"

"Because of the bad things people do on it."

"You did bad things on Samos?"

She smiled.

"How bad?"

She tugged at her postage stamp of a skirt.

She worked as a secretary at a large legal firm housed in a building near Vienna's Rathaus—the city hall. She hated the job and the lawyers, whom she called leather-skins, but it paid well enough to afford her an apartment in a clean neighborhood equidistant between the train station and her office and what could be more important than habitation? Her habitation was secure, she repeated.

We talked easily, time passed, and before I knew it, the train was starting to slow. Buttery suburban houses filled the windows with their peculiar, melting sadness. Yet I was approaching the city of Mozart, Beethoven, Strauss. Of Schnitzler, who tallied his fucks in his diary each night, and Mahler the convert, who knew how to keep the peace in Budapest, and of course Freud, and Hofmannsthal, still another convert who, with Max Reinhardt, founded the Salzburg Festival in a paroxysm of hope, and who died of a heart attack after his son too killed himself. The ear of the West heard something here it had noted nowhere else. It seemed part harp song, part harpie shriek.

As I told her about Father and Vera, the girl's small, bruised face, with its round sensual mouth, was expressive, flashing disgust, concern, and incomprehension. She said her own grandfather had been a mail carrier who'd once delivered a letter from Hitler to a woman who lived near the Belvedere, a graceful castle turned museum she urged me to visit while I was in town.

"We're the grandchildren of war," I said.

She frowned.

"You sound like my older sister. I am sick of the war." Then she added:

"The Kiss." Her flock of curls caught the late-afternoon light as the train coasted over a bridge.

For a second I thought it was an invitation.

"What?"

"Belvedere. It's where the Klimts are," she said.

"Oh, sure."

As she spoke she leaned forward again, this time pressing her palm against my arm. The tan on her cheek seemed to deepen.

Built by Prince Eugene of Savoy, who helped beat back the Turks.

I asked if she knew whether it was true that Kafka had once rented a room in Schönbrunn.

She shook her head, tilting her chin toward me.

"Not likely," she shrugged. She said she never read novels anymore. How could anything compete with the world?

The train pulled in, and I helped her with her bag, in which she must have smuggled enough stones from Samos to build her own temple.

Lately I'd taken a dilettante's interest in Vienna, because of Vera. Its importance in European history was largely forgotten even though not long ago it was the heart of an empire—multi-ethnic, relatively tolerant, sure of itself. Jews, Muslims, and Christians all had a stake in its bones. I imagined it ringed by Turkish tents, as it had been for two months in the summer of 1683, during the Battle of Vienna. The Turks—over 140,000 of them—came with ostriches, peacocks, and women. The battle was the climax of a three-hundred-year struggle to define the borders between Christian Europe and the Ottomans. The fight was won with help from the Polish king and his Ukrainian troops. Legend has it that one of the latter stumbled on a bag of what he believed was camel seed. It turned out to be coffee, and so Vienna got its first café. An earlier showdown with the Turks inspired the creation of the croissant.

Wars sometimes bring unexpected rewards.

The street outside the station was crowded. The rain was slowing; people raced back and forth between cabs and cars.

I set down both our bags and tried lighting a cigarette. Selena's legacy. The match kept hissing out until the girl cupped her palms around mine.

"Good-bye."

"I will show you the city," she smiled winningly.

I thought of Selena. Betrayal was law in the jungle of youth, and I strove to obey it. The air was ripe with opportunity. Which way would I turn?

I studied the girl's freckled, tanned face. And Selena? Eating oysters in Paris by moonlight; her thin body tucked under mine; our long talk about who we really were or might be—the charge of these memories was still fresh.

The last thing I wanted was to visit an old woman who'd been a nurse in a Romanian asylum. That was one of the things Father had told me in our last conversation. Vera's husband (who I assumed was his father, though that wasn't a word he had used) was a doctor who worked in various Soviet clinics before getting posted to an institution in Bucharest from which he was fired when the Nazis came to power. Eventually he fell off an electric tram as it rounded the corner near his stop. There was a rumor he'd been pushed, but Vera never verified it: What good would it do knowing her husband had been murdered? After his death, she continued to work, raising her boys on the asylum grounds. Countless people went mad in those years, and the facility was so overcrowded that patients slept two to a bed. Since many were incorrigible sex offenders, the nights were loud and violent and sometimes not everyone showed up for breakfast.

It seemed Vera had been a nurse in a hospital for the mad during a time when inmates ruled the world.

"Come?" the girl beside me asked laughingly.

It was amazingly easy to fall in love then. I was in love most of the time— not just with women. I loved the music of Coltrane, Puccini, and Mahler; the bird sanctuary on Plum Island; the Mad River near Sharon, Vermont; my 1975 yellow Corolla; a Carmelite church on the Pacific; a six-hundred-year-old tree along the Crystal Springs Reservoir; Keats; French roast; the word *zapatenku;* Bailey Hazen Road; the Barcelona and Paris I'd never visited and the Somerville I had; I loved even our train. Of course I was in love with Selena. Mine wasn't a lust for possession, but a glee in communion that was pure and terribly simple in its directness, a condition of ecstasy, a state of mind I took as a gift, with contempt for all social norms.

But I already had two women waiting—Vera here, Selena in England. What kind of cad needed a third?

I shook my head, squeezed her hand, and we headed our separate ways.

A few minutes later, the sun came out.

Almost at once the streets sprouted couples, children, and pensioners—as though everyone had been dressed and waiting for this break in the weather. Men pushed prams with hysterical fervor, a vendor hawked post-cards of the Lipizzaners, and a woman followed a Borzoi on a leash half a block long. Its gold mane glinted like sheared foil.

The moment I landed on the Continent, I felt its landscape in my bones. It was different from England, where my knowledge of the litera-ture seemed almost a buffer between me and the world. Here I was an anonymous part of a curious harmony. Maybe I was responding to what-ever force it was that had birthed so much music, art, and such baroque deaths. Here even the shadows crosshatching the street belonged to me in a way they never had in England or America. Synapses snapped in shocked delight before each recognition until my nerves felt like a string of fire-crackers on the Fourth of July. I'd paced these boulevards before, smoking pipes in walnut-stained cafés and chowing down on piping strudel domed with cream. Here Trakl sipped strong brew—before, of course, killing him-self in Poland with an overdose of cocaine; here Vivaldi died, mercifully of natural causes, although he was broke. I felt the residue of centuries im-possible to explain to anyone schooled solely in the clean lines and muted architecture of New England, with no thatched huts and so few castles to quicken the blood.

Crossing the Ringstrasse, I studied its balance of the monumental and the fantastic. There was a university, a theater, a museum. These were the *Prachtbauten,* the so-called buildings of splendor, offering grandeur on a human scale, so different from Rome. Gleaming façades arced across time—even though they were not yet buffed to their current state of post-postmodern presence. But with the fall of the Wall and the collapse of the Soviet system just around the corner, the stewards of capital were busy preparing their window displays.

They'd gone up at the dawn of the era of physical culture, when God, still alive, felt out of shape. Architects transformed the boulevard, origi-nally designed to guard the private palaces of the inner city against enemies from without (the Turks) and within (the poor), into a promenade for Sunday strollers. In a way, today's Turkish immigrants were a synthesis of both—the enemy without had settled within. Bicyclists sped under trees in full leaf.

I wandered into the neighborhood beyond it where, amid the gloss and grandeur, I imagined adulterous dukes in crystal calèches pulled by white mares with diamond-studded harnesses and plumed helmets adorning both animal and man. This was the inner city, just past the Hofburg, which the middle class consecrated to their social betters the way on certain holidays peasants leave plates of food out for ghosts.

When I eventually reached Vera's street, I thought a hearse was idling in front of her house. My chest tightened. Too late: Vera was dead!

The car, however, turned out to be merely one of those mile-long Mercedes limos. Its three curbside doors were open. Men in teal uniforms, the image of a winged truck blazoned on their backs, were loading suitcases and boxes from the house. I wiped my forehead with a still-damp shirtsleeve. Behind the limo stood a truck, also in the process of being loaded.

Supervising the activity was a young woman with close-cropped dark hair and a wide, fleshy nose on which sat thick-framed black glasses. She was checking off items on a clipboard.

The white marble building looked stately and decorous, blessed by a serenity bubbling up from an inner reservoir of deep money.

"You are the grandson?" she asked.

I nodded.

"This way," she said, leading me in.

My impression on entering was that I had the wrong address. I was greeted by a blow of white light: the hallway's towering ceiling dropped a brilliant chandelier. A sweeping marble stairway beckoned. Everywhere men in teal rushed about with boxes. A pair struggled to maneuver a harpsichord down the stairs. The pink marble floor reflected a gilt-edged mirror to the left tipped at an angle so that anyone entering who glanced at it found himself matted and framed on the wall. Across, hung slightly higher, the portrait of a woman's face glared at visitors. The close-up, in primary colors, highlighted a grid of lines and creased skin webbing a fleshy mouth and pale eyes looking like they'd just glimpsed something awful yet intriguing in their neighbor's window.

The young woman had followed me, clutching her clipboard.

"The study is across the hall. You'll find Kij waiting," she said.

"Entschuldigen Sie," I said, milking the last of my German. "I wonder if you might tell me what's going on."

The young woman tapped the clipboard, explaining that Vera had decided she wanted to die in the village of Prypiat in Ukraine, where she'd been born. The trip was being arranged by her two sons, who had hired a train to carry her home. A triumphal return. An Eastern Parade.

"And so we're finished here?" she asked a mover, marking her pad.

The study door was open, but there was no light on in the high-ceilinged room, which was dark and as quiet as a cathedral.

"You know the world has gone to hell in a handbasket when you have to pay the devil for water," a voice rose up as though from a well, and I heard the pop of a bottle top, followed by a soft exhalation.

As my eyes adjusted to the dark—heavy curtains draped the long windows—I saw, miles away, on the other side of the room, a man splayed across a couch half the length of a train car.

He had a large face, unshaven, thick browed, and as I drew nearer, I saw his skin was pocked and coarse. A diamond stud in his nose caught the flare from his lighter. At his age, early sixties, it was both sinister and slightly embarrassing. His nose might have been broken more than once. He wiped it with the sleeve of a chocolate brown silk jacket. Something behind his teeth's yellow glaze and the cunning gaze looked familiar.

But of course. Uncle Kij.

Like almost every enclosed space in Europe back then, the room reeked of smoke seeping from the pores of the walls, the floors, the curtains, like sweat.

"There are cities in Asia where they're already selling oxygen. We should count ourselves lucky," Kij grunted.

My heels echoed on the pink marble floor. When I at last reached the couch, Kij leaned forward, thrusting out his hand.

"Your father will have told you about me?"

His grip was limp and damp. I felt I'd been handed a garden snake.

"Have one," he said, offering me a bottle of sparkling water.

"Very little, I'm afraid." I tried keeping cool, but things were moving fast. I gulped and dropped back into a leather wingback chair, then stared stupidly at the ceiling. Framed by dark molded wood, it looked like an early Rothko.

Unmoored, I drifted between time zones, wandering centuries. The air smelled of licorice and malt—maybe the leather—taking me back to Saturday afternoons at the movies.

"You're not really poor as worms, are you?"

I'd seen some absurd houses visiting college friends over the years, but never one like this. Not quite Sissinghurst, it seemed to stretch out for miles. I could almost hear the Black Sea lapping at its foundation. Two grand pianos stood head to head near the center of the room. A suit of armor commanded a corner. The place felt like a prop room for *Citizen Kane*. As we spoke, my fingers fretted the mottled calfskin.

"Mother never stopped poor-mouthing. You were expecting a hovel?"

I nodded, wondering what else I'd been misinformed about.

"The question," he turned to the young woman, who had just walked into the room, "is just how much he knows."

I hadn't heard her enter.

"I was wondering."

She faced the window, pulling back the curtain a bit, letting a trailer of light unfurl down the floor like a runner.

A thin, jittery chap in his forties, wearing a shabby blue suit and metal-rimmed glasses, with a black doctor's bag banging at his side, walked in behind her. Nearly bald, his few strands of hair, combed forward in bangs, looked wet. His left hand tugged at the tip of a graying walrus mustache. He went straight up to Kij and kissed him warmly on both cheeks.

"Dr. Stimpleman. An oncologist who would far rather be a general practitioner," Kij said, introducing us.

"When did I last see a doctor's bag?" I wondered aloud.

"That's his booze."

Dr. Stimpleman shrugged.

"Joining us for lunch, Eric?" Kij asked.

"Afraid not. Dropped by to say I'll be at the station tomorrow. Work to finish."

"Fine."

"Nice to meet you," he bowed in my direction. "Perhaps I'll see you tomorrow?"

He positively yanked at his mustache.

"Probably not," I shrugged.

"I'll say good-bye too," Lebed, the young woman with the clipboard, said, stepping up.

"How about a real drink?" Kij asked when we were alone.

"Isn't it a little early?"

"We're lunching with Vera at noon." He looked at his watch. "That's in ten minutes. You'll want a drink," he assured me.

— 2 —

I cleared my throat and looked around. The room seemed to spread to the outer edges of sight.

"So," I said, sitting down.

Kij smiled, flashing gold.

"You'd like to know about the Viennese branch of the family?" Kij said, relighting his cigar. "That is what brings you here, yes?

"*Sancho Panza*—best Cuban around," he flourished his trophy, tipping his ash into a standing tray near the sofa.

"How much do you know about the family business?"

"Nothing."

"Of course. How old are you?"

"Twenty-five."

"And you're in Europe for school?"

I nodded, explaining I'd come to England to study history.

"You're shocked to find we're not as poor as worms?"

"Not shocked," I said. "I've no idea where Father got his information. He never talked about you, I am sorry to say. I apologize for it."

"A historian," Kij said, gesturing with his cigar. "Why not family history? All history ever is, the chronicle of a few families."

I imagined Vera with her sons in 1945: the boys would have been seventeen or eighteen then. I wondered what this man had seen. Or, for that matter, done.

"When did you move to Vienna?" I asked.

He ignored my question, so I tried another:

"Why not fly to Kyiv?"

I say Kyiv so casually now, and did then, yet the word echoes inside me as though it were a piano whose keys had all been struck at once. At the time the city didn't quite exist in the mind of "the West." We weren't sure what it was, and it was funny to talk about it as though it were real.

A smoke ring dissolved near the ceiling.

"Planes mean just one thing to Vera."

Seeing my blank stare, he whispered:

"Bombs," he shut his eyes and nodded.

"That was almost fifty years ago," I said.

He smiled, flourishing his cigar.

"A very American observation. Time for lunch."

His face strained as he pushed himself up from the sofa.

"May I ask?"

"Feel free."

"How old is your mother?"

"Not that old. Late seventies. Nobody knows exactly. Says she's for-gotten her birth date. Around the time of the revolution, so-called. She was a very young mother. But she's sick. Eric says she should have died ages ago. Calls her Lady Lazarus."

He laughed nervously, then looked around as though fearing someone might have snuck into the room.

"We've been organizing this trip for months. Isn't easy dealing with the Soviets. Even now. Fortunately, Khoriv's our inside man there, and he knows his business."

"What business?"

"Did you bring a blazer?" Kij asked.

I shook my head. A jacket? It had been my plan to sleep in the open air, on trains, on the rooftops of ragged hotels and the floors of powdery ruins, and along the beaches of calamitous seas. I came to Europe to caress its glories with my own crude hands and eyes. My jacket had stayed in England.

"You can have one of mine," he said. "Now go wash."

Washing my face, I wondered how Mother was doing. Now I was travel-ing I wouldn't have time to call her regularly as I had from England.

I needed to shave, but the mirror in the bathroom had been removed and I'd left my pack in the study. This was the longest I'd been away from Massachusetts in my life. While my classmates fucked around and traveled, I worked, went to school, moved in with Charlotte. I hitchhiked in books, straying so deep I sometimes lost sight of the difference between them and real life. I knew what that girl on the train meant about novels. The world seduces with startling images whose shadows books show: there's a gull with a cat in its mouth, a two-legged dog in a wheelchair; a man taller than a doorway; a child without arms or legs singing itself to sleep at a bus depot; a car burning along the highway; a willow in sunlight dragging its fingers over a lake while around it flutter thousands of tiny tan moths.

And in the bathroom window at this moment a horse and buggy trotted along the cobbled street as though they had no idea they'd been obsolete for nearly a century. Save yourselves, I wanted to cry through the glass.

Instead, I scrubbed the residue of travel from my face.

The dining-room door was opened by a pretty, dark-haired girl in a white uniform, hobbling noticeably. The limp made her seem both hurt and available.

"You're the new nurse," Kij smiled. "What's your name?"

"Lilah."

She lowered her eyes and stood behind the door as we crossed the threshold.

An oblong table in the middle of the room was covered in white cloth.

As soon as we sat down, a male servant in a silver vest appeared and asked what we wanted to drink. I ordered water; my cousin, whiskey.

The cutlery was heavy and monogrammed and the china painted with pink-skirted ladies under parasols.

When the door at the other end of the room opened, Kij jumped to his feet as though the Pope had arrived.

"Greetings from the very old world," a familiar voice announced in thickly accented English.

There she stood at last.

I rose.

Although she leaned on a cane, she gave the impression of a tall woman who was anything but fragile. She wore a plain black dress—she'd never shed her widow's garb, it seemed; her sparse bluish gray hair hung limp around her shoulders. She had a strong profile—thick lips, big nose, wide-set eyes. I recognized my father's high cheekbones. Whatever Vera had suffered in life, she had clearly not been beaten down by it. Or if she had, she'd sprung right back up.

Half a century rose up between us—fifty years of war, famine, destruction. Crucible moments of passion, insight, and hope. The old are time capsules. In her presence, I could almost hear the rattling of horse carts, machine guns, bells at Easter.

As I wondered whether to shake her hand or kiss it, Vera interceded.

"Give me a hug, young man."

I hadn't expected that.

Neither had I imagined her knowing as much English as she did. But then, the House of Windsor, which had ruled Britain for almost the last three centuries, originated in Hanover—and all wars between England and Germany were in a sense civil wars.

Her voice was as it had sounded over the phone: deep and guttural. She'd seen things I never would, Lord willing.

She smiled, her mouth aglitter with gold.

"You Americans all look so healthy. So nice to see you alongside my son," she sighed, glancing at Kij.

The sheer forcefulness of her features made the show of feeling a surprise.

I'd expected our conversation to flow, the reservoir of questions built up in each of us bursting forth. Instead, for the next twenty minutes we concentrated on the remarkable food that kept appearing before us dish after dish. I bit into warm bread and asparagus sprinkled with caviar and butter-soft beef and scoops of creamed potatoes, washing it all down with a Riesling. There was a Sacher torte for dessert brought straight from the hotel for which it was named, only a dozen blocks away.

My mother's recipes had cleaved close to the basics of Irish cuisine, neither Charlotte nor I had cooked much, and my experience with food was limited. To me this seemed a feast.

"Will your president drag the world to war?" Vera finally asked.

We talked about the Middle East. She seemed well informed, full of opinions.

Kij tried interjecting several times, and each salvo was met with a skeptical glance or a sharp word.

"My sons run a business. Our family has a stake in the world," she replied when I praised her engagement.

Finally, after the plates had been cleared and the coffee served, Vera asked:

"And how's your father?"

The tail of a pink scar peered up above the collar of her black dress.

I didn't answer directly. It was too soon to break the news of his death. I had to find out about *her* health first. His presence, though, crowded the room.

I said I had a letter for her.

"You'll bring it to me after our naps."

Kij sighed, dropping his napkin on the plate. He pushed himself up with effort and hurried over to help his mother out of her seat.

I stayed, while the servant cleared the table. I'd never met a servant before. Plenty of people had them back in the States, of course; nevertheless, they seemed to me throwbacks to another era, more appropriate here than at home.

"Where are you from?" I asked the young man, who must have been my age.

"Turkey."

"Istanbul?"

"Ankara."

"You've worked for Vera a long time?"

"Oh no, I was hired by Mr. Hordinski."

"Which one?"

"Mr. Khoriv."

"What's he like?"

"Mr. Khoriv is a very great man."

"A very great man!" I said. I hadn't expected that.

"Everybody would like to work for Mr. Khoriv."

"Do many people work for him?"

"Thousands. Around the world," he said, narrowing his eyes as though wondering how it was I didn't know the details of Mr. Khoriv's life.

"Maybe millions! He's a great man. You are from America?"

I nodded.

"America is very great," he said. "But it does not understand us. It is so young. It hasn't suffered enough yet to know what is the world. Turkey is also very great. And it has suffered indeed . . ."

I was about to begin a political discussion about the Armenians when Kij returned.

"She looks really good," I said. All things considered, I meant.

"You should have seen her when the door closed," Kij replied. "She crumpled. Practically had to drag her. It's like seeing Everest sag."

"She's going to Kyiv to die," I said. "Is this something she expects to happen on cue?"

"Wouldn't surprise me," he sighed. "Mother has friends."

– 3 –

An hour later, I was awakened by a knock on the door. I rose with a start, sending a leather-bound copy of Goethe's *Faust* in translation to the floor. I'd fallen asleep in the study, on the same couch where Kij had been sitting. I'd been asked to wait there while they prepared a room for me upstairs.

"We weren't really sure you'd come. Americans are terribly unpredictable, I've found," Kij had said.

Lilah, wearing white sneakers and pink socks, leaned against the lintel with a cigarette in her hand, arabesques of smoke lingering in the stale air. Back home, the nurses I knew were all smokers too.

"Vera will see you now."

So I was summoned.

"Just a minute," I said, reaching into my backpack for Father's envelope. But I couldn't find it. I opened the bag, shook out its contents. I looked under my seat. Had I lost it? Had it been stolen? I panicked—I'd come here to deliver it, after all—but then I calmed myself down.

Lilah rapped on the open door impatiently, and I got up, digging my hands into my pockets. I'd look again when I returned.

Her hips swung like a boat on the waves.

"Remember, she's more medicated than a factory chicken," Kij had warned me. "Percocet. And probably opium."

———•———

Vera's bedroom was furnished in *fin de siècle* opulence. It was as though I'd stepped into the private quarters of some nineteenth-century industrialist. A heavy burgundy velvet curtain draped the window across from which, in the middle of the room, stood a large, four-poster bed.

"Pull the curtain all the way shut," she said, switching on a lamp.

The room was crowded with richly damasked chairs. Tchotchkes littered every surface. There were ivory Buddhas from India and soapstone cats from Egypt and jade monks from China. The atmosphere was voluptuous. A cockatoo swayed on its perch in a huge yet delicate cage shaped like a mosque. On the wall hung a small oil of a boat on a river.

She leaned over to the table where the lamp stood and picked up an enamel box from which she drew a dark brown cigarillo without taking her eyes off me.

"Care for one?"

"Thanks, no," I said.

"I shouldn't either. They're killing me. Lucky to make it to Kyiv. But so what? As in life, so in death."

"You said there was a letter?"

"I can't find it right now. Money, too."

"Well, as to money . . ." Her hand gestured at the room. "But I would be very happy for a note from him. He was sweetness itself, your father."

Sweetness itself, I thought. Already the trip felt worth it.

"Sweetest of all," she repeated. "That's why I sent him away."

"Sit," she pointed to a straight-backed chair in the narrow alley beside her.

"I'd love to hear about him," I said, resolving to complete my mission.

She smiled and leaned forward, pushing her fingers through my hair, which I'd let grow all month.

"Surely your news is more recent. Your father never went bald, did he?"

I stayed silent. If I felt oddly close to this woman I'd only just met, it was partly because I'd imagined her poor and needy, my protective instincts stuck to a notion reality failed to dislodge.

"Somewhere in that box"—she gestured toward a chest at the foot of the bed—"photographs. I knew you'd come eventually. So I found a few pictures of your father. Does he still play the piano?"

The last thing I could imagine was my father playing the piano—yet he'd been the one who sent me to lessons.

"I'll take the pictures with us."

"Why did you decide to send him away? Why not one of the others?"

She seemed surprised by the question. Her sagging cheeks puckered into a fish face.

"I don't even remember, tell you the truth." She looked at the ground thoughtfully, puffing on her cigarillo.

She was lying and wanted me to know it.

"What happened to him?"

She fixed her green gaze on me.

"That's how it is in America," she shook her head. "So much distraction. Who has time to look back? Looking back is natural for us. We don't even need to look back. We just look around."

I thought of explaining that Father had draped a black cloth over the rearview mirror of memory, that as a historian I did nothing but look over my shoulder.

She shook her head.

"Don't blame him."

"Your husband was killed too," I said.

She leaned forward.

"Lots of people were," she said, wincing.

"Are you in pain?"

"Pain?" She smiled and went on. "Your father served in the British army. He had no choice."

She put out her cigarillo. Her eyes had teared.

"Lucky to have such a son. Your mother must be very pretty. An American girl?

"I'm glad I helped," she repeated, persuading me somehow the opposite was true.

"You have other grandchildren?" I asked.

"Khoriv's remarried a peasant girl. Peasant *child*. She's too young. He's too old. Unless he's managed a miracle, I'll never see that fruit. Don't put it past him. That boy has skills."

She sighed, turning her head as though falling into a pocket of space buried inside her.

Little she said made sense to me at the time.

"I remember my own mother's death," she continued. "I was six. Childhood ended that morning. I was alone in the room with her body. Her eyes stayed open. Later I told everyone I saw it rise through the roof. Fooled even myself because when I close my eyes I see it floating amid the rafters and straw. I hoped one day I'd have a little girl whose childhood I'd prolong forever.

"Empty this," she said, sitting up with the ashtray and thrusting it at me. "I'm starting to spill."

I rose, scouting a wastebasket.

"After she died, Father remarried. My stepmother hated us. She's the one who sold me."

"Sold you?"

"People were starving. Occasionally someone got lucky and met a man with money. Not half as bad as what the Chinese do to their girls. I was twelve, old enough to know what was happening. I was sold.

"He took me to Bucharest, where he was from. Man proposes, God disposes. Why He always sides with men I don't know. You look uncomfortable in that chair."

I'd been squirming.

"I'll live."

She nodded.

"I've never told anyone this story," she said, coughing. "I've heard others tell theirs so many times. No doubt life happened as they said. But things also happened the way I remember. Only I've never talked about it."

It dawned on me that few people would ever understand how the world looked and felt to her.

"Why not fly to Kyiv?" I asked.

Vera ran her long fingers up and down her neck, its creased skin like a loose, dry udder. She leaned back, narrowed her eyes, and gave me a sharp look.

"Never. Damn planes. Bloody bombs. Nothing worse. Nothing more cowardly than the pricks flying a thousand feet above their targets and dumping their load on people they'll never see—alive or dead. I still dream of the bastards. You don't forget these things. Unless you leave. Your father was smart to get away. Tell him this from me, will you?"

I sat up.

How would Vera react if she knew her son were dead?

"Tell him not to look back too much. Tell him he's right. Tell him: keep moving."

She shook her head, then smiled at me.

"Do you need anything? Another drink? A little opium?" She flashed her gold teeth. "Marvelous drug. Leave it to governments to keep it from people."

I felt myself getting caught up again in someone else's game, swept into a different world. I didn't mind. At twenty-five, a man saw wrong turns as his due, sure he'd find his way clear, led by some slutty Ariadne, like Vera's nurse, for instance, spelling *let's fuck* on his back with her nails. It was a privilege even I took for granted.

"There's a freedom you've never known," she added, her eyes on the curtain. "Living in the moment without insurance policies or laws nibbling away at you. You people plan for death right from the start. For the money of it!

"You're a generation of lawyers and accountants, I swear."

The loose silk of her cream-colored nightgown slapped the air like a wing.

"I grew up in a war. It changes you. You pamper yourselves into a stupor. Think you're doing yourselves a favor. You don't know how fast things can change."

I looked around the room. Pampered? Who was she to talk? Yet nothing ever stopped people from talking.

Pellets of rain banged the window.

"Thank goodness," she said, hearing the sound. "I was afraid the woods would burn. Been so dry."

"It's rained nearly every day."

"Really? I don't get out so much anymore."

The cockatoo flapped its wings and said something in German.

"Good, Johnson. I named it for the wife of your president. Lady Bird Johnson came to Vienna once. I was in the front row when her limousine passed. Something about her I trusted. She had depth."

The nurse limped in to say tea was ready. Did Vera want it brought in?

"No need. I'll get up."

Vera rose slowly.

"Forgive me for not dressing."

Walking, she leaned heavily on the nurse.

"Stop."

"What?"

"Stop looking at me as though there's something sinister in this. The company of a woman, even an old one, is a good thing. Always. You Westerners," she muttered.

I wasn't sure what she was talking about.

"There's half a century between us, boy. Not easily bridged. How can I tell you what you should know? You should know what people can do to each other.

"I don't consider myself one," she continued. "A Westerner. I lived in the ruins of the Ottoman Empire. Gone by the time I was seven. It's a different vision. Worse for women? Some ways, yes. But there are compensations. And what makes you think *your* women so fine? Your armies have killed hundreds of thousands of women and children, and what have your women ever done about it? Has even one ever burned herself to protest?"

"You're Muslim?"

"Of course not," she shook her large head, clucking her tongue as though chiding a child. "I'm a God-fearing Christian who knows the secrets learned only by traveling through the land of the dead."

She spat over her shoulder. Then she fixed her eyes on me.

"What I'm saying is, whoever you think you are, whatever your father and mother named you, whatever you may have learned in school to support that identity—you are not that. You are something entirely different. Your tragedy is you'll never know it. If you're not careful, you'll always stay little James."

She stared at me until I felt myself starting to melt. I wondered if she'd begun hallucinating yet. Kij had mentioned Percocet and opium.

At the same time, what she said reminded me of my talk with Selena.

"I wish I'd sent my sons to school. Instead, they grew up around my business. A different kind of education. Such handsome boys. "

"What business?"

Suddenly she looked very tired.

"We're in the service industry," she said casually, turning her head to the window.

She stopped. I studied her profile—Jeanne Moreau fast-forwarded a hundred years.

Finally I asked again: "What happened to my father in England?"

For a while she said nothing, staring at the curtain as though she could see through it.

Her eyes furrowed with a hardness I hadn't noticed before.

"What's the name of the woman you're staying with there?" she asked.

"Marian. Marian Brimsley."

"Gordon once. Ask Marian Gordon-Brimsley," she said. She was breathing heavily now.

"I already have," I said.

"Ask her again. I'm tired. I don't want any tea," she said to Lilah. "Time for bed."

———•—•———

Back in the living room, I let myself exhale. I hadn't realized how tense I'd been in her presence.

Sifting through the contents of my backpack once more, I discovered the letter embroiled in a tangle of underwear.

I stared at the strange, slanted symbols running across line after line over the graph paper on which he wrote. They detonated a minefield of complex feelings. Whatever Father may have done, I would bring it to light; I wouldn't inherit his sins—if there were any. I had hit the books, studied the wars between the Catholics, the Orthodox, the Jews, and the Muslims. The region was blood soaked. I would see what there was to be seen.

Unlike Mother's side of the family, he left me little to work with. The eighties had been the years of "the Troubles" back in Ireland. I listened often to Uncle Bill rooting for the guys in the gun trade while cursing collaborators who, in his eyes, included the third- and fourth-generation Irish American opponents of armed struggle. He quoted Heaney: "Whatever you say, say nothing," as though warning me to keep it zipped and not go blabbing the family's table talk.

As if any of my friends in college gave half a fuck.

I'd have to ask Marian again after all.

FOUR

The Wolves of Europe

In the cities of Europe, wolves are making a comeback. I take it as a good sign. The future belongs to wolves and to women. For too long now man's rule has savaged the landscape. Maybe this round, we'll watch and we'll learn.

There was a time when I kept turning to others—to Marian, Vera, my father—to tell me their stories because I knew they were also mine. The habit of gathering information and piecing it together had stuck. Now, I thought as I finished this morning's work at the embassy, my own story was entangled with the tragedies of the soldiers we'd hurled into a smoking lime pit, handing them all the wrong tools, and insisting they dig. Silvia hadn't buzzed me again, so I caught up on my reading, sifting through the files slowly, wading in horrors that should have been fictions.

On my way to the Hawelka for our noon meeting, I was followed—stalked by something more compromising than a wolf. A yellow scarf caught my eye once too often, until it seemed tied to my heels like cans to a car. Was it the person who sent the files, or someone who knew I had them, someone whom I glimpsed several times in the shadows? Then I remembered the girl at the crossroad this morning I'd mistaken for Selena.

Being followed was in either case a novel experience. It made me feel strangely important.

Entering the café, I spotted my friends in the corner. A balloon of smoke from Akash's cigar hung over our gang. Elbowing each other around the table were Lars, who worked as a stringer for AP; Jacqueline, a speech writer from the South African Embassy; Tamara, a Slovenian sculptor; Michel, whose indeterminate status made us suspect he worked for either

French Intelligence, or the Mossad, or both. Martina, an editor at the Austrian Ministry of Health, rounded our circle that day.

I approached slowly, preparing my story.

"Can you believe it? I was actually followed," I said to Dr. Akash, who'd agreed to take me to Mustafa the Bean after lunch.

Akash's decades serving the Red Crescent in the Middle East had tempered him. At sixty, he was our senior member. He alone wore a jacket, though threadbare, and a tie that flagged his bachelorhood, as no woman could possibly have picked it. His even voice, often misread as resigned, was the timbre of patience. The bleached stones of Petra and his Jordanian upbringing stressed the long view. In his pocket he always carried a trilobite fossil. When our conversations grew heated, he pulled out the stone and passed it around. "Two hundred and fifty million years old. A little bug. And it's still here," he'd say.

"What's in those files of yours? Tell us."

"Yes, do," Martina seconded.

Photographs. Depositions.

". . . signed before attorneys?" Martina asked.

"No."

"Then why call them that?"

"Because that's how they read."

"So someone's been gathering this stuff for a while?"

"But why give it to you?"

I didn't mention I had the files with me. They needed to be scanned, digitized, preserved.

"This person—or *persons*—knows you're not part of the current regime," said Lars, fiddling with his BlackBerry. As it never rang, I wondered if he was having trouble at work or at home.

Martina, who was sleeping with Lars and might have been a cause of his domestic woes, cut in:

"Maybe they're trying to trap you."

"Why? What's to be gained?" Lars asked.

"You know how offices are," Martina replied, playing with her lighter, avoiding his eyes. "A smirk at the cooler. A crack at the Christmas party after too much Liebfraumilch."

"Leaking classified documents would make a swell charge. They'll hustle you straight back to Arkansas, or wherever it is you're from."

"Maybe someone's been putting this together for a long time and needs a reliable pigeon to drop off the goods. A lot of the world is paying attention these days," offered Michel.

My friends had engaged the subject and were enjoying themselves. I didn't relish spoiling their sport. Too often my father delivered the bad news about what we couldn't afford to do, or wouldn't because he didn't want to.

"Could be the ambassador himself! Who know what he thinks?"

"So you were followed?" Martina brought us full circle.

I nodded. I hadn't felt this adrenaline since my trip to Kyiv with Vera.

"You scared?"

"Then there are the e-mails," I added, shaking my head *no* to her question.

"What do they say?"

"What Michel just did, that people are paying attention."

"Maybe it's all Michel!"

We turned to him. He smiled enigmatically behind his cigarette, no doubt wishing he'd thought of it.

"Looks like no matter what, I'll betray someone," I said.

"And save someone else."

"How do you decide? How do you choose?"

Jacqueline adjusted her engagement ring, both shamed and emboldened by the ruby's size.

"So what will you do?"

I said nothing. A woman walked in with a Russian wolfhound on a leash. She sat down at the table next to us.

Then Lars asked:

"You think they know what they're doing?"

"Who?"

"The pilots dropping their precision-guided bombs. How many would keep doing their job if they knew what happened on the other end?"

"But most people today believe work and only work humanizes them. Work is god. Fail duty and face hellfire. Can you blame them?" offered Tamara.

A group at the bar had entered an even more heated discussion. Voices were raised, glasses slammed to the table.

"We already asked these questions once," Akash pointed out.

"When?"

"Nuremberg."

In the crevice of silence I tried shifting the conversation I'd started.

"How's your mother, Tamara?" I asked.

Her mother had had a stroke recently. Last time I saw her she was returning to Ljubljana to care for her.

"Much better, thanks. Don't change the subject. Or be cleverer about it."

All right. They wanted to know. They couldn't use the information without the documents. I'd kept them to myself long enough. So I told a few of the stories. One report, from a private who printed everything in block letters, described riding through Baghdad with a group of soldiers and stopping to watch a soccer game. He and his buddies picked a team of locals to root for, cheering them on with Midwestern gusto. When their boys lost to the others, though, the soldiers grew glum. They were sick of losing. When would these towel-heads stop screwing up? Tired of backing losers, they picked up their guns and shot them. They killed every member of the team they had supported. They lowered their guns and hailed the terrified winners. And then they shot them too.

The files contained dozens of similar tales, corroborated by hundreds of men. Rape, looting, contract hits. I mentioned one other, a game played by two drugged-out snipers called "How Low Can You Go?" The object was to see who dared hit the youngest target. The winner was the shooter who scored the pregnant girl crossing the street.

My friends listened, frowning. Their reactions weren't what I'd expected. I'd spooked them. I'd spoiled their afternoon. But of course, I was an American. What else did I know how to do? They'd asked me to tell them, but they hadn't wanted to know. They didn't want to be taken seriously. They resented me for missing the cues. One by one they began making excuses. Lars had a story to file. Martina had to file Lars. Jacqueline was late for a meeting. Because, how could they use this information?

It's not like such stories were news. But who'd expected it from the Americans after Vietnam?

Soon Dr. Akash alone remained, his cigar charred to a stub. As I was brooding, Herr Hawelka carried over a cognac, put his hand on my shoulder, and sighed, *Ja ja.*

Not one of my friends had presumed to advise me on what I should do.

"Shall we visit the Bean?" Dr. Akash asked. "Real horror is healthier, don't you find? It's talk that's depressing."

The air outside had cooled considerably as the sun dropped behind a platoon of passing clouds. On the street some people had retrieved their long coats.

"The spring breeze," Akash said, drawing up his collar as we walked down the cobbled street of the Old City. "In Aleppo once I had a crush on a girl I called *Naseem*. It's the name of a breeze. She returns whenever a certain kind of wind brushes my cheek."

We were a block from the café when the yellow scarf reappeared, fluttering toward us, followed by a dark-haired woman who couldn't have been older than twenty-five. Herself a kind of breeze.

She blocked my way. She wore low-rider jeans and flashed a bare midriff below her denim jacket. Somehow the scarf was perfectly congruent. She stared at me with dark eyes framed by green shadow, whispering: "Do something. Try."

Then she whirled on her heels and disappeared.

Akash put his hand on my shoulder.

"Who was that?"

"I think I know her," I said, rubbing my thigh. "I've met her before."

So this was my phantom Selena. The real Selena would be in her mid-thirties now.

"No, no pressure at all," Akash shook his head in sympathy.

This morning I'd looked up Selena Gordon on Google: 477,000 listings for that name. Yet in less than five minutes I found her—the photo confirmed it. She's a doctor—just like her mother—based in Ramallah, working for the World Health Organization. As recently as last year, she'd given a talk before some EU group in Vienna.

"Let's grab a cab," Akash said, ditching the stub.

The Turkish driver professed not to know where the hospital was, so Akash leaned forward to guide him.

Nearing St. Anna's, Akash grunted at the driver and sat back. He turned to his favorite subject: the sanctions. The sanctions obsessed him. He couldn't get over them. He didn't understand how anyone could.

A specialist in blood diseases, Akash had come to the Children's Hospital to work in a new program developed by his Austrian colleagues. Initially the project focused on kids in southern Iraq stricken with leukemia. Trying to work in Basra where sanctions made it impossible for doctors to get the equipment they needed was, he said, like being forced to take part in the making of a snuff film.

"The bloody American on the UN Sanctions Committee vetoed everything. He knew we were trying to bring in a blood centrifuge, yet he had the balls to claim its use would be military. I asked him if he believed the insurgents intended to spray their enemies with blood instead of drawing it?"

We got out at the entrance.

"I'll get it," I said.

Akash nodded, continuing:

"But this was part of the fallout from the '91 war. Half a million died from those damned sanctions. One of your secretaries of state said on national television: 'We think it was worth it.' Nice crop of people you've harvested."

A sudden gust knocked off a man's hat, and he scrambled to retrieve it before it was flattened by the tram.

Akash paused a minute at the threshold. He adjusted his tie, brushed off his jacket. The hospital was his home. He would show it respect. The electric door waited.

Around us hummed the busy life of a sleek, open-hearted facility—here the stuffed toys are implanted with monitors and regularly check the patients' vital signs, transmitting them wirelessly to a bank of screens at the nurses' station down the hall.

Mustafa the Bean was Akash's personal charge. Akash had been walking toward his hospital in Basra when he heard an explosion not fifty feet off. On reaching the scene, he found Mustafa curled in a ball, bleeding everywhere. He understood at once the boy had plucked a cluster bomb. By the time they reached the operating room, the surgeon had to amputate. The child lost both arms and legs. All that remained was the limbless nub of a nine-year-old boy with lashes long as butterfly wings.

Yet he survived. Soon the doctors were feeling guilty and the child was trying to cheer them up by telling jokes he'd picked up living on the streets. An orphan, he couldn't explain what happened to his parents because he didn't know. One day they simply never came home. Akash, whose second language was Arabic, arranged to have Mustafa flown to Vienna. That had been more than a year ago.

To meet a ten-year-old Iraqi quadruple amputee is, tragically, not so difficult in this world. Few, however, tell dirty jokes in three languages. The doctors had been teaching the boy English and German over the last year. I was just one of many tutors Akash enlisted. He hoped eventually to send him to study in England.

"Next to Stephen Hawking, he's Rocky Balboa."

A digitally altered photograph of the famous physicist sitting around a table playing cards with Einstein and Newton hung on the wall to the right of the boy's bed.

"Welcome, welcome," the Bean cried, seeing us. "You gentlemen happy to know I vocation. Vocation right word, yes? I be translation machine," said the boy. "Like computer with tongue, what you think, Mr. Pak-man? Snip snip, Dr. Schneider said, and I fit in laptop. Voice activated. Good, yes?"

The bald boy smiled.

"You'll have to learn a few dozen more languages," I warned.

"Look," Mustafa gestured with his eyes to the night table, at a ziggurat of boxed language tapes—Spanish, French, Italian, Dutch, Norwegian, Swedish, Polish, and Czech.

"All doctors bringing their languages. I expect call from UN."

I promised to spread the word, even as I realized I'd forgotten the gift I'd planned to pick up.

After a half hour's banter, I shook hands with Akash and meandered back to the embassy, making one more stop on my way.

Back at the embassy, I pull the files from my briefcase and slip them under Silvia's stack. Then I take out the memory stick: so much information packed into one rectangular inch.

Weighing it in my palm like a stone, I wonder how long before our entire lives are scored on chips implanted at birth. Soon we'll have records of everything. Imagine the boon—and the burden—for historians. Still, it would have saved me a lot of trouble in Father's case.

When I discovered the existence of another woman besides Mother in my father's life—of several women, brothers, uncles, a childhood, a history I never knew—I felt stunned and betrayed.

I wonder why. It's not as if he'd told me this had never happened. His sin of omission from his point of view was no sin at all.

Marian was the other woman. That much I did learn from Vera. But what had happened between them I wouldn't know until returning to England.

FIVE

The London Stone

(Marian, 1936–1946)

~ 1 ~

I fell in love with Andrew even before we met the morning he got off the boat in Liverpool. He must have been ten—there was some confusion about the year of his birth; I was twelve. The day was cold and gray and the water knocked the boats against the piers. Everything—the buildings, the ships, the people in hats—looked huge, overbearing. You felt you were in the middle of a party for those invisible giants Mother warned me about when I was younger. She said they lived somewhere above the earth. We were their toys. Why can't we see them? Because they're invisible, silly. That was the best she could come up with.

He was as lost as any boy you'll find, yet there he stood in his torn black coat, a funny little knit cap pulled down over his ears so that all you saw were his blue eyes and pink mouth—the lips already thick, sensuous, though naturally nothing like that crossed my mind then—smiling! He didn't look in the least frightened.

Later I learned what he'd been through with the sailor. But at least he had the chance to escape.

At the bottom of the walkway he set down his duffle bag. As he yanked off his cap to scratch his head an officer hustled by, knocking him against one of the piers. The cap flew from his hands and dropped into the water. I watched him sink nimbly to the ground and fish it out with a piece of wire. Wringing it dry as he could, he pulled it back on.

What did I know of love at twelve, you might ask? But I knew a bit. Because of Daddy's work, we'd moved often. Each dislocation and every home taught me how fully the heart can entangle itself with the world. I'd left behind friends, rivers, and houses. Each had claimed some part of me. So much of what once stood around me solid as Stonehenge had already melted into air. The real world of grown-ups was even flimsier than the tales they told to shut us up at night. And now this boy was docking as though our family were a port of call for any ship—which, thanks to Mother, we were.

Then, on top of that, he turned out to be so clever, so charming, so gifted. He learned quickly. Father and Mother soon grew fond of him, though it was hard to say with Father at first—he was away so often, and even when he was home he seemed distant, swathed in the fog of a busy man.

When I asked Mother who the boy was, she said he was fleeing a place where the fighting between the giants was especially bad. We *had* to help him out.

Mother, I said, I'm too old for that.

Well, you're too young for history, she replied. Her manner was severe. She pushed her glasses up her nose. She was one of those women who shroud their looks in glasses and glum dresses with big collars to ward off the would-be suitors circling round in Daddy's absence.

It was clear the boy would need a protector.

How did we know him?

Daddy had met him on his travels.

It was some years before I figured out what Daddy's relationship with Andrew's mother had been—and then I wondered how it was that an army of orphans weren't living with us, because Daddy spent a lot of time helping mothers and children in trouble.

My brothers hadn't come along that afternoon—I'm not sure why—Aidan, the baby, might have been sick. In any case, I was the eldest—Mother knew that if I approved, all would be well in Hyde Park.

Lady Lindenberry, who lived around the corner in the grandest house on the block—its ballroom was said to be the largest in Europe, or at least in London—had dropped by that morning to see Mummy. She invited us to bring our charge to tea. Everyone was curious about this new Gordon acquisition. Years later, I understood they'd suspected he was one of my father's bastards.

My crucial discovery at our first encounter—and this may have been when my heart flared—was that the boy dripping water on my shoe as he extended his hand with a bow did not speak English. In any case, he made a valiant effort. He shut his eyes and tucked his chin deep into his collar, so that I could see the sopping top of his black cap, and thrust forward a trembling wet hand that felt like a frog and mumbled something that sounded like *Plechadkayfamakeacquians,* but that Mother must have understood because she immediately prompted me:

And aren't you pleased to make his acquaintance, too?

I made a face and turned away. That was how I showed my feelings in those days.

And so we took him home.

That night I lay awake in my room listening to Thor, our bullmastiff, snoring. I could feel the new presence in the house. We had over the years sheltered ducks and rabbits, as well as countless cats and dogs, but this was the first time we'd taken in a human being. Part of my nightly ritual included summoning before my mind's eye the faces of every member of the household, living and dead (both the grandparents I had known were gone by then) and imagining them standing before me, while I moved up the row, giving each a kiss. It was my way of reuniting our scattered tribe. That evening Andrew joined the procession.

There are few situations more delightful to a child than having a new companion who does not speak one's language—it's a bit like acquiring a very clever pet, who knows he's dependent on you and dare not bite.

My brothers quickly agreed with me that we liked Andrew—I didn't need to do much diplomatic work there. Bulwer and Sebastian were game, and Aidan, the baby, too young to vote.

That year, Andrew became our project.

We could bring him to school in a cage, Sebastian suggested.

Brilliant, Bulwer parroted his elder. We could have whips and riding crops to poke him just to show the others he doesn't bite. He stuck his tongue between two crooked rows of teeth.

Doesn't he? Are you so sure? I played along.

If he bites, I say we cut off his ear, Bulwer proposed.

His ear? Makes no bloody sense at all. Why would you cut off someone's ear if they bit you? When a dog bites you, do you cut off its ear?

Why, I bite it right back, that's what I do, bluffed Bulwer.

Sebastian shook his head:

Stop giggling. You sound like a girl. When a dog bites, we put it down. If Andrew were to bite one of us, I'm afraid Mummy wouldn't have any choice but to put him down.

Like they did to Schnitzel?

Schnitzel had been the dachshund we'd had in Belgrade. For some reason Daddy wanted us to know that our departure was costing the dog his life. Mother tried denying it, but I believed Daddy. He was teaching us not to be sentimental. It was the first time the idea of death had appeared before me so starkly. Later, when I learned Father had to watch the executions in Palestine, I got sick.

Despite the teasing—most of which went on between us while Andrew was out of the room—we set about doing what we could to help the boy along. First thing was to teach him to speak English. We took slabs of poster board and cut them into tombstones, and on each we wrote one of the letters of the alphabet. We called it the alphabet graveyard.

The alphabet, I mimed to Andrew—he knew how to read in his own language, so there were concepts we could build on—the alphabet was just a series of graves, I said.

He nodded politely.

We spread the tombstones out around the living room, propping them on furniture, doors, and mantels.

And you, I said to the boy, whose expression was both hopeful and wary—you knew he would be watchful all his life—And you, I said, are now in the land of the dead. Up to you to bring the dead letters to life. To do that you have to put them together to spell words. You are the sorcerer's apprentice. You want to sit? Conjure a chair. But you have to know the word for it, how to spell it. . . .

We wandered around the house for hours as Andrew learned how to animate the world around him by manipulating the twenty-six symbols we use to grasp a place that supports whales and tanks, crickets and queens.

Watching a child learn to speak is a spectacle like seeing snow for the first time, or tasting the sea. My own daughter was a slow learner who said hardly a word until she was five when suddenly sentences of exquisite syntactic suppleness began to stream from her lips.

But watching Andrew build a world with the raw materials of language was a wonder. I saw that however we may define ourselves, once we learn another language, we are changed.

One day, while Lady Lindenberry was visiting Mother, we decided to make Andrew perform for her. By then our game had evolved. He appeared to have mastered spelling with telepathic rapidity and had moved on to bigger things. So while Mother and her friend sat in their chairs, we gathered a number of objects and set them down in the middle of the room. Andrew's challenge was to make up a sentence about them. He astonished the entire company by reciting, without missing a beat, a couplet improvised on the spot:

A book, a feather, and a chamberpot:
Three semi-wise men's gifts to Camelot.

There was laughter, applause. But the fact that he said Camelot—which wasn't a vocabulary word we'd dredged up—made me suspicious. While Mother and her friend applauded the performance, I resolved to confront my star pupil.

I waited until after supper. Then I went up to his room and knocked on his door.

There was a dictionary in his hand when he opened it. But no amount of diligence could have taught him to rhyme so quickly.

You little cheater!

When he blushed, I knew I was right.

You already knew the language.

Eyes to the floor, Andrew explained that back home English studies began in first grade. By the time he arrived he knew enough to read Edgar Wallace in the original. He showed me one of the popular novels. The book was weathered and water stained.

Why didn't you say anything?

He explained that he had never spoken with a native before, and he'd worried that what he'd learned was all wrong. Our methods certainly differed from the lessons he'd received from the seventy-year-old spinster back home, who'd probably taught herself from books, and whose chief credential seemed to be that she'd once traveled through England where she'd glimpsed Queen Victoria. How was anyone there to know if what she said or taught were true, or pure myth?

He apologized for having deceived us.

Promise me you'll never do it again, I insisted.

Despite the deceit, his story touched me.

Won't tell your brothers, will you?
I looked at him, remembering his wet cap.
But you must promise to tell me the truth. Always.
The tips of his ears stained with iodine.
He promised.

— 2 —

We went to different schools, of course. At St. Hilda's I learned how little likely I was ever to become a scholar. My temperament, my teachers observed, was artistic. Today this might sound like a virtue, but then it was meant to keep me in my place. In time I learned to stifle even it—which may be why I put such stock in Selena's patient, sure unfurling. Nobody worried much about what I did—not even Mummy, who never went to university herself, yet who should have urged me on.

Andrew was sent, along with Sebastian and Bulwer, to the City of London School for Boys on the Victoria Embankment. When he was fourteen, he joined the Officers Training Corps while my two brothers both elected to sign on with the Boy Scouts. In the OTC he wore a uniform to drills twice a week and learned to shoot a .22. We watched him marching as part of the Lord Mayor's Show that year. At the same time he studied hard and took top honors in most every subject.

When the Blitz began, his school moved out to Marlborough, and day students suddenly became boarders. The boys didn't like being away, knowing the women were exposed, but Mother wouldn't leave her house and insisted her sons remain with their class.

You will have heard enough about the "great generation" back in America, I'm sure. Don't believe the PR. We were not a very great group by any measure. The history of Europe offers a great boneyard of examples, with killing fields everywhere. But, as it happened, from September 1940 until the following spring, we watched the skies for more than clouds. That was the season it rained fire. The first day of the air war, nearly a thousand planes shed their bombs. Hitler dreamed decadent London would quickly surrender. After all, we hadn't been invaded in centuries. We'd grown soft, he was sure of it—he'd forgotten the millions who'd died in the trenches during the last war in which he himself had fought and been wounded.

One night Mummy, Aidan, and I joined several thousand of our neighbors down in the tube shelters dodging the shower of bombs. The smell of so many bodies clustered together was overpowering—I felt like an old sock at the bottom of a neglected hamper. Beside me sat an older fellow who drove a bus. As he spoke about how much shorter his route had become since so many places along it had been destroyed over the last weeks, I realized I'd known all the buildings he mentioned too. I had walked by them with Mummy on our way to the hospital where we volunteered.

The next morning, when we emerged from the underground, I remember the shock of sunlight glossing my cheeks—the fact that it was still there, that it had not somehow been brought down in the attack, was astonishing. That wasn't the only shock: we found the house belonging to Jack Spence across the street from us was now just smoking posts and jagged bits of wall. After that, Aidan was sent to stay with Mother's sister in Sussex.

I remember speaking to one of the Dead End kids in Watson's Wharf, off Wapping, who organized a patrol of the neighborhood. He was a tall boy with his hair shorn to stubble and hyperthyroid blue eyes. Today I expect he'd be pierced and tattooed head to toe. A Selena. But nothing brought people together as quickly as a common enemy. He and his mates prowled the danger zones, the identified target areas, looking for and finding unexploded time bombs they would attempt to toss into the river with a hoot, and every so often one of them would get blown up, but when I asked him why they did it, he said: *Because London is our home, ma'am.*

It is, I imagine, the response of children everywhere. Because it is our home. Because we know this ground on which we stand, and nothing can hurt us here, even if it kills us.

Then came the attack of the twenty-ninth of December. All Cheapside and Moorgate went up in flames. Paternoster Row, where the bookstorehouses were, shelves on shelves stocked with millions of volumes, turned to ash in less than an hour. So many of Wren's unearthly churches gone. Everything around St. Paul's. Only the Cathedral looked on, largely undisturbed—though clipped and singed. Signs had to be hammered up so people who'd walked these streets their whole lives would recognize where they were. In several places the bombs performed a service for which later generations of archaeologists were grateful— pieces of a Roman wall were discovered in Cripplegate and behind the altar of All Hallow's Church. In the Herbarium, a Chinese mimosa that hadn't bloomed in over a century suddenly came alive.

Working in the hospital I discovered not only Londoners' faces but also their bodies, naked, broken, and bleeding. By the time the war ended, I'd cleaned the shit and piss of both rich and poor. I tended children charred to coal and a woman whose feet had been crushed by a gargoyle swooped down from a church. Every day I saw up close another life spoiled by war. There was a man who'd gone blind after his dog was hit by a lorry carrying milk that had toppled while dodging a crater in the road; milk gushing down the street was the last thing he saw.

That must have been in '44, when the Germans made one last effort with the V2s, those screaming rockets shot from Holland straight up into the air thirty miles, which dropped on London four minutes later, flattening entire blocks. They say it was the first time rockets traveled that fast that far. Who will ever forget that November day when a V2 hit Woolworths, leaving more than a hundred and fifty dead? Some of the survivors came under my care.

By war's end, a third of London had been destroyed. A hundred thousand homes gone to dust. These things changed us. Old England died as the cumulative result of the attacks.

And, to tell you the truth, we were thrilled that it did, our fear burned away by the kerosene of euphoria. That's what no one can ever explain—despite the cruelty, the terrible joy of it! No twenty-year-old expects to be hit. It was a little like being in love—a quickening, skin peeled to the nerves, senses on alert for every sound, each shadow, every smell. Walking down the street you'd be smacked by a wave of heat telling you a smoldering building belched around the corner, and the next thing you knew flames were dancing on the crossbeams of a church familiar since childhood. You'd prayed in its pews countless times. Sat there as a girl contemplating the threat of hell's pit yawning just out of sight. Instead, hell opened and gulped down the church in your place.

Strangest of all was the realization of how weightless things were. It was like watching your life in a mirror: you couldn't feel what was happening, only see it. Maybe you wept, yet something inside you asserted itself in a way I can only describe as religious—a voice saying, *Don't be afraid! This material world in flames around you is nothing, and so can never be destroyed.*

It was different when someone you knew died, of course. Then you felt yourself torn up from within.

If even girls grew fearless under fire, imagine how the young men took the challenge.

It was worse later, when things got quiet and the boredom set in. You learn to crave the buzz. The bombs hurt, but they also kept us awake. They droned like dragonflies. Thousands fell in ten months at the start of the war, and thousands more at the end—and ultimately those who survived were determined to live and forget and remember. All at once.

On holidays, when we both happened to be home, Andrew and I liked walking through the city early mornings—just past dawn was our hour. How does that Wordsworth poem go? *The very houses seem asleep and all its mighty heart lying still.* The becalmed heart of the smoldering giant made room for us then somewhere among its many chambers. We felt ourselves grow expansive in the open air. Sometimes we'd walk through the park toward Buckingham Palace or Westminster Abbey; or we strolled to Trafalgar Square, where Andrew pulled out the sack of crumbs begged off the cook for the pigeons. Andrew called them the Angels of the Somme, in honor of the boys who died there in the first war. He developed an elaborate and sentimental fantasy—he was a very romantic young man, I must tell you, though the conditions of his uprooting had left him keen to the fragility of things. He pretended that the birds were the souls of the dead English soldiers come back to guard their loved ones as best they could—and if they couldn't stop the bombs falling then they would go up in flames with their kin, knowing they'd probably be right back in Trafalgar feeding on crumbs in no time.

Didn't pigeons sometimes fly right into plane engines, bringing them down?

Anyway, we'd sit there while the city started to stir—first the double-decker went by, then a couple of cabs. A bobby watched us to make sure we weren't spies semaphoring the skies.

We talked about all sorts of things. For a period this alphabet boy turned talker.

Once my uncle gave me a gift of five quid for my birthday. It was an enormous sum—our family was more than comfortable, and Mother had all kinds of posh friends, but there seemed an awful lot of us at the trough, and everything in the way of treats and entertainments we dedicated—by design—to the war effort. Before dinner on Boxing Day we did a roll call to acknowledge the foods missing in action—plum pudding, for the war effort! mincemeat pie, war effort! turkey, the war . . . until Mother walked in and shouted at us for dishonoring those families who had actually lost someone. We soon shut up. We knew how well off we were compared to most people on the Continent. I kept thinking of how it must have been for the French.

For all this, I didn't give Uncle's gift to the orphans. Instead, I took Andrew to a performance of Cyrano, put on as a fraternal gesture toward France.

Afterward Andrew began calling me Roxanne. I called him Nose (*What can death be like, I wonder,* he'd ask with a flourish). Like everything else about him, his nose was a little larger than life.

What has the Nose been sticking itself into this week? I'd ask.

And he would, like Cyrano, deliver his version of the "Gazette," which he called a newsreel.

On Friday morning around 0200 hours the Huns began to lose their courage—which they showed by shedding bombs. Of course the Huns are blind as brickbats—or they have something against water and abandoned warehouses, seeing as how that is where most of their bombs fell. In other major developments, Vera Lynn announced to the listeners of her radio show that the White Cliffs of Dover were, as long suspected, a private reference to her lover's buttocks. Moreover, the Queen has promised to stop feeding beef au jus to her pooches until all the dogs of London can once more afford beef au jus, and their owners be damned. More locally, young Andrew has won a prize for his paper on Wellington's Station in Life after Waterloo. That is all for this, the 30,000th day of the Blitz in the Year of Our Lord 1941.

Anyone seen much of Our Lord lately? he asked as a follow-up.

To which I had no reply.

———•·•———

As the war at last came to an end, Andrew began putting his skills as a linguist to use—not yet for Daddy and the King, but on behalf of something far more important and difficult: I mean life's finer feelings, which for most men constitute the one unmasterable tongue.

We were waiting for the sun to rise over the Thames that dawn—might wait a month, you know—when Andrew said:

I know a spell that might yet bring this lazy sun a-running.

Through the iron gates of life? I asked, recognizing his allusion.

Exactly. And he put his hand on mine.

So it was I learned by touch just how large the borders of our being really were—how our body is hardly our perimeter, how it is more of a dotted line, proposing not a boundary or a demarcation so much as the outline of a convenient harbor, while our true self has no walls at all, but extends out to the trees and the houses and the sky and other people—to as far as we allow it to go.

All this he taught me that morning so that when we kissed I felt as though my lips had touched something made of clod and steel, sunlight and cloud.

I don't think your father will like this.

Not even the backfire from a bus carrying soldiers managed to startle me out of the moment. The world receded to backdrop, where it belonged.

Bugger Father, I said. Anyway I think you're wrong. He respects you, Andrew, far more than he does my brothers.

It was true. My older brothers disappointed him. Bulwer hid inside theological studies. Meanwhile, Sebastian had fallen under the spell of Lord Russell and his pacifists. Right up until 1940, he supported appeasement, leading to terrible rows at home. Luckily, by the time of the Blitz, Russell had come to his senses and brought his followers into line. His sons were a great heartbreak to Daddy. Aidan alone inclined to soldiering, but he was only a boy by war's end.

Andrew was Father's favorite, and I wasn't surprised when Father took him along to Germany to serve as an interpreter after the fighting.

Let's walk, he said suddenly.

The sun had not obeyed us, but we offered no further petition.

Where to?

To the London Stone, of course!

What's that?

My dear, what kind of a native are you? he gassed as we picked up our pace.

Andrew knew our history far better than any of us.

The city was rumbling to life. A milk lorry worked its way up the street. In its wake trailed a cadre of cats.

Oh my dearest, my collop.

Your what? Watch yourself.

It's London's foundation stone. Brought here from Troy by the grandson of Aeneas. You remember St. Swithin's on Cannon Street?

Lost in the Blitz.

Not the Stone.

We were across from the railway station that stood there then.

There it is, he said, pointing at a piece of black stone less than a meter high.

It used to mark the center of the city, he said. As long as it stays unbroken, London stands.

You even know what a collop is? I asked, not wanting him to have the upper hand.

Rhymes with your favorite nineteenth-century novelist?

George Eliot?

But would you want to marry her?

What?

I'm just asking.

Why? Who wants to know?

You have to say just one word.

What's that?

That Barkus is willing.

That's three.

Just *willing*, then. That's all.

People's intellectual limits, I've discovered, are more often than not defined by their social ambitions than by their native abilities. In society it doesn't pay to be too clever. One must learn to go along with things—to live that half-life of which one can die. I worried Andrew might not play his part as wholeheartedly as was called for by the times. Victory was a shining concept but a mercurial reality blinding you to the loss, isolation, and money fears—the whole caboodle of miseries—inside it. No war ends cleanly.

The hot, dry summer had left the Thames low and sluggish. I lit a cigarette. The world had turned and rediscovered its peaceful season, its cloudless sky safe for pigeons again. I was twenty-one. Andrew was almost twenty. He would soon be leaving for Germany with Daddy.

One period was over; the time had come to turn the page.

Stopping the Career of Laughter with a Sigh

I have drunk, and seen the spider.

WILLIAM SHAKESPEARE

– 1 –

I remember the day he returned. The world was changing yet again. The kaleidoscope had been given half a turn by one of the giants. The Atlee government was nationalizing industries: coal, gas, even the Bank of England. Then came the National Health Service. As I was still volunteering at the newly rebuilt Chelsea Royal, that was news. I listened to doctors complaining how this would ruin them, but all the while I was thinking of those people crowded together in the tube shelters during the bombing. "Fair shares" was the cry after the Beveridge Report: no more boys working in mines or on the Clyde sixty hours a week. No more special treatment for doctors or lords. *The people* had arrived.

At the same time we were staggered by the photographs that had begun appearing from the camps. We'd heard about them for years. One of Mother's cousins, a rabbi from Scotland, visited the family during the war raising funds for survivors. Daddy sponsored many refugees, most of whom wound up settling near Grasmere and the Lake District.

My brother Aidan was the only one home besides myself to greet Andrew. This must have been right after the incident with his brother at Braunschweig. What began as an imaginary illness blossomed into a real one. It left him permanently fatigued, and at last he was sent home.

He stood at the door looking half dead. His face was gray as the ash on the windows. I thought immediately of the wet-capped boy on the docks. He practically collapsed in front of us. A little like you, come to think.

Poor Aidan inched back toward the stairs. Even Thor looked worried.

Normally he'd have knocked Andrew over. Instead he sat there calmly and licked his hand.

We hugged, but it was awkward. He didn't seem inclined to speak, never mind crack a smile.

After getting him to bed, I sent Aidan out to fetch the doctor and put some water on for tea.

Everyone was still in volunteer mode. Mother was working that day at the hospital. Sebastian was in school, fighting for a lasting peace. Bulwer had interrupted his theological studies to travel with a group that was visiting all the camps. When he finally returned he looked as though he'd just been released from one himself.

My own response to the camps and the war was different. To me they had nothing to do with God. The way men ordered their lives on earth was their own doing. And I use the word *men* deliberately. Even in the middle of this hell I believed in the power of kindness. But everyone said I was sheltered and naïve, so I kept my thoughts to myself.

They were wrong of course—the things I saw regularly at the hospital were precisely what most of those who judged me feared above all: the pussing, open wounds, lost limbs, eyes clouded by terror, what they call the casualties of war. These were sights they spared themselves, and so in my eyes gave up their single legitimate claim to any authority.

For the next two weeks I stayed home nursing Andrew. We were supposed to be getting married. It was what we'd talked about, what we'd repeated in letter after letter. Afterward, I hoped at last to go to Cambridge. I'd done my service. Now I wanted to study literature, with the intention of one day writing radio plays for the BBC. I'd deferred my own life long enough.

But by the time Andrew was well enough to go out, I'd realized that there was in him another wound not even I would be able to heal.

----·•·----

The first time he yelled at me I felt like a child who'd come to Daddy begging a kiss, and he'd replied by slamming the door in my face. In fact, I had entered his room while he was shaving—and I had wanted a kiss. This was a few days after his return. Our reunion had been so odd. And he didn't exactly slam the door—he hammered his fist into the wall. Where had this come from? I had no idea. I had no experience of men's anger. Daddy may have studied the corpses of executed men in a day's work, and he was certainly firm with the boys and had raised his voice at them more than once, but never at me. Never at me.

He'd been standing before the mirror in his T-shirt. His arms were thin as strings. His handsome face showed too many angles.

His outburst was a land mine. I felt shattered. He had been my only refuge in these terrible years. It was the Blitz all over again, only this time I alone was the target. Some terrible poison had seeped into the room.

I turned and ran out.

Eventually I recovered.

It happened once. Why expect it again? Look how much the city had withstood.

One morning we were driving out to Cambridge where I had an interview. We were going to drop Aidan off at the home of a friend. Mother had bought an Aston Martin to replace the old Morris that had been melted into scrap by a buzz bomb.

The boy was looking forward to it. He was a cheerful, sensitive child. He was twelve—an age when he could still enjoy excursions with the family, though he might be loath to admit it. Andrew had been like an older brother to him, and I thought it healthy for Aidan to be in the company of someone who, unlike Sebastian and Bulwer, had risked and sacrificed for his country.

In that grainy, postwar world Andrew was my London Stone. As long as he stood by me, I knew where I was in the world. So I told myself late at night. I looked forward to our picnic on the Cam. And the next day I was to meet one of the tutors with whom I hoped to resume my studies the following year. I remember wearing a new orange scarf that fluttered in the breeze.

The drive began chipperly enough. Aidan was full of some great adventure he and his friends had embarked on involving a ring of Russian spies—Russians had suddenly replaced Germans in our imagination as the latest specter over Europe. It was remarkable how quickly that happened. Aidan's high spirits issued in a stream of comic patter. For a while we listened to him prattling on about various secret codes, Moscow, and MI5 when suddenly Andrew turned around and snapped:

You stupid little brat. You think it's all games. You think Moscow is some kind of Mordor, a public-school fantasy?

He was shouting.

Andrew, I said, putting a hand on his shoulder. He was driving, and I watched him veer side to side. His nose and cheeks were red.

And you—you think you're an angel of mercy because you put bandages on the wounded. Yet for every one of your people you saved, a hundred of mine died or are dying.

I wasn't exactly sure what he was talking about. I had of course heard about Stalingrad and the casualties on that side—half a million men, I believe. Much later we all learned about how Stalin had tortured his people, how he had starved them while our Socialists and our Fabians rooted him on. It hadn't occurred to me to try to understand how Andrew felt about that—I hadn't for a second thought he might have been worried for his family. Because he seemed so much a part of mine, of me. I'd forgotten about his mother and brothers.

He'd told me about them, yet there'd been a certain withholding when he spoke. He resented his mother for sending him away—as though she had done it out of meanness. I told him, It's not like she indentured you, but I knew the boy had been beaten and worse on his way here, and somehow the sailor's behavior tangled in his mind with his mother's intentions.

He had come to seem to me one of us, and it came as a shock to be reminded that he wasn't.

His roots lay elsewhere, and they sank deeper than any of us had imagined. He had learned to speak and write beautifully—though he had an odd way of talking about himself in the second person as though he didn't want to take anything too personally; and he stuttered a little, especially among strangers—like Aidan, as a matter of fact.

The boy didn't mean anything by it, I said.

That's the goddamn problem with you people. You never mean anything by anything, and people die because of it.

He was still shouting. There was no need for it, and I told him so.

Need, he shouted. Need? What do you know about need?

I couldn't stand it anymore.

Turn the car around, I said.

What? His wild look only unsettled me further.

Now. Andrew, take us home.

The thought of spending the day in the company of a lunatic—that was how he seemed to me—after all we'd been through, all I'd looked forward to, was unbearable. I could feel Aidan squeezing against the cloth of the backseat, trying to make himself invisible. That crushed me even more.

Then Andrew turned to look at me. His mood had changed; he appeared repentant yet he couldn't bring himself to apologize, and so his silence was echoed by mine.

I want to go home, I repeated.

As soon as we returned, Aidan mumbled something about friends and rushed out of the house. I left the picnic basket in the car and hurried straight to my room.

On my way up I ran into Sebastian, holding a book in his hand and mumbling to himself.

Sebastian, what are you doing here? I thought you were at school fomenting peace?

Hullo. I thought you were going to be there yourself today. He shut the volume, which appeared to be an Arab phrase book.

Change of plans.

Me too. What's wrong? Pretty scarf.

Thank you. Nothing. What brings you to London?

That's a very red-eyed nothing, darling, he said, putting a hand on my cheek. All quiet on the eastern front?

I shrugged, veiling my face with the scarf, trying to seem playful. What are you doing here?

It's only that I've received an appointment.

An appointment?

I'm supposed to help out some subminister. In Palestine.

You mean Israel?

What's in a name?

Everything, I mumbled, thinking of Andrew.

The thing about a family is that everyone has a story going on at the same time as yours only you forget it, and when you intersect periodically you're reminded of the common ground.

The thought of Sebastian going to the Middle East, where there was still fighting, made me despair even more.

Suddenly I began sobbing. My poor brother tried wrapping his arms around me, but I pushed him away.

I hurried to my room where I hurled myself across the bed, mourning the world of men in which I'd awakened. Surely there were universes better ordered than this one.

After a while, there was a gentle knocking. I sat up.

Come in.

I expected Aidan or Sebastian. It was Andrew. He had brought the picnic basket and some flowers. For the first time since coming back, he smiled. He crossed the threshold slowly. I sat up in bed, hugging my knees, suspicious, but hopeful nonetheless.

The next morning, lying alone in my bed, I thought about Andrew. The day felt strangely sullen. I listened for the birds that normally assembled in the copper beech, but they seemed to be on strike. I realized then that something had happened at Braunschweig, something irreparable. It had altered him. You often hear that an individual's character is pretty well set by age three and that's possible. But people's situations are so various. Presumptuous to claim with certainty that characters reveal themselves under pressure because we never know exactly how many different kinds of forces shaped the man. I couldn't know what Andrew was feeling. I couldn't know how his mother had treated him or imagine what it was like to have her send him away to a strange country without saying why. I thought of London's own children during the Blitz. They'd been sent out to group homes in the Midlands for safety. Then, to our amazement, every week thousands—literally—walked back on their own, hundreds of kilometers if necessary, sniffing their way back like abandoned dogs. What a sight: children too young for school with haversacks on their backs, hastening to reenter the city of fire—because at least here they knew who they were.

Andrew hadn't been given that choice.

Unfortunately, Andrew's anger was local and specific, directed above all at me and my family.

Within a week he had moved to a cold-water flat in Brixton.

I tried to get on with things, rescheduling my appointment at Cambridge, talking to Mummy. Daddy wasn't back yet, which was fine as he was useless in domestic situations. Mummy urged me to give Andrew room, saying he wasn't the only one chewing nails after this war. Hospital wards overflowed with troubled men who'd seen things they'd not soon forget, and who perhaps had done things for which they might never forgive themselves.

So I gave him room. But rooms open on corridors and corridors lead to stairs and stairs eventually leave you standing outside the house.

One afternoon, some six weeks after he'd left, I found myself at the doorstep of his new flat. I had news. It would either change his outlook entirely, or lead to something awful for both of us. I couldn't imagine anywhere in between. I trembled. Before leaving the house I'd tried on two shades of lipstick and changed dresses three times before settling on something simple but not black.

One more misjudgment.

He'd lost weight. The shadows in his room couldn't mask the ones under his eyes. The very air around him was murky.

Can we go out? I asked.

He looked at me a long time with those pale eyes.

Why?

Because it's stuffy in here, I thought. And depressing. Because it smells of your cigarettes and because you haven't taken out the rubbish in days. Because outside there are people every bit as wounded as you who have understood that the only way they will get better is by helping each other and maybe that will wake you up.

That was what I wanted to say.

What I said was:

Because I want to.

He shrugged and grabbed a key off the hook by the door.

We settled down in some grimy pub—most of London was still robed in grit and ash. You couldn't forget that the ash was wood and cloth and human flesh. Twenty-five thousand dead in London alone.

Andrew was missing a button on the sleeve of his white shirt. That was something he would never have permitted himself before. He labored so hard to be correct.

His cheekbones seemed on the verge of breaking out of his skin.

Do you know why I'm here?

At the table next to us, a group of drunken men were rehearsing Vera Lynn's entire repertoire. There were few songs I detested quite so passionately as "The White Cliffs of Dover."

He answered with a stony look.

You're making a difficult thing impossible, I said.

I decided to gamble. I leaned across the table in that smoky room and covered his hands with mine, just as he had done that morning along the Thames.

Andrew, I'm pregnant.

I had imagined the different ways in which he might respond. What I hadn't expected was the barely articulate rage. His face grew redder and redder, like a coal someone was blowing on.

Well, you'll have to kill it, won't you?

I wanted to die then. What had happened to that beautiful ten-year-old boy I'd taught the language in which he was now cursing me? Not just me: our future, *the future.*

We'll meet again, Don't know where, don't know when, the men sang.

You don't mean it, Andrew. This is a grand thing. New life in the world.

Is it? Why? Because it's an English life? That why it's valuable? Is that the measure we're to use for everything now?

Then he leaned forward and hissed:

I will be skinned and skewered and fed to damn rats before I do anything to bring another little British bastard into the world.

With that, he pushed away from the table, and was gone.

———•·•———

I wandered around the city, through Lambeth and Southwark, up Blackfriars Road and across the bridge near Temple. It was humid and smoggy, and I stopped and looked at the river and considered that not so long ago he was playing Cyrano, and how had we gotten here?

Everywhere there were cranes and lorries and muscled workmen with shovels, picks, and hammers. The rebuilding of the city had begun. New life was struggling to rise from the rubble. New life was stirring in me as well.

I crossed Fleet Street and saw St. Paul's up Ludgate to my right. I'd read a cynical writer who said he hated children because in their pinched faces all he saw were the features of future murderers, of tyrants in their infancy. It was best to abort while one could. That was how deeply Hitler's evil had stamped itself on our hearts.

Yet as I began to feel the physical presence of the life inside me, the abstract grievances paled.

I turned up High Holborn to Kingsway. Did I dare to bring another heart into this world? I would be spurned by most of my family. They'd turn me out. I knew that. On the other hand I imagined the child being born in a new London, part of a new generation that would have learned the lessons of war once and for all and would never choose violence again.

I rested my hand on a beech on the corner of Kingsway.

I paused outside the gate of the British Museum and thought of all it contained—they were still returning treasures that had been shipped out of the city for safekeeping: the Rosetta stone, the marbles, the books and manuscripts from the Reading Room. The genius of the world lay inside those heavy walls. What advice did its bones have for me? What had we learned from our time here on earth?

Walking down Oxford Street toward Hyde Park, I understood at last that I was alone.

– 2 –

Back home, I brooded over his words: he wanted our child dead, swore he'd tear it out of me himself if he had to. Said he didn't want another English monster walking the face of the earth.

We were all a little crazy after the war, I no less than anyone. Andrew may have been tough, but I'd been raised by a man ten times harder. Not only wasn't I afraid of men, I enjoyed fighting with them. I took pleasure in standing up and denying them whenever they thought they could tell me what to do.

Father was not a sentimental man. It took its toll on all of us. I once asked Sebastian how he could hold such extreme views—his opposition to the war and everything—and he replied, *Look at Father. That man has not enjoyed one day's peace in his life. He does what he believes he must as a British citizen. My loyalty lies elsewhere.* Although he would have denied it, Sebastian was the only truly religious member of this household.

When Andrew wrote saying he was leaving for Canada—he planned to find a way into the United States because he'd never serve the King again—Aidan chose to avenge me.

One day—and this is where things get complicated—because we had stopped seeing each other by then, so I know only my own part of this story—one day Andrew received a package. I can only imagine how he felt when he opened it and saw the jar.

SIX

Boundary Conditions

– 1 –

The streets of a city remember their origins. They never completely erase them. There's always something of the past that remains: a hitching post in an alley, a public square once pasture, a plaque heralding the birthplace of Confucius. The best boast of it, like the Etruscan tomb I saw alongside the Internet Café in Cortona recently. Out of the blast furnace of Nagasaki you salvage a streetlamp, the stones from a temple, a watch. Once, on display at MIT, I gazed on two of Buddha's teeth. How many pilgrims each year visit Jesus' tomb, the Wailing Wall, the Dome of the Rock? While researching the Russian Revolution over the last years—undaunted by past failures and unearthing information in archives newly (and for who knows how long?) opened—I've visited Ukraine often and found its urban centers much transformed since my first brief, aborted stop there. The underground shopping mall below Independence Square in Kyiv (once the Plaza of the October Revolution) today rivals the glitz of Fifth Avenue or Via Veneto—albeit it on a more modest scale. Does it matter that the bling of couture illuminates our fantasies without necessarily adding shine to our character? Who has benefited from this material transformation is hard to say—though the freshly gilded churches are beautiful. But that summer, things looked very different indeed.

Beginning with the trains.

~ 2 ~

Kij's insistence that I travel with them made me uncomfortable. While I wanted to go—I had so much to say to Vera, so much to ask her; it had been naïve to think I could settle my business as if I were borrowing books from the library—the ululating force field around my uncle made it impossible to relax, and I thought twice before agreeing.

"Three days," he promised. "We'll fly you back from Kyiv."

"Three days," I said.

It was late evening by the time we reached the border. I was sitting in a private compartment down the hall from Kij and his lover Eric Stimpleman—Vera had her own wagon, a scaled-down version of her bedroom; there was also a dining car, as well as a separate one for the servants, including a priest, whom I wouldn't meet until just before our arrival in Kyiv. I'd been reading Blunt's *Secret History of the English Occupation of Egypt* when the train ground to a halt. Scratching grime off the window, I pressed forehead to glass to study the shadows.

Outside, a door opened. Someone's heels clicked onto the platform. Male voices barked in the rain. More tapping up stairs. The door shut. Then the whole train lurched forward as new cars were added.

It was a very long train now. Lanterns of cigarettes dotted the windows.

I wasn't ready to sleep, so I stepped into the hall.

In the open area at the other end, Kij sat with his leg hurled over the back of a chair. A fan of playing cards rested above a bare knee gleaming under the loose folds of a violet satin robe. The fluorescent light overhead flickered. A bottle of vodka surveyed the table. Of all things, Aerosmith sounded on the cassette.

Stimpleman hunched in the chair across, staring intently into his hand. He wore a rumpled blue velvet jacket and tugged the nib of his mustache in an obvious tell.

At that moment the conductor walked in. A red stain streaked his left trouser leg above the knee.

"We're at the border," he whispered. "Passports ready, gentlemen?" He smelled of camphor or coal; his arms hung stiff at his sides.

This was in the days before the European Union, when the United States was still admired in some parts of the world for its exemplary openness. To me, passports seemed the relics of a paranoid European nationalism.

"I thought it had been taken care of," Kij's voice crackled with annoyance.

"Maybe," said the conductor, "but this is another country. You never know what they might ask."

"Thank you," said Kij. "I thought Khoriv had fixed it," he repeated to me when the conductor left. "I'm sure he bribed them, but you can't know how they'll be taken. They will be taken. But whether in good faith is another matter. Makes you want to riddle the pricks. One day I'll mow them down like wheat."

He shook his fist at the ceiling.

"You have mowed wheat?" Eric asked.

But the bribes must have worked because no one bothered us, and before long we were moving again.

"Want to play or not?" Kij's thick hand opened toward the empty chair.

"We've already passed through Hungary, Romania, and Moldova," Eric said. "Made mechanical adjustments."

"What for?"

"The Tsar controlled border crossings by laying a broader gauge of tracks inside his empire. Used to have to change trains altogether. But these are special cars Khoriv had outfitted with dual gauges. They've also added the local carriages."

"Engineer Melnikov, 1842," grunted Kij.

"Kij's an expert on trains," Eric said. "Miles of track run through his apartment. Even the john. What's that station called?"

Kij shrugged.

"So? He likes shoes, if you want to know."

Eric made a face.

Their banter drew me into a world where I couldn't relax. The waters were cold and dark; just out of sight, sharks. But my fieldwork had taught me to stand back and let things reveal themselves.

"We're mapping the border of the old Ottoman Empire," I offered.

"That explains everything," said Kij.

"Sure, I'll play. Have to pee first. What's the game?"

"You call it *stud*."

Eric's long flat face framed the Cossack mustache as if it were some kind of exhibit, contrasting sharply with his comb-over up top.

"Hot," I said. "Can we open the windows? Air-conditioning broke?"

"They're open. Wait until the train gets some speed."

"Feel it?" Eric asked.

"What?"

"The changes. We've just passed into a different world. Boundary conditions."

"Never heard of it."

"Tell him, Eric."

"It's physics. Figuring out what happens along the frontiers of the universe. The behavior of matter at the edges of space and time. Helps scientists understand the order of things nearer the center."

It always surprised me how fluently Europeans tossed ideas around.

Kij slapped down his cards in disgust. "What's that smell?" he asked. "What's burning?"

"Look," Eric said.

A bonfire flamed by the side of the road surrounded by trees. I didn't see any people.

"You like England?" Eric asked, adding: "I have a cousin in Manchester."

"Finally," he said, wiping his brow as the train picked up speed, and the wind cooled our foreheads.

I told him of my passion for history and explained that English literature was unlike that of any other country that I knew of—in it, self-reflection had been refined into a secularized spiritual practice.

"Must be a girl in the house," he winked and tugged his mustache.

"Why do you say that?"

"History's all well and good, but the spell of stones works best on the calcified." Then he said: "Imaginary time."

"What?"

Kij dealt the next round. Eric scooped his up in one go. I was still standing.

"When you're experiencing boundary conditions, there's no imaginary time."

"Meaning?"

"Most of us live in imaginary time. Fantasyland. In our heads: our dreams, hopes, neuroses. Not here. Here, things get real in a way we're not used to. Pay attention, or you'll get hurt. Here neuroses find bodies. We think the universe is closed, contained, self-sufficient. In fact, it's wide open, and no matter how you try, you can't keep this reality out."

He gestured sit.

"I've got to pee," I said.

"Now that's real."

On my way, I bumped into the Turkish servant I'd spoken with in Vienna. He was carrying a tray of food to Vera.

I asked him his name.

"Tariq," he smiled.

I told him I hoped we'd have a chance to talk. I was interested in hearing about his life and the work he did for Vera.

"Are you really?" he smiled.

"What?"

"Does Christian peoples care what people like Tariq think?"

He smiled, shrugged, and walked away. I could see this Christian thing had not made a particularly positive impression on much of the world.

When I returned, Eric continued speaking at me.

"You have any idea how invested we are in being modern?"

As if to punctuate his point, something pelted the window. We looked over and saw a whitish spray quickly washed off by rain.

"We hate civilizations that work at the agricultural or pre-industrial level. Even low-tech sets us on edge. They show us ourselves as we had been. For which we feel contempt. And guilt. It scares people to see peasants in huts without floors alongside animals they later eat. They remind us of origins. All we've lost or spoiled. We're in the business of destroying the past. And I mean *business*—most of the money's in selling newness, the future.

"Of course, another reason I'm uncomfortable in the land of my birth is because I'm a Jew," Eric added. "Being a Jew hasn't always been a good thing to be around here, and I can't forget it."

"Life is suffering," Kij said, drawing on his cigar, eyeing his cards. "I'll take one."

Eric obliged, sliding it toward him with his finger.

Kij's expression gave nothing away.

"What's it like being a Jew in Austria?" I asked.

"You don't know where to stand because whichever way you lean, you're alone."

"Give me a violin," Kij said, spitting into his handkerchief. "For the rest of us, life is easy. Austria after the war looked so pretty."

"And whose fault was that?"

Then he looked at me:

"Mother offered you opium?"

"She did," I lied, for no good reason.

"You weren't tempted?" He smirked at Eric.

"Sure."

"I recommend it."

"Where are we?" I asked, gesturing at the darkness outside the window, at the vast, empty steppes.

"Nowhere," said Eric. "Land of Nowhere. Fields."

"Fields can be very beautiful," I said, remembering the summer I drove through the Midwest, across Ohio and Missouri and Kansas and Nebraska, on my way to visit Charlotte, who was staying with her grandmother in Utah. Many days I'd park the car on the edge of a cornfield and walk outside and just stare at the miles and miles of green and the crows circling above, the deep sky with the occasional cloud, and I felt this sense of majesty I'd read about. Only greater, much greater. I knew the farms belonged to some agribusiness corporation based in the Caribbean. Certainly there were chemicals on the crops. They might have been testing nuclear weapons right under my feet. But, for a moment, it appeared as though the amber grain were real and the scene as nice as it looked. The fantasy fizzled the moment I saw the Archer Daniels Midland logo on the combine.

"Americans," Eric said, "always look for the good in a thing. In death, in war, you search for the positive."

I shrugged.

A wave of unease shuddered through me. I couldn't get a bead on what these men were up to. I felt out of my depth in a way I'd rarely known. At home, work, and school, I was the savvy insider. My parents' style of child rearing had taught me to sail the whirling winds of each moment. But not this.

"You think I'm complimenting you," he smiled. "That's how self-centered you are."

"What does any of this have to do with my being an American?"

"You people are so overwhelmed by the fear of losing what you'll never really own, you can't see things for what they are. So you react by commodifying everything. Your entertainments, your medications, your media all have one goal: to distract you from the death hurtling your way at full speed."

Kij put down his cards and spat again into his handkerchief.

The tape had finished, and the silence gave Eric's words room to grow.

"You're a very political thinker," I said.

"Irony becomes you," he answered. "You've no idea what it's like outside the empire. Here's a question for you. Quick. Emancipation Proclamation: moral milestone or capitalism's calamity? Everything turns on your point of view."

"What?"

"Many people in your country hate the inconvenience of life without slaves. It's worse than you know. Bet you haven't a clue how much gets done for you. Mainly outsourced, a million miles away."

"You grew up in Vienna. Don't look poor to me."

This time, Kij spoke:

"We began on the grounds of an asylum."

The cold copper of his eyes reflected frosty tundras, the vast ice hills of Siberia, and centuries of unrepentant gulags.

"These things leave a mark. Remember: I'm over sixty. I can smell my own death. In the charmed circle of your America, people will soon live for hundreds of years. It's biblical. Epic. This is the outer dark; here we survive however we can."

"You're rich," I frowned.

"Now," he nodded, "yes. But rich isn't something you do once, then quit. Getting rich and staying rich are two different things."

Kij fingered his nose ring.

"Think I'm joking? That's because you live in America. Everything's a joke for your Lenos. You play, we pay.

"And so," Kij smiled, "let us go and trade jokes."

He heaved himself out of his chair, leaned forward, and grabbed my forearm. His hand was large, and suddenly his sweaty bulk pressed against me. Up wafted a bouquet of earth, vodka, sweat, and cigars. I don't think I've ever met anyone as massive, or who inhabited his body as fully as did

Kij. It was as though he'd pushed himself into every crevice, pore, and knob of flesh padding his bones.

His robe fell open, and I saw to my dismay he wasn't wearing underwear.

I flinched, but his hand leeched onto me and wouldn't let go. His nakedness seemed unimportant.

"Walk with me," he said.

Under our feet something rattled like loose marbles, but Kij ignored it, so I said nothing.

"See the rest of the train? Love to."

The moment we stepped into the unrestricted cars, things changed. Here the seats were packed. Not just the seats. The aisles brimmed with people—men in haunted fedoras and ratty, tan, fourth-hand suits. Thin women with straight black hair wearing embroidered shirts, hands limp at their sides, stared into the night. Pretty women, their features straight and fine, their deep-socketed eyes turned inward. A man in shiny black pants clutched a chicken to his breast, stroking it feverishly.

All seasoned travelers outside the overdeveloped world know such sights by heart, but after my weeks in the bosom of England, the vision felt ruthlessly stark.

I looked away. We walked around a family eating dinner on an over-turned crate and a couple embracing on the floor. A dog lay curled in a heap. A compartment for six held a dozen or more paper-thin bodies rubbing shoulders and elbows. A blind man played a sopilka—a simple flute, almost a reed. The musician's lids hooded his eyes. When he looked up, I saw that in fact he wasn't blind at all.

A pale-skinned boy, hairless as though from alopecia, hoisted his crutch in a strange greeting. I waved back, feeling his eyes linger over my face like flies on a cow patty.

I'd walked into Lourdes or the charity ward in a hospital.

I picked up my pace. These people radiated no more anger than the pigeons in a city square. I've traveled some since, but the composure of the poor rattles me wherever I go. Why do they take it?

These are like cattle cars, I thought.

"Who are they?" I asked.

"People," shrugged Kij. He seemed not to notice. "Some sleep on the trains. Trains are cheap. They live like birds. Ever seen a bird cemetery?

They keep moving. Sometimes they sell rags they find in one place at the next stop. Swap potatoes from their yard for apples from orchards hundreds of miles away. The train's like a caravan."

Smoke clouding the cars made everything ghostly and seamless. We were bats in the sun, boats in a fog-lathered harbor, visitors in a dream, hearing a midnight cry from another century, passing the corpses of Carthage, the poor with us always, but veiled, hidden from sight, kept from disturbing us by the skilled use of smoke, mirrors, and restricted cars.

What havens did these people have? God's special wards. Had to be. Without that, what else? I didn't know then, and still don't, what more to do with the perplexing presence of the poor. Their passivity may be part of the cause of their poverty, but what causes that? Oh, I can work up a lather on so many issues, and its foam will scald who?

"Your problem," Kij said as though hearing my thoughts, "is that you pity them."

"This is my problem?"

"What you should be wondering is how to use them. The poor are a resource, like coal. They're material. They know they are. They're begging you: use me. Give me orders. Jobs. Money. A kick in the ass. Think of them like bricks or lumber for building your dreams."

Such were the lessons of war Kij had gleaned.

"I thought Eric said fantasies don't play in imaginary time."

"We're trying to change that. Be more like you."

As we entered the last car, Kij announced that this was where they showed movies.

The scratching at my throat persisted.

"That's progressive," I said. "We only show films on planes."

I began sweating. I was a scholar. I hadn't studied for this. My fever was back.

Kij nudged me forward.

Inside, the smoke was even thicker. I could barely see the picture on the screen at the other end, but I heard moaning and, as my eyes focused, I saw a couple fucking on a waterbed. Grainy porn from the 1970s. As the pair rolled about, the handheld camera whirled with them.

Kij noticed my shock.

"You don't have this in America?" He smiled. "They always show porn after midnight. I've seen this one. Not very good."

I thought of my thesis about idealists who tried to style the world to their private dreams. More than two hundred years ago, the German poet Hölderlin, as Bulwer reminded me, knew the project was going badly. He wrote about the fading traces of the Greek gods, and he entered into the spirit of Saint John composing the Apocalypse holed up in a cave on the island of Patmos: *near God is, and difficult.*

I surveyed the faces in the car: bone-thin, gray-skinned, glazed eyes gazing hungrily at images of others having their sport.

"Liberalization," Kij explained. "Never used to show such things. Censors wouldn't allow it. Had to be high up in the government to taste Western porn. Progress," he said, clearing his throat. "Like I said, we're learning from you."

The train was slowing.

"We're in Odessa?"

"Not for hours. Must be a problem with the engine, or the tracks. Sometimes a cart gets stuck. Cow dies on the cross-ties. I'm tired. Let's go back."

I took a last look at these soon-to-be-democratized citizens and sighed.

"Be good to see Khoriv," Kij said. "He's a character. Always talking us out of jams. I remember cops coming to arrest Mother for something, and Khoriv got up on a chair and began singing the Romanian anthem. Their jaws dropped. They forgot why they came. Then they laughed and left us alone. I swear."

I looked at him.

"Come on."

"He's like that."

We walked swiftly back through the train. I looked for the boy with the crutches, but it was late. The lights had been dimmed, and he had melted away into the hot, empty night. The importance of Uncle's revelation dawned on me later, as I lay in my claustrophobic compartment, unable to sleep. I saw almost in a kind of vision the legions of the vanquished scattered over the plains of the earth. The losers in the vocabulary of the world. And I stood between them: the wraiths of need on one side, while on the other men on horseback whirling swords.

How could I not want to change history? In what direction would I need to turn to succeed?

So began a slow metamorphosis of the heart that in time led to Vienna and other fiascoes.

For the moment, I was trapped on a train surrounded by the sound of snores and whimpers, squawks of a hen and bleats from a goat, echoing down this barnyard on wheels bearing us back to the place where my father was born.

I remembered the night he took me walking on water. It was New Year's Eve—he and Mother were heading to Uncle Padraig's annual party on Beacon Hill. But first he insisted we have our little outing in the newly fallen snow. With great excitement I struggled into my boots and zipped up my coat. Mother yanked my cap with the earflaps down till I could neither hear nor see. We walked out into the night, where the wind hurled swarm after swarm of dry flakes into our faces. We clambered over the snowdrifts in the parking lot behind the restaurant at the ocean's edge. Then I plopped down on the sled, while Father took up the handle and off we went, right onto the water. Together we stood on the frozen whitecaps of Cape Ann looking back at our town on the Massachusetts North Shore. Even half a mile away the lights appeared close and bright as tropical fruits, and I was tempted to reach out and pluck every one and deposit them in the sled on which he'd dragged me. Our load might weigh us down, yet I knew he could bear it. He was king of the waters, Neptune of the North Shore, slayer of cod, tuna, even shark.

Father said: Look, there's Devon House and the Schooner Restaurant and the Gull Café. Although he didn't mention it, there was also the fish cannery where he sometimes worked. Standing beside him on the ice, I felt myself safer than I have anywhere since. We didn't talk much. I stared back, imagining Mother in the kitchen behind one of those windows making soda bread and mincemeat pie for tomorrow before putting on her rented gown. While I gazed longingly landward, Father turned both ways: toward our house, and toward the sea. Had we glanced down, we might have noticed a web of cracks forming under our feet.

It was years before the fissures finally shattered, setting us adrift in different directions, but the causes for the breakup were already there. They were the causes whose effects I've lived with ever since. Another name for it is *history*. My father. Vera. The money. The gun.

That evening we returned from walking on the ice to find Mother already stuffed inside her rented taffeta gown, orangish red to highlight her hair, drumming her fingers on the kitchen table, cigarette in the ashtray.

"You have any idea what time it is?"

Growing up in the Dunkin' Donuts and No-Name Gas capital of Massachusetts, where cyclone fences were as chic as the resin-based dwarves they protected, and working variously as a nurse's aide or an administrative assistant at Badger Country Day School, Mother longed for a glimpse of the world beyond Devon, Lynn, and Revere. She loved visiting her rich brother on Beacon Hill one or two nights a year, where she could act the grand dame she should have been had the world been fair, which it wasn't, so she had to adjust, which she couldn't. Her beauty enabled her imperious impulses, and strangers jumped when she called. If I wasn't with them on their trips to the fancier parts of town, she always made sure to bring back some exotic hors d'oeuvres. (And yet she was the one who objected to my going to England. This was after Father had moved out, and she was living alone. She'd wanted me to go to school locally. But I assured my tough-minded Irish American mother, whom I could hyphenate until monkeys typed *Hamlet* without getting any nearer to putting her in words—dark-eyed, white-hearted, small-breasted, acid-tongued, loose-lipped, and tightfisted, for starters—I assured her that England was where the original masters of the universe lived; Oxford was where their masters, the masters of truth, were to be found. Yes, the real masters of truth all lived in England, from which America derived its strength—England was the source. Or so it seemed to me then. In the end, Mother relented and told me to be careful crossing the street.)

I went straight to my room only to emerge a few minutes later when I heard shouts from the kitchen. Father's head was thrown back. He breathed heavily through his stuffed-up nose. His eyes were shut. His arms, thick from hauling nets and hoisting crates, knotted over that chest I so often used for a trampoline.

Mother, always feisty, a chaos of hair lashing her shoulders, leaned across the table with a letter, perhaps a bill, in her hand.

"We can't afford this," she said emphatically.

"Yu-yu-you aren't being fair, B-B-Barbara."

Father's stutter, along with his English accent and his odd style of speaking about himself in the second person most of the time, as though he couldn't fully acknowledge his own experiences unless you too participated in them, endeared him to people. Sick, he'd say, "Your b-b-body needs a little rest now and then like you want a bit of b-b-beef on Sundays." It made for some comic moments in restaurants, as when he'd say to the waitress: "You want a good p-p-piece of fried chicken now and then." "Yes, you do," she'd reply. "So you'll have the chicken?"

Now Father, who had managed to put on his tuxedo, tilted his head farther back, as though dodging a blow.

It took both of them a second to acknowledge my presence—because their relationship was a place apart. They were a universe unto themselves. One on one, they could be the best of company; together they generated an exclusionary force field. Yet I couldn't take my eyes off them. They looked as though they'd stepped from the screen into our humble living room. I wasn't sure whether to flee or ask for an autograph.

"Why aren't you in bed, James?" Mother asked, sipping her whiskey as though she hadn't seen me come home just ten minutes before.

"It's New Year's Eve," I reminded her.

"Listen to your m-m-mother," Father murmured.

And they resumed arguing. They fought until it was too late for the party—which was, I suspect, why they carried on in the first place.

When my parents saw they were going nowhere that evening, they finally quieted down. A rickety kind of peace descended. The three of us spent the night on the couch in front of the television watching Guy Lombardo conducting the New York Philharmonic while the great ball dropped on Times Square.

By then, they'd abandoned the phony decorum of glasses and were drinking straight from the bottle.

But it wasn't until I went abroad that I learned why Father had recused himself from the world.

– 3 –

The train rocked gently. I blinked out the window. A ragged, velvety darkness, pricked here and there by the light of a star, covered the countryside. Had I really slept all day?

Eric's voice echoed down the hall.

We chugged slowly past outlying cottages, their moon-soaked stucco stained black by factory chimneys on the horizon yet guarded by shoulder-high sunflowers. Chickens strutted up and down the dirt paths, the first line of defense, followed by railroad yards full of ancient-looking abandoned cars, in one of which I thought I glimpsed two eyes pressed against the window. I rose, laced up my sneakers, and headed to the bathroom to wash.

We were approaching Odessa, that fabled port designed by the French, built on the bones of Cossacks by the German-born Empress of Russia, Catherine, who used their bodies for landfill yet whose ruthlessness didn't stop my fellow historians from extolling her strength and her wisdom because she liked speaking French. My favorite writer from here, Isaac Babel, who wrote about the Jewish gangster, Benya Krik, had been an informer for the Communists. Eventually he too was shot. The city's dead gave it depth.

Kij and Eric appeared as I'd left them, sitting around the table with cards and a bottle of vodka lying on its side. Kij had put on the same brown silk suit he'd worn in Vienna.

I wondered what Khoriv would be like. I also couldn't shake the image of the boy on crutches. I thought of the kids back in Devon—the poorest had toys, television, a bicycle. Here was need at a level I'd only heard about. I thought of them in relation to Aidan, Marian, Selena. Hard to see them all on the same planet, which was now small enough to feel like one room. The one-room planet Earth.

Now the train floated past brimming green Dumpsters and rusted cars with broken windows on parallel tracks. A world of parallel tracks. They might have been sitting there since the Revolution. The incomprehensible graffiti was in Cyrillic. I began to sweat. As in Vienna, only this time much more intensely, I could feel the past tightening into a fist, getting ready to strike. The cold corpse of history was slowly reassembling itself, gathering strength, a hybrid half Lazarus, half Frankenstein's monster returning to life. In the deep of night, I could see its demented eyes starting to flicker.

"Believe me, when you consider what we've had to do," Kij said, waiting for the train's door to open, waving his cards in the air. "Odds against us, how we fought to hang on, I'm amazed we're still here. One day we'll wake with our balls in our mouths."

When he turned his head, I marveled at the thickness of the veins in his neck.

The train sighed to a stop.

A short man in a cobalt uniform boarded. I thought of how many uniforms had marched through my life lately. They were rarely linked to happy enounters. A long strip of blue plastic stuck to his heel like a little tail. Under his arm he held a package wrapped in brown paper.

"Kij Ivanovich?" He asked Eric, who gestured toward Kij with his cards.

Kij folded his hand neatly and set it down on the coffee table. He rose, sinking both fists into his jacket pockets. His large, pocked face turned severe.

"Something I can do for you, Sergeant?"

I looked out the window. The dimly lit station swarmed with people. There were tents on the platform.

"I am to give this only to Kij Ivanovich."

Kij towered at least a foot over the young sergeant, whose loosed belt dangled down his thigh.

"That's me," Kij narrowed his eyes, keeping his hands behind him. "Who from?"

"The gentleman said I should tell you it was from Khoriv."

"He said he'd be here. He's never late."

I wasn't sure whether Kij addressed the remark to the policeman or to us.

Kij drew his hands from his pockets very deliberately, so as not to upset the cop, and rubbed a palm over a face wrinkled from smoking and lack of sleep. Then he pulled on one of his front teeth as though making sure it was screwed in tightly enough.

"Not true," Stimpleman said, stretching his long arms. "Remember Istanbul?"

"Istanbul," Kij said. "Okay."

He put a hand on his belly and rubbed it.

From outside came what sounded like the braying of a mule. The air seemed charged with new intensity.

Then he said:

"Possible he's flown there on his own. I don't deny it."

The policeman blurted in a nasal voice:

"Are you Kij Ivanovich? You accept this? You have documents?"

Kij stepped forward, pulling an Austrian passport from his pant pocket.

The policeman examined it carefully, eyeing the photograph, Kij.

Satisfied, he handed him the package along with his passport, executed an ironic salute, and hurried off the train.

I followed him to the door, where I stared out at the ragged crowds standing like sheep arrived to find their meadow replaced by platforms on either side of which trains rattle by: What shall we do, Mother, where shall we go? they bleat. A thousand pairs of eyes stared at me. This, I thought, is what people see getting off the boat in the underworld.

"Maybe he sent a letter," Stimpleman said.

A pigeon hurled itself against the window, and we paused a moment to stare.

"I should look," Kij said, sitting down.

The package was webbed with thick string.

"What's this," he muttered, shredding the paper and cutting the twine with a Swiss Army knife. His hands trembled.

Inside was a box he tore open, pulling out a bulky white bag, which he turned upside down.

Out dropped something none of us quite recognized at first. Whitish blue, it appeared to be a dirty glove. Then, as my eyes focused and my mind caught up with what it was seeing, I recognized that lying there on the table, cut off at the wrist, was a human hand.

Nobody said a word.

"My God!"

Kij looked at Eric.

"Khoriv's in trouble," Kij finally said.

I couldn't take my eyes off the thing, its thick pale fingers curled half shut, a wedding band glinting, dried blood in the stump.

"Why?"

"This is a message."

In what language? I wondered.

The moment swelled.

"I'll talk to the engineer. We've got to push," Kij announced, heading off.

Eric turned to me: "Life is suffering," he shrugged.

— 4 —

A few minutes passed as the horror worked its way through my body. I felt my own fingers spasm in sympathy.

I'd like to imagine the decades have hardened me. In this age of organ sales over the Internet, what's the big whoop over a hand? Two kidneys, two eyes, two hands—who needs more than one?

"Look," I said, "I don't know what's going on. This trip wasn't part of my plan. Enough. What's going on?" The world gets reappraised.

My voice had risen a register.

"We haven't given you much."

Eric stood up and paced the narrow corridor, glancing uneasily at the crowds on the platform.

"What's happening here? Whose is that?" I pointed at the hand lying quietly on the table.

"Well, I can't say for certain, but I think it might be Khoriv's."

And what was I to do? I was a graduate student. I'd come to study history, not witness a dismemberment. I'd been so accustomed to being a student, I expected that was how everyone else saw me. It was a shock to find no one fretting to protect my fragile self.

"Why aren't you screaming?"

"Why aren't you?"

"I am. You just can't hear it."

"I'm not. In our line of work, these things happen."

Finally I blurted out what I'd been wondering from the moment I stepped into the house.

"And what line would that be?"

Eric drummed his fingers on the window.

"Women."

"Women?"

It took a moment.

Then I got it. I sank down into the hard chair.

When Eric decided I'd digested his news he said:

"Vera started it. After the war, everybody was starving—you have no idea how devastated Austria was. It's a fact they don't feature on television. There were soldiers everywhere. Sure, people had choices: gifted people, rich people, people with family or ethnic ties . . . but Vera had been snatched from her home. Her husband bought her when she was twelve. Dragged her to Romania. Near the end of the war she wound up in Vienna, with us to raise. I was one of several kids she cared for, on top of her own. She knew I was a Jew, and it didn't bother her. She was a beautiful woman with no education, but smart as anyone I've ever met."

"You're talking about my grandmother?"

I had turned the chair around so I could lean my chin on its back, but I found myself sitting upright, heart pounding, sweating again.

"Exactly," he said.

A gang of Odessa mosquitoes kept us flicking our arms and faces.

"The number of rapes in the Russian quarter was unbelievable," he went on, fingertip polishing the table. "And the Americans were no saints. It made sense to organize around the demand—supply abounded.

"She began by selling herself. Later she helped other girls break into the business. She started letting her friends use her apartment, for a fee, naturally. And then she rented a bigger apartment. She even gave her business a name: the House of Widows. Because of all the war widows working there.

"At first she'd take us off the premises during business hours. Eventually the place grew big enough so that we could play in one wing while her friends lounged in bras and strutted before soldiers in another. We'd only see them when we wanted to get Vera mad.

"Anyway, we grew up inside it. It was natural for us to continue her work."

"Natural?"

"We've lived with it since we were ten—by the time we were fourteen, it seemed normal. Screams from the bedroom became routine. Most of the time, people behaved. Occasionally things got crazy."

Eric paused a moment and tossed back his head.

"Like now."

His eyes narrowed as he took a long drag on his cigarette, then he rose and paced up and down the car.

The train must have collected its passengers and was starting out of the station.

Someone twisted the sky's lid a half turn to the right.

"By the early 1960s, Vera wanted a rest. Got sick. Nearly died. That's when we insisted she retire.

"At her peak, she rivaled Madame Claude of Paris," he said, assuming I understood the reference. "More than once that legendary bitch called us to supply her with the kind of girls favored by the Shah of Iran and his sideshow of freaky pricks.

"When we were older, we began recruiting from our own circle. Girlfriends, neighbors, friends of friends. People wanted money, especially dollars. Later, after Khoriv, who lived in Kyiv, hooked up with the family again, we had access to a steady supply of girls."

He turned to the window as we pulled away.

"Look," he gestured.

"What?"

"All those houses. Full of new people. Millions slaughtered yet they keep coming back. More than ever. How is it possible? Each one needs food, shelter, a job. Real estate at the cemetery."

It was true. The houses seemed to fall over each other. Mile on mile. Despite all the work of the exterminators. Houses of wood, stucco, mud and straw, of brick and cement, the urban planning of chance, cash flow, and war.

"We took over at a transitional moment," he said. "Vera doesn't know how big it is. When she stopped working, she stopped asking questions. Likes to pretend she knows what's up. Truth is, she's clueless. Blonds are an internationally desirable product, competition's nastier, and the business, never gentle, a lot rougher. We may have branched out a little too far. Some people don't like that. This is the price."

"Khoriv's hand?"

"It's a message."

"So you said." I rubbed my eyes. My heart was pounding; I was afraid any minute I'd burst into tears.

After a moment's silence, Eric picked up the deck of cards.

"Play a hand?"

———•———

The train raced ahead with all the purpose of a bullet hurtling through the night toward a target it couldn't afford to miss. Again we'd plunged into a flat grassy landscape lined with rows of poplars whose whitish trunks gave them a metallic sheen in the moonlight. They'd be easy to replace with artificial ones, I thought. Nobody would know the difference.

Kij returned agitated, face tight, teeth nibbling his upper lip, flexing his own fists, grateful to have them.

"Look, why don't you go sit with Vera," he said to me. "This really isn't any of your business."

I shrugged. Vera was why I was here. Vera, who loved her sons maybe too much. I had come to deliver a letter from a dead man. That's all.

"Go," Kij insisted. "Just go."

~ 5 ~

Vera was asleep when Lilah let me in, gesturing toward a chair near the bed. A dim light shone inside a cone of yellow silk.

As I passed Lilah, she gave me a look and ran a finger along the rim of her shirt button. Then she bowed her head forward so that her hair covered her face and only her nose was visible.

A feather of longing brushed across my temples, the bird of desire in flight. Lost in a landscape without landmarks, it scouted for prey. Selena seemed part of another world entirely, Charlotte a ghost.

Vera snored loud and free as a child, no worries, conscience clear. Maybe it was the narcotics pumping into her from the IV in her arm. My heart beat fast. Morphine, I presumed. I crept forward and settled down in a chair next to the drip. Her mouth was open. Her teeth floated in a water glass. I imagined them starting to speak: something was coming apart, a world dissolving.

Sitting there, I thought: every woman I've ever been with will eventually look like this, swaddled in sagging flesh, trafficking in cures for time. Even pierced Selena. In time, if I'm lucky, I might look like her myself. Before me slept the fate of the world. What could I learn from it?

I turned away.

My eye fell on the painting across the car and I rose for a closer look. It appeared to be from the school of Caspar David Friedrich—a melodramatic nineteenth-century landscape in violent, roiling browns, yellows, and reds, showing a bearded man—a Christ figure, clearly—in a rowboat carried by a torrent toward a waterfall. The man's hands are clasped together, eyes turned to a sky in which a sun struggles to break through.

As though hearing my overheated fragments, Vera opened her eyes and with a quick heave hoisted herself into a sitting posture. Her hair was in a bun webbed by a net, her cream-colored nightgown slipped from her shoulders. Without her makeup, Vera looked like what she was, a very sick, toothless old woman.

Wild with unwashed dreams, her eyes fell on me hungrily.

"I will tell you," she lisped. "I will tell you exactly what's happening here." Her head turned slowly from side to side as though to make sure no one was eavesdropping.

"I'm dying. Couldn't leave my boys to fend for themselves alone."

Her voice was gravelly and weak.

"If they weren't murdered by strangers, they'd have eaten each other. You don't know what our lives have been."

I remembered one of the few stories Father told me. It was supposed to be a bedtime tale about a mother who eats one of her sons. I'd never taken it literally. Now I wondered.

She nodded.

Rubbing my jaw, I leaned closer. How to speak to this woman about whom I suddenly knew so much? I wasn't shocked by Stimpleman's revelations. We were a sheltered generation. Anyone who'd been in the army, in Vietnam or the earlier wars, had seen so much more than us. What they saw made them want to keep us out of things as long as they could; what they didn't account for was our need to see. How else could we know what they were talking about? A place I'd visited with friends back in college called the Golden Banana on Route 1 in Danvers had naked girls in cages doing anxious, asexual dances for a dollar. Were any of them Vera's? I'd bought girls drinks and twice found they were students at the same university I attended. One girl, however, was from Prague. I never got her complete story, but she told me she once danced for Havel, then president of the country. Men don't see the same world women do. Even still.

"My neck hurts."

"I thought Austria was a socialist state," I said.

Again I felt out of my depth.

"Austria! I don't blame the state," she said, her voice rising. "This was up to us. I refused to ask for help. I had to find a way to make money or my sons would die."

"And you couldn't type?"

"I typed. I swept. I washed the rotting bodies of the mad, the dying. None of this helped. It didn't help me to save your father. And it didn't stop the soldiers from taking what they wanted when they wanted."

She plucked off the hairnet, spilling filaments of quicksilver across the white pillow.

"You don't understand what governs this world. How thin my hair is. My fingers fall through it like it isn't there. Our bodies were our only assets. Then came the bodies of others. Men had guns, but we had tits."

A bolt of pain jolted my molar.

"That's the hard thing," Vera said. "Once I accepted the changes—teeth, hair, eyes, and heart, life started up again. What a relief, to stop worrying. I had survived. Leaving is easy. Relax.

"Look at this," she said, pulling a photograph from under her pillow.

I dragged my chair closer and leaned forward into the sour-milk-and-wet-cotton-wad-and-piss smell encasing her.

The picture showed a spoon-eyed blond of twenty in a snug white nurse's uniform leaning against a wall, shoulders forward, hips back, a cigarette in hand, chin tucked into her collarbone, as if taunting the cameraman.

"This is at the asylum?" I rubbed my bottom jaw with the heel of my hand.

"Exactly. I had no reason to accept things as they are. What's the matter?"

"Nothing. A tooth. What things?"

"Such an American. No history. Teeth can be terribly difficult," she said, gesturing toward hers in the glass.

"Actually, I'm a historian," I said. "You're dying, and you want me to bitch about teeth?"

"I am, darling. It's a natural occurrence. Let's not get carried away by a word. Let's not get too proletarian about it. Teeth hurt. Living hurts. Death is a great painkiller."

I asked her what she meant.

She patted the bed.

"Sit."

I rose from my chair and perched on the rim.

"You know how sentimental our people are. Schmaltz and cognac. Then they want to hug and groan over what's sure as rain. I've had enough. From here on I insist people say only useful things to me."

"And what would that be?"

"If I knew, would I still need to hear it?

"Imagine men on horseback," she said, closing her eyes. "Imagine it's a movie. By their red hats and blue coats you know they're soldiers. But they aren't moving. Neither are their horses. And neither is anything in their landscape. Which is white. It dawns on you: they're frozen. Look closely and you'll see red ribbons streaked across their chests and temples like lipstick. Kissed by bullets. Dead in their saddles, boots frozen on.

"I saw this outside my mother's cottage one morning when I was a girl. I remember watching someone trying to hack a pair of boots off with an axe. They'd been protecting the town, I forget who from. Now I don't remember the details. Just the men, frozen solid till spring."

Her eyes gazed inward. She rubbed her long fingers over her face.

I'd seen my father do the same.

"Hand me that."

I reached for the silver-handled brush on the small dresser near the door.

"If you must have ambitions, let them be grand," she said, running the bristles through her tarnished tinsel. "Only those stand a chance. Who knows why? It's the law, that's for sure."

She winced and reached over to massage her left shoulder.

"Now bring me that chest," she said. "A woman still has a few choices in this world."

"I've heard it argued both ways."

"I'm not afraid. I've been expecting this."

"You're not worried?" I asked, holding a box inlaid with what looked like carved ivory wings.

"You mean, my conscience? Is it clear? I lived in the twentieth century, darling. Of course it's not clear. You want me to enlighten you?"

"Vera," I said. "I've traveled a long way. I've gone through some things to be here. You're why I'm here."

I pressed my hand to my jaw. My tooth throbbed as though in sympathy.

"Aren't you afraid?" I asked again.

"Of?"

"Soon you'll be gone. It will be as though you never were."

"I'm scared," she squealed in a phony falsetto. "Poor me, poor me, I'll be the first! First to visit the land of the dead!

"Or maybe . . ." she went on, dropping back to her normal register. "Maybe this happens to everyone? Maybe you should take heart?"

"I want to know about my father," I said.

"Death isn't a figure of speech. Figs for consistency. When you get where I am, words fail. Go blabber on. Lights approach, they leave. Thank God for drugs.

"Some people die quietly: they pass in their sleep; drop heads on desks and never raise them; sink into chairs after dinner and turn on the television where their wives find them, eyes open, watching cartoons to the end. There are endless ways to die. But can we choose how we go?"

She picked up the photograph of herself and stared as though wanting to thrust her old soul back into the young woman's body.

"Anyway," she said. "Death was always my nearest neighbor. War stole my friends young. I saw Slava Lastivka take a bullet in the eye. Part of her brain landed in my lap. Four cousins were killed all at once by a bomb."

She put her fingers inside her mouth. Her cheek looked like a knit purse being probed for loose change.

"It feels better without the teeth," she sighed. "But then I can't eat."

From the elegant, bronze-handled chest she removed a bottle that was either tinted green or filled with green liquid. She unscrewed the top and hoisted an eyedropper. She then picked up a glass and dribbled what I assumed was some kind of tincture of opium into the water.

She held the glass up and squinted. The liquid had turned a whitish green, the color of fennel.

"Hand me my teeth."

It took a few seconds to fit them.

She brought the glass to her lips. A stream of green liquid dribbled down her chin, and she wiped it off with her nightgown.

"Have a sip," she said, tipping the glass toward me. "It'll help your tooth."

Remembering Kij's advice, I thought why not, it would be something to write about one day.

I raised the glass to eye level. In the dim light it looked like melted emeralds.

The liquid tasted bitter.

Her lids fluttered. She seemed to be falling back into herself. Her voice grew faint.

"You should think about life. Religious people tell you to get ready for death. But do it without fear."

"What?" I felt remarkably clear. My body turned to glassine. I thought about the severed hand lying like an ashtray on the card table.

"I found Father's letter," I whispered, but she had already slipped off.

The train raced on through the night. It seemed to be riding a little above the ground, on rails of light. I didn't feel stoned, exactly. Everything around me had turned transparent. I'd awakened inside a lucid dream. I could see my room at Oxford through the train window. I felt I could melt through the wall and be back in England at once. It would be good to return to my project. To kiss Selena again. See Marian; start making my own decisions about who I was and where I was going. But, for another moment, having turned, I had to let go and be carried, and hope for the best.

The door opened. A slash of light sliced the room.

As though sensing a change in Vera, the nurse appeared, hips swinging despite her limp.

I stood up and moved away from the bed.

I watched as she bent over her patient, drawing the blanket up to her neck and brushing some tinsel strands off her forehead. Her hand lingered, checking her temperature.

Vera snorted. Her lips flapped open, flashing her dentures.

The nurse turned to me. Lilah's nose was plumb and square tipped. Her irises were brown and damp as loam. She looked to be in her early twenties, with clear skin tinged slightly orange, a mango, light down on the back of her hands, and long eyes. Although her blouse bunched up around her skirt, I could see she had the waist of a child. Only the tiniest tattoo on her wrist suggested the spirit within wasn't Mother Teresa's. Except for that one night with Selena, which had ended so uncertainly, it had been a long time since I'd really held a woman. The last year with Charlotte had been like cuddling with a crocodile; I was starved for a touch.

Since opium is an anaphrodisiac, I assume whatever I drank was something else. It carried me past the bounds of any familiar world, racing across a country where I didn't speak the language, surrounded by family I'd never met, all of whom seemed to be mad.

The train rocked and wobbled as though it might tip over.

She said nothing. Nothing needed to be said. We'd been speaking in code from the moment we met. A raised brow, parted lips, a look, a look away, a smile only half suppressed: a thousand messages had zipped between us. I rose and moved toward her, and her arms opened to embrace me, and her eyes took me in. Our tongues touched, and soon we were on the floor in a tangle. Her cheek smelled of rubbing alcohol and saffron. Her breasts were large, soft, and lazy, as though they'd just finished feeding. A spray of desire cocooned us. We rolled over the floor and I buried my face in her nape and her hands tightened around my neck until I thought she wanted to choke me and maybe she did, so I fought back and we wrestled to a draw under the painting.

I sat up, keeping my eyes on the disheveled face below and I ran my finger over her wet lips. Then I raked my hand over her leg, encircling her foot, which had a thick knot of muscle between ankle and heel. I slipped a finger under her arch, pressed my nose to hers, eyes shut, and kissed her lips. Then I leaned back.

I sucked in my breath.

Vera was sitting up, watching. Her mouth was open. Silver fronds hung down her face. Blotched skin draped the high cheeks.

"Very nice," she said. "Very nice. Wouldn't want to go again, would you?

"Don't be shy! Every human on the planet's here thanks to what you just attempted," she said tenderly. "Don't you love her? You're ashamed?"

I looked at Lilah, lazily shoving her breasts into her bra, buttoning her shirt, smoothing down her skirt. Her hair hung in a tangle over her shoulders. Sensing my gaze, she looked up and smiled.

I tried standing up, but my head was ringing and my legs wobbled like springs.

"You shouldn't be watching."

"Why not? It's the same if I'm here or not," Vera laughed. "Think there's more to love than you had with her?"

"I do," I said.

"You know this firsthand?"

"Yes," I answered.

"Well, I don't," she glared as though the fault were mine.

I said nothing.

"What's more, I don't believe there's anything to it," Vera rasped.

I realized in that moment that sex yanked me into the cycle of desire, pursuit, fulfillment, boredom, and failure, which kept me from having to look at what else was going on around me. I hadn't told Vera about Father's suicide. My father had killed himself, I'd just seen a human hand drop from a bag, and everything was far from all right.

The carriage rattled.

Vera coughed and pointed to Lilah:

"You like?"

She smiled at the girl, who kept her eyes on me.

I ignored her. It was a mother's embrace for which I longed. No mistaking it—as pure and clear and raw as that.

Vera rose, putting one foot down on the floor, then the other, but she couldn't quite push herself up.

I was on my knees now.

"What if she were your daughter?"

Vera's finger stabbed the air. She'd worked herself up into a rage.

"You want her messing around with a punk who uses her, then cuts her loose?"

Kneeling, I stared at this woman moving toward us: halting, hunched, in a froth. Was she hoping to join us in a ménage?

Suddenly Lilah was at my side, helping me up, leading me forward, into Vera's arms, which embraced me like water.

Then the train whistled and screamed to a stop. Lilah and I fell backwards. I lifted my head in time to see Vera, who seemed to sink in slow motion, clutching at her chest. Her eyes widened: something inside her wanted out and was hammering at the gate. She clawed the air.

Lilah and I rose in unison and scrambled toward her.

She was large. She fell hard.

Watching her crumple, Charlotte's face blazed into my mind. I had made so many mistakes with women. When would I learn?

I stared at Vera's pale cheeks while the nurse took her pulse.

Then she looked up at me and said:

"Stimpleman."

Suddenly sober, I hurried out.

Kij's face grew darker. He paced up and down the narrow corridor, mumbling to himself. He buried both hands in his pockets, then he took them out and rubbed his face. At one point he had three cigarettes going at once. Watching him calmed me.

The hand had been swept from sight.

When Eric returned and said that she would recover, Kij cried, "My God!"—whether in alarm at the gravity of her illness or at the prospect of her survival I couldn't tell—then hurried down the corridor to see her.

Alone in the car with Eric, I asked:

"Isn't it time for her to die?"

"Of course," he said softly. "Long ago. But we dare not think that."

I nodded.

"What happens in Kyiv?"

"Now, who knows? Depends on what Khoriv wants."

"What if that was his hand?"

"I never worry about Khoriv. Who should worry are the people who sent the message. Khoriv doesn't scare."

"I repeat: what if that's *his* hand?"

"Then may the Lord have mercy on those who sent it," he said, crossing himself.

"What's Vera going to do?"

"Exactly what she planned to do. She's returning to her village. Khoriv bought her a house there. The places where we've suffered turn dear to us later. She'll depart from this world in the town where she was born and about which she never had one good word to say that I remember, but who knows? There's always a lot people don't tell you."

The idea of departure was on my mind too.

"Is there a plane from Kyiv to London?" I asked, realizing I had no visa to be in the country in the first place.

From nowhere, calm descended. I'd been thinking more about my theory of the turn. Over the last two days, I had been through something with these people. I'd walked into the middle of their lives, and they had carried me far out of my way. They'd opened up a huge part of the world for me. But I needed to get back to England, where I'd finally learn the answer to the riddle of my father's death.

"Through Frankfurt," Eric said.

"I don't have any papers."

Eric shrugged.

"In this country, papers grow on trees. If you know where to look."

When Kij returned, he said:

"We're going to need you in Kyiv."

"What the hell for? I'm not going."

"What?"

"Wait," Eric said.

"I need to get back to England. This is your business."

"No," said Kij. "You're coming with us."

"Who the fuck are you to tell me?"

"Your host, that's who," he said, his voice genial, yellow teeth flashing. "Under the circumstances, given how rarely you're likely to visit, don't you think you should seize the occasion? Come to Prypiat."

"What about Khoriv?"

"My brother can handle himself."

"What makes him so tough?"

"Twenty years in Siberia. For deserting, my friend. After the war. Trying to get over to your side, in fact. That's a better education than Oxford."

"I may not have enough money to get back home."

"Not a problem," Kij said, slumping down into his seat and staring out the window.

After a minute, he turned to the task at hand.

On the table stood towers of coins he began sweeping into a bag.

"Kij is about to play Santa Claus," Eric explained.

"Whenever Khoriv does business, it's always Christmas," Kij added. "He's known for it. Spreads it around. People would notice if he didn't. You're not a businessman, are you?"

He sighed, heaving his bulk out of his chair and heading out.

Eric shrugged, lifted the vodka bottle and turned it upside down. A few drops dribbled to the floor. Then he opened his black bag and took out a flask of Jameson's.

"Drink?"

I shook my head.

"Poverty," he said confidently, "is nothing but the sign of an under-nourished imagination."

"You're such an expert, doctor."

He frowned.

"I've seen what I've seen. And what I've seen is that money can help. And so can religion. I'll drink to that."

He turned the bottle up and took a long drink.

We were approaching Kyiv. Goats grazed alongside the tracks. A horse-cart heaped high with hay ambled along.

I thought of the boy on crutches. He felt more like family to me than either Kij or Vera. How would my work ever be useful to him? Today, leaning back in my chair, I wondered how to answer that question. In the gap between idea and act spring guilt and government agencies. My only response must be in what I do, what I keep doing despite my doubts. A book, wrote Boris Pasternak, was nothing but a burning, smoking piece of conscience. I am here, alone, writing my "oral history," trying to understand everyone's point of view, because it's the best way I know of being fully present among people. In the company of others, I dream: alone, I quicken to life.

And somehow I believe the answer to what I should do with the files is written in the palimpsest of what happened before.

– 6 –

Approaching Kyiv, Kij hunched over the CB on a table facing the window (in the prehistory of cell phones) while Eric shuttled back and forth between us and Vera, reporting on her progress. He downgraded his initial prognosis from mild heart attack to coronary incident and said she needed to sleep, but that she would certainly recover. Her perfect death remained on schedule.

"Look, I want to hear about Father."

"That was so long ago. Who remembers? I'm busy."

There was no reason for me to stay. They had no interest in helping—and why should they? They had problems of their own. Fine. I'd settle this for myself.

I remembered Vera saying she had photographs of my father. Tracking them down might give me some answers.

Alongside us, the silver-dark Dnieper shimmered like a vein of mercury marbled with blood, and for a second it seemed we were skimming the waves.

Lilah was sitting at Vera's bedside and reading a book.

"She's going to be fine," she said. "Don't feel bad."

Vera's snores filled the room.

I shrugged, wondering just how much of what happened I would tell Selena about, and if she'd care.

Below the painting sat several cardboard boxes intended for the house in Prypiat.

Inside the largest was a smaller one held together by a rubber band. I forced my finger under the cardboard and poked around. I was in luck.

I picked it up and walked to the door. Passing Lilah, I lowered my gaze. Why was I the one who felt ashamed? When it came to sex, women always trumped men.

Instead of returning to the common area, I ducked into my own cabin where I settled on the bed to examine this photographic record of my father's past. I drew up the shade for light and turned the box upside down onto the green woolen blanket, spilling a mountain of black-and-white pictures. Most had serrated edges, like huge stamps.

What I found puzzled me. The first I saw were of Vera. Some, on hard stock, in sepia, must have been from early in the century. One showed what looked like a single-story, two-room house with four children lined up in front of a white gate. A goose fleeing the camera's grasp succeeded only in pushing its neck from the frame. The children, two boys and two girls, were shabbily dressed. They appeared to range in age from five to twelve. The two boys looked gravely toward the future. Young Vera, barefoot, stared into the camera as though she wanted to eat it.

Who had taken the picture? This hadn't been a household whose residents owned Kodaks or even Leicas. Maybe an itinerant photographer traveling from village to village was documenting the state of his nation for the children of the future to see. Or maybe he traded his pictures for something to eat.

Another photograph showed the unmistakable young Vera at roughly eight. This time she wore a traditional embroidered blouse and a look of early insouciance. She stood before a well with a roof like one of those funny broad-brimmed Chinese hats that rise to a point. A wreath of flowers sat on her head at a jaunty angle.

I picked up a handful of photographs and scattered them around. Vera, her childhood home, her parents.

I poked at the pile.

The slow sting of despair was more than the aftermath of my aborted fling with Lilah. After Father's death, what did history matter? How could knowing what had happened to him help either of us now? I imagined Stalin, Roosevelt, and Churchill at Yalta. Three men horse-traded the destinies of hundreds of millions. And what kind of men do we really know them to be?

A train heading in the other direction whistled by.

Light shone, but why, and for whom? The world was in the grip of a seemingly incurable meanness, and we appeared powerless against it. Greed and fear steeled us, while the poor, the mad, and the broken were hurled into the streets, and undesirables disappeared and nobody knew where they'd gone and soon everyone forgot they'd ever existed. What did my personal grief amount to before so many powerful foes?

Our age itself was evil, but what could *I* do about it? About anything? I did this and that; yet it was as though I did nothing. "I" was a pronoun, a label pinned to a succession of apparently random gestures. And yet "I" was at the same time responsible for the world in a way I couldn't explain. This was my first direct insight into what Vera meant when she said I wasn't merely my name or my circumstances. Writing this, I try to keep in mind that the self isn't a fixed entity but rather a pattern of perceptions in vital and ever-shifting relation to everything on which it gazes. Easier to say than to do, I'm afraid.

My attention was snared by a photograph showing an older Vera, full figured, in her nurse's uniform, standing proudly in front of three cribs.

I prodded this house of cards to which the past had been reduced. There were more pictures of the boys, some with Vera, others of just the three of them, or the two, or alone. The boys were better dressed than I expected.

As the boys aged, I began to recognize them. There, unmistakably, was Kij—his face thinner and longer than that of his brothers. The tall one smoking a cigarette had to be Khoriv. And the other, looking like Khoriv's shorter twin except for the eyes, which were wider apart, and the slightly less forward chin, was most certainly my father, Andrew.

Unmistakable: my father in short pants on holiday, just as Vera had promised.

———•—•———

The train began slowing down. I longed to walk out into the air, free again. Why should I obey my criminal uncle? He wouldn't hurt me—I wasn't afraid of that. This wasn't a prison cell, I told myself, leaning back in my seat. I had put the photographs away. My backpack sat across from me.

On the other hand, the prospect of finding myself stuck in a strange city where I didn't speak the language, without any papers, and only a few hundred dollars left, overwhelmed me. Were I to go to the American consulate—was there one?—I might have to tell them about Kij, Khoriv, Vera. The hand.

I understood now that Father had never really left home. In his heart, in his imagination, he'd remained with his mother. Mother and I were less real to him than his memories.

Yet these memories were no longer abstractions, as they would have been had I not traveled to see this world for myself. All around us stand trees in parallel forests, and when one falls, even though we're not there to hear, it makes quite a sound. This was small consolation to Mother and me. Each of us carries a cache of utterly singular images shared by no other being in the world. That's what we are—bundles of memories unpacked by a mysterious stranger.

I yanked up the window: tight, but I could leap out, backpack in tow.

As we approached the platform, I stuck out my head. It was mid-afternoon, not a cloud in the sky. Despite everything, my mood brightened.

A handful of people milling about turned to us with stunned looks on their faces, as though the train's arrival had caught the entire station by surprise.

Near the middle of the platform I noticed a familiar, gray-haired man wearing a leather coat. He too had noticed me and was waving.

I waved back. What else could I do?

There, standing on the platform in Kyiv, beside Lebed, the girl with the clipboard from Vienna, waiting to greet me, was my father.

— 7 —

Before the shock of seeing him registered fully, a voice behind me said:

"Why not travel with me?"

I turned to find the bearded priest standing so close behind me I could smell the mint on his breath.

"The ambulance will be waiting," Kij, who'd just walked in, said in German.

"She needs a hearse," sighed the priest. "The little boy I just saw back there on crutches needs a mother. And I," he looked at us wearily, "need a drink.

"This is the nephew?" he said, turning to me.

"Guten Tag, Vater."

The priest smiled:

"So few Americans speak a second language," he replied in flawless English. "Where are you from? Wouldn't you like to see a little more of this city than you might if you stayed with your boys here?"

"I don't know, Father."

Again somebody else was dragging me into his story.

I kept thinking of my father out there, but was too confused to say anything.

"Father, we're in a delicate moment here. Let's play it by ear," Kij said.

"That is why God gave us ears, my son," said the priest.

I couldn't contain myself any longer.

"That's my father out there, Father!"

"Your father?" Kij asked.

He bent down and peered out.

"Your father? That isn't your father," he half smiled. "That's Khoriv. That's my brother, Father," he said to the priest.

A white limousine idled vainly at the curb. The burly chauffeur in a ginger-colored uniform, visor shielding his eyes, leaned on the hood. Behind stood the moving van, ready to go.

All right, I thought, why not face it head-on? Why not insist they take me to the House of Widows? I'd seen too much and understood too little. The only remedy for the state it had left me in was to insist on looking squarely at everything.

Stepping off the train, I was confronted by the specter of my father again, though it seemed obvious, now that he stood directly before me, that Khoriv was several inches taller. He had the same Roman nose, the caterpillar brows, the startling blue eyes. Unlike my father, Khoriv wore a gray suit with a two-button jacket under his leather coat.

He surprised me with a quick bow.

"I'm happy to meet Czek's son at last."

He offered his right hand. His left arm, I noticed, was sheathed in a cast.

I couldn't restrain myself any longer.

"My father's dead," I exhaled. "He killed himself."

Khoriv nodded.

"And I know why."

SEVEN

The House of Widows

We were sitting in a dimly lit room on the top floor of an old apartment building on the northern edge of Kyiv when the lights and air-conditioning went dead.

"Fucking power station," Khoriv grumbled, rising and going over to the desk where he opened a drawer, pulling out two red candles that he planted like a pair of horns into holders on the sill. As it was late afternoon, and the sky was bright, this suggested hours might pass before power was restored.

"Ever since Chernobyl, nothing works right around here. May a duck kick me. As my mother used to say."

Sweating and dazed into silence, I gazed around. Lost. I was lost. At the same time, I was excited to be here.

The building was a blank concrete pile from the Khrushchev era, named in his honor, and embodying the Soviet aesthetic (contempt for idiosyncracy, suspicion of beauty, the flattening impulse of all authoritarian systems, a distillation of life to brutal basics, cut to the root, a proud reminder of our days in the cave). Like public housing from the same period in the United States: a cruel architecture, reflecting contempt for whoever was poor enough to live there.

They'd knocked down walls between the apartments to create an open space, still unfinished, with wires and pipes dangling like minimalist sculptures so you had to step gingerly lest you lopped off your head or poked out an eye. Yet the leather chairs were Italian, and the art on the walls, if real, was money. Windows on the south looked out on Kyiv, with its romantic onion-domed churches and vast stretches of green amid the high-rises.

163

To the north lay Chernobyl, followed by fields and forests bleeding into Russia.

Vera, Kij, and Lebed, the girl with the notepad from Vienna—only three days had passed since I walked into this nightmare—had driven directly to Prypiat. Vera refused to hear of an ambulance. She gave me a hug at the station, saying I had to promise to carry her love to my father in a separate suitcase all its own. I never even told her he was dead. Then she slipped into the ghostly limo. The ancient mariner herself. I imagined the men in teal suits unpacking her furniture and setting up her house. I never saw her again.

"I told you Khoriv could take care of himself," Eric winked, squeezing my hand as he got in after her.

"Listen, my American friend," said Kij just before I walked off with Khoriv to his chauffered Mercedes. "Your job is to tell the family's history. Write what you saw. We're quite something, no? Remember, don't drink the water. And don't worry. We're just doing our jobs. Khoriv will explain." And he climbed into the car alongside the priest, who waved to me ruefully, smiling through his beard.

Then we were here and the air conditioners died and we began to sweat.

In the fifty or so apartments below us nested "the girls," as Khoriv called them. This was their dacha, their retreat. Punk and disco made the loose panes tremble. The House of Widows catered to the higher end of the human consumer market, which meant their girls were treated relatively well. They weren't kidnapped, not enticed with ads in newspapers or flyers stacked in Laundromats advertising bogus gigs abroad, the way competitors netted their women. After all, Khoriv reminded me, the first piece of merchandise in the House of Widows had been Vera herself; subsequent partners included many of her friends. From the start they ran a "humane" operation centered on the principle that a woman's body was both weapon and asset; it leveled the field; it was the one way she might wield enough power to balance a man's.

Khoriv saw nothing wrong with this arrangement. That he was a man running the business was incidental—after all, for decades Vera had managed every aspect of the work herself. His mother was also his mentor.

That the hotel where the girls rested between assignments, when they weren't on their backs at the flagship bordello near the center of Kyiv, was less than stellar wasn't his fault. Lord knows he'd spent a fortune on trimmings. But the fundamentals were off.

"Our architects are fools. It's all they know," he explained as we walked up the stairs because the elevators had stopped long before the power went out.

On our way up, we paused now and again to visit one or two of the girls. All smiles, Khoriv, who knocked and waited, introduced me as his nephew from America. "Studying at Oxford," he added, waving his stump in the air like a proud father and enjoying the palpable awe that lit up the room at the mention of America. The women were skinny and too young, and some were beautiful, with thick lips and long-lashed Tatar eyes that glinted in the sullen glow of lava lamps at sunset. America seemed part of every girl's mythology. An American could make out pretty well here. The hope of gold at road's end was coded in the very letters of the word America. America America America, I repeated to myself. Are other countries as in love with the sound of their own names?

We passed a playroom full of children watched over by one of the girls. "Hello, Ada," Khoriv called.

She looked up. Her unsmiling face acknowledged the greeting wordlessly. She had a gold star on her cheek, planted, I assumed, by one of the children.

The House of Widows itself. At last. It wasn't at all what I'd expected, but neither was anything else. No guards, bars, wires, or fences staked the place, isolated on a ragged shred of postindustrial plot, amid abandoned machinery so abundant you thought it was the cash crop—cars, motorcycles, trucks, forklifts, empty shipping containers. Blighted as a project in East St. Louis, but safer.

The women had worked miracles with their digs, which were the only privacy they had left.

Tamara, a fair-skinned blond, certainly under twenty, wearing a red halter top, was watching a Russian soap opera when we knocked. She smiled at Khoriv and invited us to sit in the living room she'd plastered with posters of Madonna and Prince. Since she spoke no English, Khoriv translated.

"She wants to get to know you better."

"Tell her I think she's very beautiful. But I'm married," I lied.

The smile turned to a pout.

"Married? She wants to know why you're not wearing a ring."

"Never while traveling. Afraid of losing it. Too precious."

"She says you don't look mean enough to be married."

"Tell her thank you. I think she's very beautiful."

"You've already said that," my translator admonished.

Stung perhaps by my dismissal, the girl flared. The translator didn't fail in his duty:

"She says you don't see her as a woman. She's not just a whore, she says. I think she likes you."

In fact I was on the verge of hysteria, a breakdown. Visiting the House was my choice. I wanted to face things, tack toward the truth, but maybe sometimes it was best to look politely away. In the heart of a country where I didn't speak the language, in the company of criminals who spoke too many, I resolved to act. Only the habit of fear kept us from shaking the trap of circumstance, I told myself. It was a profoundly American view, born of radical privilege, which I'd universalized into a principle without imagining how things felt to people raised in a world where "no" was the national anthem and everyone counted on failure to keep them free. To the women, hope was a threat. Hope promised trouble. Hope led directly to grief.

Still, my panic, born of the distance between what I expected and what I found, was outweighed by my curiosity. I was so close to learning what happened to Father. I had only to keep pushing.

Khoriv was telling me, in some detail, about his childhood. He talked unsentimentally about Vera, the asylum, the war, his years in Siberia, the traumatic postwar period.

My face must have reflected my agitation because he interrupted his narrative.

"We're not going to hurt you," he assured me, which scared me more than anything he'd already said because it meant he sensed my fear. "I just wanted this chance to, you know, talk."

Then he added: "What you don't understand is that you Americans are the scary ones. Everyone's frightened of you. Who knows what you'll do next? God on your side, you kill millions. Then you blame them for forcing you to save them from themselves. Yet you don't see this. Strange."

I know, I know, I thought. We're a ruthless rabble, and if you don't slap us around in our own tongue, we'll never hear you. And why should we? What do we care what you think when we can squash you like bugs? But we love praise—praise us enough, we might not bleed you. Then, again, we might.

"I'm not worried," I said to Khoriv. My voice was clear and strong. I almost believed myself.

"Good. I want you to understand. Your father asked for my help. I did what I could."

"What are you talking about?"

He ignored me. Maybe he was imagining his mother getting out of the car and walking into the house he had bought for her in the shadow of Chernobyl's reactor, where she wanted to go to die, amid the several dozen old people who continued living there because it was home.

Eric said Khoriv had even imported an ancient woman from Japan, a survivor of Nagasaki, to serve as Vera's companion.

Khoriv rubbed the nub of his hand. Or maybe he was looking farther north, at his now and forever permanent neighbor, Russia, whose role in his life was so large and yet, to most of the world, so invisible. Khoriv spent years in Siberia, punished for not wanting to stay here. Precisely for wanting to leave home. Yet it was clear in the fading light of the red sun sliding down a slate sky that he'd made a place for himself. Deputy Minister of Transportation, no less.

Was I to spend the night?

I imagined Khoriv orchestrating a warm orgy of welcome.

"Fifty years I waited to tell someone. It's because of me. Because of me your father was sent to England," he began, his voice tensing.

"Because of you?"

"I was the oldest. One day Mother took me aside and said that things were getting bad, there was a war coming. She said she wanted to send me where I'd be safe. But I refused. I couldn't imagine leaving. I said I wouldn't go, that she should send Czek. That was your father's name. Mother's small joke. We're named for the founders of Kyiv. You didn't know, did you? Anway, I didn't think she'd do it. Send him away. But then, you see, she did. She sent him away so she could be sure at least one child survived. So when we got a letter from your father more than twenty years ago . . ."

"He wrote you?"

"He wrote Mother a long, bitter letter. And he sent money. He thought she was poor. He had no idea. And I couldn't tell him because he didn't know about me yet. Mother was in Vienna, while I had moved to Kyiv after Siberia. By the time I reconnected with her, I was working in the government. When I began in the Ministry of Transportation, I recognized the possibilities. I saw how I could help her. I began finding ambitious girls from my side of the curtain. Always plenty of candidates eager to live in the West and earn cash."

Suddenly I remembered Father's letter and the money I'd forgotten to give Vera.

Khoriv brushed his thick brows with his fingers.

"When your father found out about Mother's business, he must not have grasped how well we were doing because he kept sending money."

And so my head, already spinning, orbited into a still stranger zone.

Just then a girl wearing only a bra and panties raced in. Her left knee was scraped; blood trickled down her ankle.

She screamed something I couldn't understand. It was about Ada, the woman watching the children.

Khoriv leapt up.

"Why? What from?"

The girl pumped her right thumb between her fore and index fingers in a gesture saying *needle.*

Khoriv picked up a walkie-talkie and barked something in Ukrainian.

"Max will be there in a minute. He'll take her to the hospital. What room?"

The girl told him. He repeated the number into the walkie-talkie. Then he draped his arms over the girl's shoulder.

"Go back to your room, sweetie. She'll be okay. Max will handle it."

The girl, who didn't appear comforted, turned without looking at me and walked out.

Returning, Khoriv didn't let up, either.

"May I ask you a personal question?"

I stared at him.

"You don't have to answer. What are your political views? You don't seem to me the typical American."

I said nothing.

"Politics are a delicate subject for you people, I know. Let me guess: you're a soft Socialist. You believe people can be better than they are. That the world will become better—if only it listens to you.

"You live in a dream."

His eyes felt like the infrared scope on a rifle.

"I live in this world," he said defiantly. "It's the only one I know, and it's enough for me. I'm grateful things are as they are. I don't believe in change. Why waste your life chasing illusions? My girls have taught me. I spend hours with them, and when I come back I feel I've done something useful. You'll say I'm exploiting them. Maybe. It may surprise you to know I've had these discussions with Kij and Stimpleman. I don't see it that way. I'm helping them trade what they have for what they think they want. How is that different from what everyone does? It's the factory girls you really should worry about."

"You think you're helping these girls? Your new wife approves?" I said, finally finding my voice and remembering what Vera told me.

"I know I am. They tell me so. But you are of course determined to change things, even though you have no money, no clout, and, forgive me, kid, not a clue. You don't know shit from shinola when it comes to my world. And you never will, yet you'll spend your life trying to fix what you don't understand. Very American. I'd invite you to take a few days, get to know my girls. But you're desperate to race back to your little cave with its pencil fights and paper wars, aren't you? You're all children, you big thinkers. Don't worry, I won't stop you."

By now he sounded both haughty and hurt. He threw out his arms, tugged a shirtsleeve, checked a button, and turned his head. I stared at his profile. A birthmark on the right side of his chin looked like a flattened fly.

He waved his bandaged arm in disgust. Waste of spirit, talking to me.

"Here's the thing," he said, yanking off his jacket and loosening his tie. His white shirt was soaked.

His voice dropped. Suddenly he sounded vulnerable.

"I'm sorry for causing your father's death. Never my plan."

The silence deepened. He glared at me, confused, off balance, then he sank down into the chair and dropped his head between his hands.

"He approached me. He and his friend Mr. Aidan. From Interpol."

"Mr. Aidan? From England? Aidan Gordon?"

"Yes, from the UK, which incidentally you shouldn't discount as a world power; they're doing an excellent job managing you Americans. We should all be so smart in choosing our big brothers. Ha ha. I read George Orwell. In Ukrainian. And as you know, we have the original big brother"—he gestured to the north windows—"always ready to help. I work with them sometimes. Business is business."

"Aidan approached you?"

"Through your father."

"To do what?"

"Help him."

"How?"

"Vera got a letter for me from your father. She passed it on without reading it. She hadn't worked in the business for years by then. In the letter, he said he wanted to meet me. In London. He said he knew what I did and he knew I was in trouble and he could help me. I had never mentioned a word about the family business to him, and I had no idea we were in trouble, which made me think he knew things I didn't. Besides, I wanted to see my brother again. So I agreed. It wasn't easy getting to London in those days. I had to go to Riga and then to Helsinki, from which I was able to fly without being recognized. Remember, I worked in the government. I played poker with the president. I spoke a little English already. Getting around London was no problem. After Siberia, everything else has been easy.

"We met at a bar in a neighborhood where he said he once lived. When I saw him I wanted to cry. I think he felt the same way. But we didn't. We'd been alone only a few minutes when a stranger appeared. He was a stranger to me, but not to your father. It was Mr. Aidan, from Interpol. At first I thought your father had tricked me. That Mr. Aidan was going to arrest me. After shaking hands, he sat there quietly while your father and I talked in Ukrainian. I don't think he understood a word we said.

"Your father explained. He was trying to help me. Interpol had been watching us for a long time. They could have arrested us. But they preferred to target other gangs. Not all our competitors run their businesses as cleanly as we do. In return for information about them, the police would leave us alone.

"To be safe, they didn't want to risk dealing with me directly. Instead, I'd write, or more likely fax, your father. We'd been in touch for years, so there'd be nothing suspicious about that. And he would pass the information on to Mr. Aidan.

"So I began sending your father information—by fax, sometimes by mail. I told him where others got their girls. And I let him know when guns were part of the shipment. We never trafficked in weapons.

"They were a lot more interested in weapons than in the girls. Not for the reasons you'd think, either. Wasn't guns going to terrorists worrying them. It was their own companies. They were losing business, and they didn't like it.

"That was the only time your father and I met. We were supposed to meet again a month ago."

Khoriv stared at me.

"But then he killed himself."

He said it as if it were an accusation. I remembered Aidan's charge, and looked away.

He sat up. His confidence returned.

I tried to imagine my father flying to London to meet with Aidan and Khoriv.

"Now, unless you say otherwise, I'll tell Max to take you to the airport. You'll find a ticket waiting."

My interview was over. I could either say that I wanted to stay, or I could brush myself off, pretend I wasn't ready to scream, and walk out.

At that moment another girl carrying a tray with a bottle of vodka and two glasses on it waltzed in wearing a pink nightgown.

She brought the tray to me first. Her small purple mouth seemed locked in a permanent moue, and her waist was cinched by a broad purple belt with a buckle painted to look like Cher. Her face and arms were doused with glitter.

This must have been what it was like growing up around Vera, I thought, remembering the scenarios Eric described on the train.

"Drink? Why not? We have to wait for Max anyway," Khoriv urged.

I reached for a glass. The girl smiled shyly.

We drank. We waited. At least we didn't sing.

Still no Max. Who knew where he'd gone after dropping the overdose at the hospital? If that's what he'd done.

And then I remembered the letter. I reached into my pack and pulled it out.

"Here," I said, thrusting it at him. "I was supposed to give it to Vera. When you're through, explain it to me, will you?"

Khoriv paused. He blinked. Sweat beaded his face as though he'd been running. He was a little drunk.

In any case, it felt good making the first move for a change.

He took it.

"Always wrote long letters, your father. Why don't you go down a flight? There's an empty room near the stairs. It's not locked. You can sleep. Have another drink first."

The girl, pale as though powdered in sugar, glittered, refilling my glass.

————•—•————

Alone in the room, drunk, I brooded.

It was dark. A candle aimed its flame at the ceiling. American disco echoed below. But the bed was comfortable, the sheets Egyptian cotton. And Khoriv no longer worried me. He was a businessman, and I was no threat.

For some reason I remembered how in college a woman I dated briefly accused me of having had a happy childhood. I took the charge seriously. I was then drifting in a bohemian milieu, and at that age neuroses and articulate despair were evidence of superiority and sophistication.

The city in the distance flickered like fireflies in the sultry summer night.

"But it all went bad," I protested, hoping for points.

Doesn't matter, I was told; it's the first six years that count.

Now I admit without shame: for a while—no matter how briefly—my childhood of beach plums and thorny bushes and biting winds and storms had been lit by the kind of wild light you find growing up near the sea, reared by two characters who had their differences, but who knew how to take their pleasures, too. Downstairs, our neighbor Ms. Johnson sang opera in amateur productions in Beverly, and many nights I fell asleep to arias from *Aïda* or *Carmen* wafting up through the vents or open windows, accompanied by foghorns. The tenant on the first floor was less nice—he was a mechanic who drank, fought loudly with his girlfriend, and, as we found out when he was arrested, sold heroin to kids at the school up the street.

That period of my life was long over, and another was about to end. There was some internal border I'd crossed. I felt the change with a clarity I hadn't known since childhood, when every birthday seemed a rite of passage, and you never knew what as yet undreamed of longing might well up inside you. Who remembers the morning a girl became more precious than a toy?

This place in the world to which I'd come had shown me ways of being I'd never dreamed of. There was no going back.

Outside, the ancient ancestral city slept like a drunken god, skull rattling with memories—of King Tor and the other ones, Perun and Dazhboh, who ruled before the Vikings fell to earth.

Wedged on the cot in a room one floor below Khoriv's office, I was falling asleep when I was startled by a knock on the door.

Khoriv. Drunk. Shirt unbuttoned, eyes red.

"I never knew this," he said, throwing the letter at me. The pages scattered across the floor.

Then he began to sob.

Vera was right. These emotive Slavs!

I sat up, embarrassed.

"It's okay," I said awkwardly.

His bloodshot eyes bulged as he shook his head muttering, "No."

EIGHT

The Translator

Was I completely unable to stop this terrible
traffic in human lives? At first it seemed so . . .
GEORGE S. N. LUCKYJ

~ 1 ~

Braunschweig, 1947

You've been given a mission, assigned as a translator to the Fifth British Infantry Division Headquarters in Braunschweig, Germany, less than forty miles from the British-Soviet demarcation boundary. Many of your people have fled the Soviet army, thrown themselves on the mercy of the Allies. The Brits don't know what these emotive Slavs (the word has the same root as slave) are saying: they babble among themselves, they sulk, they plead, they weep. They write letters to friends and friends of friends and relatives in America. A few have family in England, but that's rare. We've never let too many in.

Listen to yourself—you've been in England what? Ten years? But you've learned, you know the language, you navigate London like a native. You've studied at university. You have certificates. You have papers. The papers are everything: you are a citizen, with rights, and above all, obligations.

You are not what you once were, not what they still are. This is no one's fault.

You remember your mother leaving you with the sailor who took you to England. You were ten, eleven, twelve? You don't know exactly since your mother celebrated birthdays when convenient. Sometimes it happened three or four times a year; then, years went by when life was too busy for birthdays. Good God, there'd only been three of you, you'd think your mother would remember the moment. But it was a strange life on the asylum grounds.

You remember the sailor taking what he wanted from you, and then you remember, you choose to remember, little until waking up in Liverpool, whiff of salt and spoiled fish in the air, amid the hurly-burly of the docks, ships, a biting wind, and needing desperately to pee while people questioned you in a language making as much sense as the chatter of starlings or grunting of boars in the Bucharest zoo.

Then someone walked by and knocked your cap out of your hands into the water, and you had to drop down to retrieve it.

There was a woman waiting to meet you. Beside her stood a little girl. She wore a floppy white beret like someone in a book. You'd never seen a hat like that! The girl frowned. Then her mother said something, and the girl forced the corners of her mouth into a phony smile. The woman, who was herself dressed like a queen, with a long soft gray coat, and a handbag big enough to sleep in, said something you hoped she knew you didn't fully understand. You guessed she was telling you to come along with them. So you picked up your duffle bag and went.

You didn't have enough of the language yet, no words for what you saw. You were all eyes, and life was a foreign film without subtitles. The year was 1937.

You gawked at your new family, people Vera somehow persuaded to take you in.

Ever since your mother handed you over to the sailor, you haven't known what to feel. Fear, rage, and confusion? You missed your mother and your two brothers for a time, but then even that feeling died.

But war changes things. You no longer count on anything. Not even your mother.

You walk into *Nevada,* the nickname for the barracks where they housed the Ukrainian deserters from the Soviet army. The deserters' code name is "Friend." A good name. You assumed it meant they'd be treated like friends. Allowed to stay. You looked forward to returning to London surrounded by people who spoke your language, with whom you'd rekindle memories of places fast fading from the face of the planet.

Standing inside *Nevada,* you are aware of who you are. You are a young man with an identity card. Before you, sprawled across bunks or gathered in whispering crowds, speaking the language your mother spoke to you, are men who have neither a card nor the language of their new masters, on whose mercy their lives depend.

That is the difference between you. A card. And it is everything. Signature. Seal. You cannot get over the power of a simple rectangle. It is a key to another world, and you have it.

These men too were once bundles of wind and light, boys staring at their own faces reflected in transparent streams where newts swam and peepers bellowed in the reeds.

You stare at the ragged, yellow mugs—unshaven, scarred, eyes patched, noses shot off, thick tongued, sallow, stinking of onions and potatoes and such well-seasoned sweat it could be peeled with a paring knife—and you see something familiar. You squint. You stare. You suck in your breath. You can't believe it. There, amid the mob, the anonymous faces of your tribesmen, you see Khoriv. Your brother.

Freeze. Your first impulse is to turn away. Turn! You want to run out before he sees you—though there's not much danger of that, he's lying on his bunk with his eyes fixed on the ceiling.

You recognize his chin and his nose (strange, the hundreds of thousands of chins and noses you've seen in your life, and yet there's only one set like this—how is it possible? You'd imagine nature would have run out of combinations).

Your brother is in *Nevada* among the deserters from the Soviet army. He is seeking asylum. He is looking for something you are here to provide.

Maybe. You don't know. You don't know the secret orders issued from London. How many will be let in, why, who returned. The men themselves tell you, over and over, that, if they're sent back, they'll be shot or shipped to Siberia. You've explained this to your superiors (but you scorn that word, you have no superiors, God alone is entitled to that), tried making it clear that these men are scared.

They've deserted the Soviets for a thousand reasons: because they never wanted to fight in the first place; because they were badly treated, beaten, kicked; because they were told to shoot children; because they did it and will never sleep peacefully again; because the officers who commanded them spat in their faces and threatened their mothers and wives. Because they knew what waited for them back home was slavery of another kind. They would die like bugs in the dark.

So they ran, deserted, raced into the weapon-laden arms of the Brits or the Americans, full of trust that these men had not only been allies in war, but were also bearers of a new way of life: they came from countries where men were free, and human life held an absolute value, and where it was possible to live with this thing called dignity, which you learned about in your British school, but had also heard about from your mother before. You are a human being, she said. Made in the image of God. Act accordingly.

She had several such formulas she trotted out daily, recipes to quiet you and your brothers at table, or at night, when you went too far with your roughhousing.

You liked this concept of dignity. In your language the word is *hidnist*. There were words for the same thing in all the languages—five or six—you've studied. It's why you feel so warmly toward strangers, who will never bother to learn more than a few words of your tongue.

Once you'd mastered their language, you explained that dignity had a counterpart even in your mother tongue. *Hidnist.*

Isn't that fine, they said, smiling. It seemed to impress them. Or maybe what amused them was that you cared enough to explain, that it mattered so much to you, you almost teared up pointing it out.

You love your job as a translator. Translation is a miracle, like the city of London, airplanes, or the Alps.

The job's not easy. Especially now you've found your brother among the deserters.

Your task is to translate during interrogations. The captain, major, or colonel for whom you're translating (depending on the deserter's rank) is usually polite, formal, aloof. Even your adoptive father, Colonel Gordon, wants only facts: how many bombs the Russians have, how they feel about Poland, what the prisoner knows of plans for disarming. To their captors, the men themselves are mere news-bearing mules.

As if any of them know a thing. They can tell you what guns and ammunition their units used, certainly. But they live on the ground. They're not the ones hidden safely in castles or fortified imperial rooms plotting strategies, planning world domination. These aren't the men who sat drinking and smoking at Yalta, congratulating each other, scheming for advantage—personal and national—savoring the cognac, reaching agreements that changed millions of lives. Who signed a secret protocol agreeing to repatriate all Soviet deserters.

The men in *Nevada* choose to believe that if they tell their captors all they know, they'll be welcomed as brothers. Once the Brits see them as men just like them, who believe in the same things they believe in, who care enough for the Allied cause to betray their homeland—once the British discover, with help from the all-important translator—that every word in their language has a counterpart in yours and that you've more than adjusted to their way of life—will they have any choice but to throw open their arms and embrace them?

You see your brother is there, but you don't approach him. You don't make a move. Not right away. Not at once. What would you say? Hello? *Guten Tag? Bonjour? Dobrijden?* You may not recognize me. I'm the brother mother palmed off on that sailor a decade ago. She sold me just as she herself had been sold.

You remember her saying to you:

You must not get too attached to me. You have other things to do.

What these were you never learned, though you would never lose that sense you were here—on this planet, on this earth—on special assignment for your mother.

Do all children feel that way?

Before you moved to the asylum you lived in the city in a small apartment belonging to your father's family where you and your brothers shared not just a room but a bed. Because you were the youngest you learned to claim your corner, to kick and punch back. Even sleeping, your brothers wanted what was yours. Or so you thought.

You don't know if your mother is still alive. You don't know if your brothers survived the war.

You used to weep, thinking they were dead. You were sure of it.

Now you're not sure of anything.

Whenever you stand still a minute and turn into it, really tune in, you hear everything: your mother's voice singing to you, your brother insisting spiders tasted good while dangling one by the leg in front of your nose—Khoriv, the older brother of legend, the natural leader, a man of the people, your hero and nemesis both.

Your brothers built a snow fort, then hitched you to the sled in which they sat, laughing, whipping you with a string. You were their servant, their slave. You heard the stream rushing outside town where as a boy you fled from your brothers, where you discovered all that lay curled inside space, the dimension of waves and nodes called silence. Silence was the heart of God. You lay on your back, head pillowed on moss, and stared at a hawk tracing circles in the sky, lost in the sun. Watched a grasshopper balance on a blade by your cheek, staring at you. It saw you, knew you—not your name, something more essential, that boyness. Only things in the wild understood that. To your mother you seemed not so much a boy as a problem: one she showered with kisses sometimes, certainly, whose hair she combed and nose she wiped, but you could see behind her eyes a part of her sorting things out, trying to understand, wondering where you belonged—in that chair, or in the one next to Kij?

How is Kij? How is Mother? How did you survive the war? What will you do now? Can I go back with you? Would you like to join me? How did you leave Mother behind? Is Kij with her? Is this part of her plan? Can we help her? Can I?

Every child stands as a question before its parents. *You brought me here why?* But your mother was always too busy to answer. Taking care of strangers. Her job. Sometimes you imagined disguising yourself as a patient—then, maybe, she might have noticed you. Instead, you ran off the asylum grounds, by yourself, while your brothers tormented those poor men who walked around talking to themselves, spit spooling from their lips, limbs trembling involuntarily like shirts on the line in a breeze. When you left all that behind, the black steel fence around it, fleeing into a countryside that, especially on summer days, seemed to go on forever, the chant-almost-roar of cicadas in the languorous heat and the dust rising up behind you as you kicked the ground with your small bare feet, rushing to the stream-almost-river, you felt you weren't yourself anymore, you were something else, as though sunlight and wind mingled with mud to make this thing that looked like a body. No one in particular. A boy, with no answers.

You're alone. For some reason, you have always been alone.

You cannot bring yourself to go up to him. You walk out quickly. You go to your room, an eight-by-eight cell with fleas and a smell of vomit mixed in with the paint. You lie on the bed in your clothes and look up at the ceiling and say the Twenty-third Psalm in English. You love the Twenty-third Psalm—who does not? Lo, though I walk through the valley of the shadow of death I shall fear no evil for Thou art with me. You tell yourself there is no evil here to fear. You are in God's world, among just men committed to seeing His Kingdom come on this earth.

It comes to you as though from above: you must save your brother. You must get him admitted. He must break through.

Because once the officer has exhausted his questions, sucked all he wants from the prisoner, this deserter for whom, you have discovered to your everlasting sorrow, the British have only active contempt though they try not to show it in front of you, he is discarded.

There are many things you don't translate: the modulations in the interrogator's voice, the hissing contempt, the quick looks.

These British are subtle yet proud. They have stood up to the Huns. Again they have won. Their victory cost them—more than they are accustomed to paying. Enough for them not to want to know too much about how others contributed. After all, the Brits were the original targets of Hitler's rage—once he saw they wouldn't join him—even though they were cousins, the Windsors were originally Hanoverians, the two nations shared roots, and values. They were a strong people on a small island, and they had conquered much of the world on their own. When they recognized Europe wasn't the place to go picking for spoils, they turned elsewhere: to Asia and Africa, then weak and beckoning.

But it cost your people too. This you know. Brits like numbers, and you, working in the office, have them. British military dead: 382,000. Plus over 60,000 civilians. In your country the numbers were: 2,500,000 soldiers and 4,500,000 civilians. More losses than Germany. Each one a soul. Each with a family. And it wasn't your fight. Your people never asked for this war.

Among your kinsmen there are subtle men too; you're sure of it. They haven't all been killed, have they? But these geniuses are not among the deserters. Your brother is certainly not one of the subtle ones. Unless he's changed since you last played soccer together on the street while the grown-ups shot at one another from the hills all around.

You begin to strategize what you'll say to the colonel, who makes most of the decisions, though you've heard him lament more than once that everything is out of his hands, that the important decisions are all made at Whitehall.

When you're done, they take the men back to the barracks where they're kept under arrest until word comes from the Soviets. Then they're put in the back of a sealed truck so they can't see where they're going and driven on the autobahn to Helmstedt. There they're met by a Red Army guard, at which point they cease to be our concern. Most are shot, or sent to Perm, in Siberia.

You toss in bed. Light a smoke. If you could you would smoke a hundred a day, but cigarettes are precious and ten are all you can afford. You ration yourself. You are disciplined. You calculate. You consider how much capital you have with Colonel Gordon. Suddenly you're afraid. You hadn't been until now. You've done an excellent job. Even though several times, afterward, in the mess or on the street, on a sunny warm spring afternoon, with swallows swinging up and down across the sky the way swallows do, in a wave, you've asked Colonel Gordon if something else might not be done. You have told the colonel what you've heard: that most of these men, who were our *allies* and fought alongside us against the Germans, will be shot. And they're not bad men; the colonel can see that for himself.

The colonel sees it. The colonel sees everything. The colonel likes you. The colonel adopted you—basically bought you from your mother—so you think of it. He paid for you. He raised you, paying all the way. The colonel's daughter, Marian, likes you. She likes you a lot, enough to make sure her father takes you under his wing, brings you with him to Germany, where you're treated with respect and dignity by the other officers, not to mention the men (you are a lieutenant yourself, in the club, as it were). At night you read books to improve your language: Dickens, Austen, of course Shakespeare. You love Shakespeare. You can't get enough of that crazy language of his. You don't recognize half the words until you look them up in the dictionary, but then you know them. You have that kind of memory, which makes you perfect for what you do.

So you count the capital you've accumulated. You've pled a few cases, asked the colonel to take into account some of the things a man might have told you—yet has the colonel ever let a man off thanks to *you*? No.

It's not that the colonel is cruel or inhuman—he is terribly human, with a very pretty daughter, who loves you. Say it: she loves you. She wants to marry you. She desires you. Just as her father desires you. Just as her mother does. But the colonel believes in rules, in laws, in orders. He believes it is obedience that distinguishes us from beasts.

And you agree with him, you nod, you say yes. You agree with him up to a point. Because you do argue back, you have enough confidence for that, you have not studied in vain, all those thousands of hours, nights reading dictionaries and cramming for tests, drilling yourself, reciting vocabulary lists to the man and the cat, to the pebbles in the stream, to the devil himself whenever you've felt his presence enter the room. You sweep all thoughts of your mother and brothers out of your mind as you study, so you can have more room for crazy words like *incarnadine* your examiners believe you need to know in order to do your work well. Return on investment. The seas *incarnadine*.

To do your work well is the highest duty that you, a man with dignity, can perform.

So you have argued back, your line a simple one: sometimes rules and laws and orders are bad. Wouldn't he agree that the orders German officers gave their men were evil, stripping them and their victims of dignity?

Well, you press forward, thinking of your brother now—because you've gone ahead and taken that step, you've decided to make the case for him—without telling the colonel who he is of course, and without ever revealing yourself to your brother because you are afraid of the confusion of feelings that arise whenever you think about him. (You want to embrace him. You want to weep. You want to spit in his face for letting your mother give you away.) Isn't it possible that this order for repatriation is a mistake? Can the King really wish these men, who've suffered much already and only want to lead free lives, with dignity, can the King really want them tortured and killed? Is this what Mr. Churchill intended when he signed the treaty at Yalta? Or is it possible this clause slipped by him? That he didn't stop to think about what the words actually meant for flesh-and-blood people. You don't blame him for not taking the time to imagine it fully—after all, these weren't his people to worry about. He had taken very good care of *his* people.

His people. Your people. Our people. How does one turn into the other? The awful power of a pronoun.

You pause, stare at the floor, keep from cracking your knuckles, hunch up your shoulders the way you do when you're scared. He had won a victory for them, kept them from being enslaved by the Nazis. But if Mr. Churchill had had a little more time in between cigars and Armenian cognac there at Yalta, and someone had been around to explain things to him, surely he would have seen the flaw in the clause; he would have recognized instantly that the paper he signed might be misinterpreted by evil men, by men with less natural dignity and high-mindedness, in ways that could hurt others; he would have recognized that the law could be read as reflecting a callous indifference to the integrity of the individual, to all the primary values on which this civilization rested.

You see, Colonel, it is probably difficult—difficult? No, impossible—for a man of your education and quality to understand the way things are done elsewhere in the world. You could not understand that a government might force its own men to fight and then shoot them when they got tired of killing on command. You are English, after all. You have a beautiful daughter, whom I will one day marry.

(You were once that naïve. You were.)

Why does the case of this man interest you so much?

He's from my village.

I see. A neighbor!

It begins to make sense to the colonel. Lights are starting to go on in that great dim warehouse of a head—dim only because it's so large, it would be impossible to shine a light on all the things stored there. Your heart's beating fast. You think you might, with another well-placed word, perhaps an allusion, break through. The wall has almost been breached. You're sweating.

A dog's bark far away triggers a round of howls across the countryside. You love that sound, just as you do the sound of cows heading to pasture in the morning on the farms outside town where you go whenever you can, just as you did when you were a boy living on the grounds of the asylum, sneaking away to play near the water in peace. You have never left the grounds of the asylum. This you know.

I understand you, Andrew, the colonel says. He smiles slightly—he's almost embarrassed by it, you sense it and immediately you cringe for pushing him too far, making him show feeling. It must be excruciating. He's already made so many allowances for you.

He puts his hand on your shoulder, kneads it a little, lets it linger there a little too long.

He looks into your eyes, cups your chin; you're starting to feel very uncomfortable now, trying to keep yourself from wriggling; that would look bad, you know the colonel prizes comportment, dignity, control. I do, he repeats. But you must understand our circumstances. If one, why not all? And if all, then what will we tell the Russians? No, Andrew, this is a moment to be strong and keep in mind the words of no less than Mr. Anthony Eden: "One cannot be sentimental about it."

There it is. The verdict. The wisdom. The distillation of centuries, millennia of breeding, empire, and culture. One cannot be sentimental about it.

You heard it not as it was—a knife in your heart—but as you wanted to hear it: the word itself, the law interpreted by a being of a higher order, whose logic you couldn't hope to fathom. Don't try. Your duty is simple: to obey. Obey.

You have tried. You took a stand. But the decision's not yours. You have no power. What choice do you have?

Because you have not slain the slave inside you. Not by a long shot.

One cannot be sentimental about it.

Of course not; that is where all problems begin, with sentimentality. The world cannot be run by sentiment. It must be organized around laws. What are laws after all but the codification of perceptions and observations about how things happen in the world? That is what laws are. If you are so stupid as to disobey or not recognize them, well, you will suffer the consequences. Because that is what happens.

Yet it seems tautological and doesn't quiet your sense that there's more to things than *the* law allows: that Mercy, Pity, Peace, and Love are not merely words in a poem but realities in the world.

But you don't know how to make that case, and you fear you are being sentimental yourself. It scares you, this penchant of yours for sentimentality. It muddies all thought. Sentimentality, you read somewhere once, means showing more feeling for a thing than God himself does—like putting a sweater on a cat. You think God must be a little unfeeling because in your mind you are constantly buttoning up sweaters on cats. You must get a grip.

You are still standing there, looking at your future father-in-law, utterly oblivious to the little black seed of hatred that has just been planted inside one of the wet, red chambers of your heart.

You nod in agreement.

Yes, master.

You don't say it, but you feel it. Because you are a fucking sentimentalist.

The matter is decided. You have consulted the oracle, and the oracle has spoken.

Let the dogs bark, and the cows low, and the starlings twitter. Gun the engines and load the guns. Step aside. We are coming through. Do not be sentimental. Spit in your eye. Up your bum.

You thank the colonel for his time and go off, back to your room. Say it: to your cell. Tomorrow you are supposed to translate during the interrogation of your brother.

You cannot do it.

There is a water stain on the ceiling you've been staring at every day for the several months you've been here. You've been trying to figure out whether there's a leak in a pipe running between the ceiling and the floor of the room above you. It is a perplexing question. If indeed there is a leak, something must be done so that it doesn't get worse. If, on the other hand, there isn't, then you don't want to bother people who have better things to do. The war is newly over, and there are many more important things to do than to fix leaky pipes. Yet, if there is a leak and it's not attended to, there will be the devil to pay down the road. If there isn't a leak, then how did the stain get there in the first place? You imagine explanations. For a long time you thought there might have been a plant on the floor above which someone watered sloppily. Or maybe someone had dropped a glass or a broken a bottle. But you have in fact been to that room above you—it isn't a room at all. It's a closet. There is a room attached, but the area under which the spot is to be found houses a closet. This deepens the mystery. If above you stands a closet, then how the hell did the stain get there? It is not inconceivable that someone had broken a bottle. Far from impossible. That's true, you acknowledge that. But it is not likely. For who would have been there in that room who would have felt obligated to go into the closet to drink? This building you are living in was once a schoolhouse, and the room in which you are staying had itself once been a closet. All the closets on all three floors line up neatly. Of course, it comes to you: they were supply closets. They kept buckets there, with mops. Which were probably— in emergencies, in haste—not wrung dry but dumped into the closet wet. That's the best explanation, the one you hold on to.

Because the other thought that comes to you is that it's the urine of a small animal dwelling in the crawlspace between the ceiling and floor above. And you would prefer not to imagine such an unhygienic scene.

———•—•———

The next morning, time to wake up, yet you lie in bed, eyes open. The stain is still there, perhaps a millimeter larger. Yes, you're sure of it. As soon as you're well, you'll investigate. The point is, you're not well. At all. Sick as a dog, that's how you feel, if truth be told, if it still gets told anywhere these days. You allow yourself the cliché because you are too frightened and confused to think up anything clever, although you know how the British hate clichés. You pride yourself on always trying to use fresh, personal language.

There is a knock on your door. You ask who it is. It is the corporal. You explain the situation to him. You tell him that today you will not be able to do any translating at all. You need to stay in bed. The corporal understands, he is only a year older than you—though you are a lieutenant, and a foreigner on top of it. Whether it is the desire of the lie to become the truth or whether something came over you last night, you really do feel sick. Your throat is sore and your temples throb and your tongue, your professional instrument, as it were, which has turned so many phrases of gobbledygook into the King's English, feels tumescent, swollen as though bitten by a bug. Your eyes burn. There is no way around it, you even want to throw up but you are too weak to move, so you lie in bed and stare at the stain. You lie there all day, wondering whether they got the guy from the next town to come in and do the translating in your place. You imagine the Russian-speaking translator interrogating your brother. Your brother is taller than you. He has the build of a circus strongman. You can't see how you shared the same mother. Or maybe the father? And he took advantage of his size. Throughout your childhood, he tweaked you, he pounded your arm, he called you Snotnose and Poopypants and Pisspot. Your brother was not your best friend. But then you remember one Christmas. Your father was still alive. That was a good time. The time your father, who was not always very nice to your mother except at holidays when he would be transformed, took all four of you, the three boys and your mother, to the forest to watch while he cut down the Christmas tree you then all helped to drag back to the little house where you lived. Your eyes fill with tears and you are flooded with understanding: as long as your father was alive, your life was very good indeed. Your father kept the peace among you. He wouldn't let Khoriv push you around. He made Kij, who was older, share his soup with you that time you accidentally knocked the bowl to the floor. Your father had noticed you listening whenever there were musicians around, and he deemed you were worthy of piano lessons so you could hammer at the ancient Kablehus in the living room and which had once belonged to his mother—to your father's mother. The thought of a grandmother you never saw clogs your throat; you see the human chain, generation on generation, reaching back and back beyond sight into the dim mists of history and ending where but with Adam? It was only after his death that things got harder. You now see why. It was not easy for your mother to take care of three boys by herself, especially before a war. Your beautiful mother. Every one of your friends—not that you had many, but one or two, now and again—was in love with her. Her long braid and big eyes and the elegant fingers with which she stroked your hair. Your brother, who has deserted the Soviet army—how did he get drafted there in the first place? But during the war people moved around a lot, running this way and that, like animals trapped in a burning house. Did he leave her alone or with Kij? For that matter, was she still alive? For years now you've had no idea if your mother is even alive and no idea how to find out. Then it occurs to you: your brother would know. You don't know for sure, but you doubt your mother sold him too. Or maybe she did. You have been away from home for ten years: it is 1947 and you are almost twenty-one, probably. By now your mother might be in her grave, dead in a concentration camp, or rotting on the street in a bombed-out city. You don't know, and if you don't ask your brother, you may never know. You will live the rest of your life—ten years, or fifty—in ignorance, always wondering what happened to your mother.

You won't be able to live with yourself. You can't do this. You can't let your brother be interrogated and then shipped back to the Soviets to be shot. It will haunt you forever.

Besides, your mother didn't sell you—she used to tell you that your father had bought her from her parents—she turned you over to a Ukrainian sailor married to a British girl whom she paid to take you to England so you could get away from the war. She said she knew a man who was willing to help—her and you. The sailor drank, he beat you, his wife beat you, but you took it in stride. You had already learned to read English in school. Your mother loved you. And you love her. More than anything.

You shoot up in bed, sweating. You have to save your brother. Whatever it costs, as much begging and tears as are needed. Even if it means losing the colonel's daughter, you must save him.

You've made a terrible error. Alienated from yourself, brought up by people with no clue about who you were, had been, must remain—you've let your human feelings decay. They've nearly rotted away.

Even as you struggle to dress, fingers clumsy, thick as the truncheons MPs wear at their sides, you argue with yourself: Are you just being sentimental? Would God do this, if he were you? You really are feverish, though now you suspect it is a moral fever that's burning you up like Dresden, the body's deep knowledge that you have committed an error. You have made the gravest of mistakes, a bad decision you won't blame yourself for too much because the complexity of your situation would have bewildered the keenest philosopher.

You run down the hall, throw open the door, stand on the stoop of the school in the rain. You knew it was raining; you'd heard it in your room while watching the stain. Nevertheless you have forgotten not only your raincoat but also your shoes. The water on the brick puddling between your toes feels cold.

You hurry back to your room—you don't want to look like a madman when you go to the colonel—and by now you are determined to hold yourself up to your full height, as it were, to stand tall, to force him to take full account of you in all your dignity, to understand that you will not let him send your brother back to be shot under any circumstances, even if it means going with him yourself, back to the other side, back to your mother.

You think of the colonel's daughter, Marian, whom you love. You grew up with her. She was the pretty girl in the beret standing beside her mother at the dock to greet you when you first arrived. The war had not yet begun, though things were looking bad. She was your first English teacher. She had teased you, forced her lips into a smile. She smiled and told you her name. What's yours? Her mother smiled and said, His name is Andrew. The colonel became your stepfather—he was only a major then, and he was away a lot of the time, but you admired him; he was tall and direct and kind.

You thought that—think that—despite what he did. Both things were true. Most of the time he was kind.

When she was sent to St. Hilda's, while you attended the C of LS, you lost touch but she was never far from your thoughts. When your paths crossed on holidays, you took walks together. All across the city, even when they were bombing. Once she surprised you while you were reading a geography text. She came over and put her hands over your eyes. You knew right away who it was. She asked you how to spell amaryllis, and you felt your heart open like an amaryllis even though it was winter outside.

Together you went to the British Museum, a place that thrilled you not just because of all it contained but because of the people you knew who'd been there before you: Darwin, Marx, even Charles Dickens!

You loved the way her black hair ended in curls that pointed at you like hooks. Her way of putting her hand on your forearm—even when she hardly knew you. She was the very first girl to touch you. You don't know how that was possible, yet it was. You had been terribly quiet and standoffish growing up. Not your fault. Since your father's death you'd been afraid that other people you cared about would disappear—and behold, it had happened, the nightmare had come to pass: *everyone you grew up with had disappeared.* And here you were, being smiled at by a pretty English girl. The next thing you knew you were kissing her—this girl you'd known for years.

By then, the war was on. The British were training as many people as they could, educating them so they could send them out to fight the enemy. You quickly decided that you would join the battle yourself. If you were killed, you would die with a line of Shakespeare on your lips. You had by then fallen in love not only with the girl but also with the language in which she had addressed you. One of your favorite English novels was *The Prisoner of Zenda* by Anthony Hope. You thought maybe in your own country you had been a prince. Maybe after the war you would be restored to the throne, and you would bring your mother to live with you in the castle. A thousand years of peace would follow.

You enlisted. You wanted Marian to admire you. She was already moved by your story.

You did not tell her you suspected that in your country you had been a prince.

You remember with horror how you joked you'd never bring your brothers over, they were such lugs.

You are outside in the rain, shoes on, running to the colonel's office on the next block.

You rush into the building, then you stop and go back to the mat and wipe your feet. You take off your slicker and brush down your hair, which has a tendency to stick out from the sides like a porcupine's needles. You stop at the desk and ask the corporal if the colonel is in.

He is, and he is happy to see you. He welcomes you as though he were waiting for you all along. He has heard of your illness of course, and he's delighted you're feeling well enough to step out. Although the truth is, you do not look well. You don't look strong at all. In fact, you look yellow. There is a yellow film coating the whites of your eyes. Have you been checked for hepatitis?

His voice is full of concern.

Suddenly, in the glare of his warmth and the aura of his subtle presence, which you know judges all things and measures all things on scales so finely calibrated you can't even imagine slivers of dust light enough to balance them, you are caught short. Your mouth is dry. Your intentions are less clear. Your resolve starts dissolving.

No, you will push through your fear. After a minute of agonizing small talk, you ask the colonel if he has interrogated the man they spoke about yesterday. Khoriv.

As a matter of fact, just this morning. Sullen sort.

You snort, a sullen sort, that's right, that's your brother.

But he cooperated in the end.

You smile, though you're not sure if you feel pride or shame, or anything at all. You have been translating other people's words for so long, standing in between like a bridge, giving yourself over to serving the selves of others; the truth is you're no longer sure what you actually feel.

You say you would like to see this prisoner.

Ah, that's impossible.

And why is that?

Because it's Thursday, man. The truck for Helmstedt left before lunch. It would have left earlier, but the interrogation had gotten off to a late start—because their translator was ill and they had to borrow one from next door.

He smiles, his kindliest smile, and tells you not to worry, no one will hold it against you that you were sick. You are a very gifted young man, and everyone knows it. In fact, the colonel had a letter from Marian just that morning asking after you, suggesting you might expect a letter from her yourself as early as tomorrow.

You stand there smiling, because what else can you do? Your chest has been kicked by a horse. Your brother is gone. It is as though he had never been there at all—why worry about it, you tell yourself—it was only a coincidence you'd seen him in the first place. If you hadn't seen your brother, you would not have had all these worries, not have counted the hours in widening circles of rat piss.

But you did see him. You stood an arm's length away. And now he's gone. And now you will never see him in this world again. Of that you're certain.

Problems spawn progeny like those fish grown so full of eggs they simply drop them in looping chains for days wherever they go. A new string of woes presents itself to you. You are desperate to tell your future father-in-law what you've done: let your brother be taken off to be shot. You look at the man with his slicked-back hair and his smile and his slightly creased jacket and glistening shoes. You want the comfort of a father's arms around your shoulders; you long for a morsel of sympathy, of warmth, which would go a long way toward helping you calm down.

Aren't fathers the bearers of wisdom?

You hardly knew yours.

You look out the window and see fellow soldiers standing around, smoking, making jokes.

But how can you tell him? What if he decides your actions were monstrous—that your surrender to fear was unmanly, not at all the characteristic he'd like in a son-in-law? More than anything you fear that cold gaze of judgment you have seen on his face time to time. As when the home secretary said something so stupid it was too arduous even to think of correcting it, yet one need not enjoy being governed by fools. The look that comes over his face when someone mentions the names Hitler or Stalin, about whom you have heard him go on at some length, explaining the ignorance and the beastliness with a withering analysis of the small man's infinite lust for power.

You say nothing. You say you think you are going to take yourself to the infirmary now.

He nods. Good idea. He has a reasonable faith in modern medicine.

Andrew, he says as you open the door—for a moment you think—

hope, pray—he's noticed you're trembling, so weak you can barely stand and in fact are leaning on the door for support.

He has fixed you in his gaze.

I understand this "my village" business. Believe me, I do. After you left I wondered how I would have felt in your shoes—if, say, someone from Sussex were in the same position your man was. You did the right thing. I would have done the same. Fellow feeling is a virtue.

It's only just that it's war, man. And when it comes to war, this once Mr. Eden had it right . . .

One cannot be sentimental about it. You finish the sentence for him, adding: I know, sir. Thank you, sir.

You stand a moment and wonder if you mean it. You wonder what Sir Anthony Eden *knew* about war, what he ever lost to that god.

And you walk out into the rain. This time you forget to put on your coat and let the water wash over you until your clothes are heavy and wet. You stumble back to your room and lie down. You shut your eyes.

You hope you will never wake up.

But you do. In the infirmary. Around you, smiling people rush about. How can you be angry with them? They want to help you. They've saved your life, over and over. Who are you, that your life is so blessed? Why wasn't your brother as lucky? Or is life not a blessing? Is it perhaps something else?

------·◆·------

When you came back to England, Marian was waiting. She'd stayed true to your vows. She'd spent the war working as a volunteer at the Chelsea Royal Hospital. Surely she had opportunities. Her life was full of opportunities. You were the least of her options, the poorest, not by any means the sharpest, maybe even the most difficult in light of the events that had unfolded. Yet she had stayed true. It moved you.

At the same time, you were confused, unhappy.

That afternoon driving to Cambridge you got angry with her. Angry enough to sleep with her.

Afterward, you told her what had happened.

My God, she said. Why didn't you tell my father he was your brother?

You think he would have done anything different? You don't think he would have said, *You're being sentimental*?

You people with your privileges and your principles. You people are so guilty, so scared of facing the consequences—I won't say of your actions because mostly others act for you—there's the tragedy. You'll go to any length to destroy the evidence of your cruelty. God, I hate you people.

You made love again. The next morning you felt good neither about what you said nor about the lovemaking. Love ended for you that night.

Not, however, its consequences. You moved out of their house to your own flat in Brixton.

Weeks passed. One afternoon she stopped by, wanting to talk. You immediately guessed what it was about. When you sat down at Burl's, even before she could say anything—because you could see there was a light in her eyes again, and the old warmth playing across her face, and you knew she was about to turn on the charm, about to try to seduce you again, and you weren't sure you could stand up to her. So before she could get a word in, you said:

Before you say a word, you should know that the last thing we want is a baby. Anything contaminated with your father's genes is poison to me. You know what you have to do. Let's not be sentimental about it. Kill it. If you want me to give you the name of someone, no problem. You know the names of many skilled butchers. If you want me to do it myself, I will.

Her face went so dead a chill went through you.

That won't be necessary.

She got up and left.

These were the last words you said to each other.

A few weeks later you received a package in the mail. It arrived on a bright April morning. There was no return address, yet you knew the source. At first you almost threw it out. You thought it might be something you'd forgotten when you left. As it was, you ignored it all day and only late that night, as you were preparing for bed, did you pick it up again. You would never have opened it had you not thought it might be a book you wanted back. It was heavy, tightly wrapped in newspapers, with strings around it. You cut the string with your pen knife. You felt something cold made of glass. Unwrapping it, you saw it was a pickle jar. A pickle jar! What did she have in mind, you wondered?

It was dark at your desk when you opened the package and carried it over to the light by the bed and saw:

Small, unmistakable hands and fingers.

She had sent you your child.

———•———

After that, what could you do but leave? How could you even dream of staying in the same country with her? You went to Canada first—part of the Commonwealth. But somehow you couldn't find a footing there, though you worked steadily, in many different jobs. While washing dishes in a restaurant in Toronto, you met a fellow from Boston. He had moved to Canada to escape the draft, but he missed his home. It was all he talked about: Boston Boston Boston. He said he'd never be able to return. So you did it for him. It was part of the great migration: entire nations and races of men and women crisscrossed continents, seeking a place where they might start over again, far from those places spoiled by war. As one group left—or was most likely forced out by roving predators—the predators moved in. The displaced were driven to wander the face of this very wide world, condemned to looking over their shoulders at where they'd been, damned to remembering all they had lost, their lives were a permanent scratching toward home.

If only you could cut out your memories. You tried for years. Eventually, you had a family of your own, a wife and son who loved you, whom you tried loving back, even though you could not, you admit it: it was impossible for you to feel love for them. Whose fault was it if they weren't as real to you as the memories of Marian, your half brothers, Vera?

All of whose lives you had ruined.

You came to Boston. It was the 1950s, the world was bustling. You got a job at the Parker House, washing dishes, and a room in Scollay Square, near the strip joints and burlesque, which you went to when you could—anything to distract you, to keep you from sitting still, because that was when the memories were at their loudest. You could not easily drown them out. . . .

~ 2 ~

Devon, Massachusetts: 1979

You watch the water boil. You are sure it's boiling faster because you're watching it.

He has just left. What he told you is in the room with you. It will never leave. Information huddles in the corners, its mustache drooping. Information wears a bow tie. Information glances at you slyly, seeing through to your organs. The defects, the risks.

You turn the boiling water off and pour it over the tea bag. But something in the window catches your eye. There's a blimp in the sky above the harbor. It seems so festive and playful, reminding you of all the Red Sox games you meant to go to and never did. For a minute you forget your troubles.

You walk outside. Forsythia explode against the side of the house. At first you think the yellow flares will burn out, but they don't. Spring announces itself. The heralds of summer are everywhere: in the tulips and daffodils, the fat buds, the birds. Outbursts of ocean spray over the rocks down the hill. Jets of diamond. You are dazzled. You feel you've never seen this before, never looked at your world clearly. Have you ever really looked at your own hands? You have; you know what they've done. Where they fail. But for the rest, you can't sustain the intensity.

You are dazed because it's less than an hour since you've spoken with Aidan, and you don't believe what he said.

You never expected to see him again, never mind host him in your forever-new home.

You walk faster toward the water. Water has always been your ally in this world. From boyhood days by the stream. Water is most of what you are—that's another place the authors of the Bible show their ignorance: you are not ashes or dust. You are water.

You think in strange ways, but you can never get it across to your son or, for that matter, to your wife. They act as if they know you. But you know they don't. You have been certain things to them: you have helped sustain them physically, you think, raising your collar against the wind, wishing you'd brought a scarf. You have tried to say kind and helpful things to them, but you haven't always succeeded. You know that. You wonder why. It's what you wanted: to start a family of your own, far from the violent world you left behind. To create in the new world what seemed so impossible to do in the old.

But nothing ever seems to get left behind. Everything finds you. One day.

You imagine millions of footprints in the sand, all heading your way, converging. They are your thoughts, your deeds, your words. You believed you were done with them.

You pass by the pharmacy where you see your neighbor who used to teach your son piano. She is discussing something serious with the pharmacist. You know she has been ill. Cancer. She also has arthritis and hasn't offered lessons in years. She was once full of laughter and stories about growing up in Georgia, visiting her brothers and sisters in Harlem and Matappan. You see her sometimes sitting on the porch of the apartment below yours, and you know she is waiting to die. And that is her right, you tell yourself. You wonder sometimes that more people don't do it. Or maybe that is all anyone ever does—dies when they're ready to go. You wave to her, but she doesn't see you.

You go on. You look at the cars. They've grown smaller since the gas crisis some years ago. Suddenly there are Japanese cars nipping at the fins of Detroit, zipping among the German imports. You wonder what, if any, significance to attach to the fact that this country's former enemies eventually become its leading trading partners. You have wondered a lot about such things. Datsun, you say to yourself. Volkswagen. Could these be the secret weapons we fail to recognize, which will explode when we're not looking?

You keep on. In the window of the only bookstore in town, you see a blown-up photograph of the president's wife. You think of how the world must look to her. She seems a decent woman, you think. Then you begin weeping. Soon you are sobbing. Something's not right. No man should convulse this way in public. Your shoulders rise and fall, and now you are running to reach the water, hoping nobody sees you.

There is no information like what you catch on the wind. The wind is the breath of the world, sweetened with shellfish and sea spray. The wind has known you forever; it has dried your tears before; the wind is your mother.

You have questions for both: for the wind, and for your mother. You want to know: Does a person do what they do because of who they are, inside, or because of what they are made to feel they must do by those who have power over them? How much power does anyone have over us, in the end? Sometimes you feel the power of the world is immense; other times you find that you can stand up for yourself, and then you know no force in the universe can move you or change your mind.

You stand on the jetty and stare out at the water and think of what Aidan has told you.

You condemned your brother to this. You sent your brother back. You turned him into a slave dealer, a pimp. Your arrival in this world, your mother's desire to see you survive—see one of her children survive—cost her. She gave up everything. She did it for you. And you turned your back on them. You can never do that again. Never again. You told yourself you needed to grow strong, needed to establish yourself first. But in doing that you erased who you were and in erasing yourself, you also wiped her away.

When Aidan told you they were going to arrest your brother again, you could no longer avoid the implications of your decisions. You were contacted, and you had read your Confucius. Confucius had written: *And if your brother commits murder, what should you do? You should shelter him.*

All this stirred up memories about Marian. You wondered if she knew what Aidan was doing.

When, years later, your son began asking about all this, you felt horror and relief. You wanted him to know what happened at the same time that the thought of his knowing, along with the memory of what you had been through and done, disturbed you so fully you could only imagine killing yourself—how could you live with it if your son were to know everything about Vera, Khoriv, and Marian?

You couldn't bring yourself to tell him no matter how much you wanted the relief of knowing at least one other person knew what you had been through. The only way to be sure he understood was to make him feel his way there by himself.

You wipe the spray from your face.

The blimp has disappeared from the sky, replaced by clouds a thousand times larger and more beautiful at which you marvel as though they were made by human hands.

No, that is the point: what makes them beautiful is that humans have never touched them.

The worst is knowing you can't go back to change a thing. But what do you do when you can no longer move on?

NINE

Must There Always *Be* an England?

What is precious is never to forget
The essential delight of the blood drawn from ageless springs
Breaking through rocks in worlds before our earth.
STEPHEN SPENDER

~ 1 ~

"You're back!"

Seeing me, Selena seemed startled. She stopped in her tracks, arms at her sides, and looked me up and down. We were at the head of the stairs in Marian's house. The hall clock began striking four. But it felt much later.

I'd returned from my European adventure two days before, haggard and spent. I'd slept most of the day and was on my way to tea with Marian.

Selena wore a clingy black cotton dress, her crescent body's every hopeful curve on show. She smiled. Her quick grin showed she'd lost her lip stud.

While I had done my best to smear the memory of our one night together, looking at her now, it came back to me, all our talk about identity and history.

"Hey," I said, not knowing whether to embrace or shake hands. "Going down?"

"That all right?" Her voice was suddenly tentative.

"Of course. Walk with me later?"

She slowed then said hesitantly:

"Why not?"

And so we stepped out into Marian's garden together.

I'd thought of it often over the last weeks. Knowing such a walled Eden waited in a world of troubles it couldn't completely divorce itself from went a long way toward sustaining a man on his travels.

203

Marian sat in the old spot with her back to the roses. Her face was shadowed by oak leaves and ivy. Lavender sweetened the air.

Selena poured the tea.

"Did you find what you were looking for, James?"

There was a note of irony in her voice I'd not heard before.

So I rehearsed parts of my trip, speaking from a script I'd begun preparing on the flight home.

I watched Marian's face closely. Her eyes widened and narrowed as she took the stories in. Yet an undercurrent tugged at my heart, belying the surface calm. In my absence some deep shift had taken place. Neither Marian nor Selena seemed themselves—they felt windswept and alert, as though they were standing on the edge of a storm.

Finally, I asked about the jar. Why would Father have saved it?

Marian took off her glasses and rubbed her lids.

"Aidan insisted on sending it. With a fetus inside. I'm sure your father thought it was his child."

"It wasn't?"

"It was the fetus of a girl in the second trimester, with fingers, eyes, a mouth that never learned to smile," she went on as though she'd not heard me.

An airplane droned overhead. I remembered Vera's revulsion at the sound.

"What else could he have thought?" I asked.

She shrugged, lips trembling.

"It was all so bloody awful."

"Did you ever hear from him again?"

"Never. It was my brother Aidan who got in touch with him. In 1979."

"Aidan?"

I pretended to have no idea what she was talking about. My oral history was nearing completion.

Nineteen seventy-nine was when Father began his weekend hunting trips.

"Two terrible things happened that year," she said. "The first was that our daughter died."

"What do you mean *our daughter*?"

"I told you my daughter was killed in a car accident?"

I nodded.

"That young woman—she was not yet thirty—had been the child Andrew believed I'd aborted."

"In the jar? But you remarried."

"Hugh and I never had children. I had raised Vera . . ."

". . . Vera?"

"I named her after his mother. Whether to hurt him or to salvage something of the past I don't know."

"So all this time my father thought his child was dead?"

My half sister. The smell of freshly turned soil leavened the warm August air.

"It was what he said he wanted. His child dead. Aidan stole the fetus from a lab at the hospital."

Marian let it sink in.

I wondered if she'd invited Selena to help keep my cool.

"And after she died?"

She paused and looked at Selena, who met her gaze. The women studied each other.

"That was when Selena came to me."

Something about Selena's confident chin and worried eyes made me anxious. Her chest rose and fell under the black dress.

"Aidan hated your father," Marian continued. "He'd been around when Andrew returned from Braunschweig and was being so bloody to me. And he was there when my own father, on learning I was having Andrew's child, cut me out of his life.

"I moved to the same dim little neighborhood in Brixton where Andrew had lived. Aidan, who was still a boy, brought food our cook prepared on Mummy's command. Mummy herself stayed away, out of deference to Daddy."

At that moment Bulwer emerged from the house, gin in hand, wearing a fedora. He was about to say something, had opened his mouth, but after one look our way he stopped, stepped back, and turned, shutting the door behind him.

"Unfortunately Aidan and your father crossed paths again," Marian resumed her story after Bulwer's retreat. "Aidan worked for Interpol. By then he'd been assigned to the task force on human trafficking. It became his area of expertise. He claimed there's a human supermarket in every city."

I recalled a conversation I'd had on the train with Tariq, Vera's Turkish assistant. As we were pulling into Kyiv, he rehearsed the city's history, how it had been founded in the eighth century by three Viking brothers who'd sailed down the same time as their kin fell on Ireland, England, and the Americas. It was the Vikings who started exporting slaves from the region. You know how Swedes are about sex, he joked. By the twelfth century Kyiv was the seat of one of Europe's most powerful empires. His own family had been involved with it ever since the first wars between Kyiv and Constantinople, Turks against Kozaks. The word Kozak itself is Turkic for *free man*. The winning side always took spoils.

Everything in the world has a history, I thought, watching Marian's fingers throttle a napkin.

She looked up toward the roof of the house where a pigeon perched on the gutter like a gargoyle waiting to swoop: an Angel of the Somme.

"It's easy to feel lost in a new city, even in a new house," she continued. "But once you have a name, a destination, a focus, everything narrows. Aidan had no trouble tracking Andrew in the States. After all, Andrew himself had managed to trace his mother and brothers. He was sending them money. He thought they were poor."

"Poor as worms."

"What?"

"Phrase he used."

She looked at me. I, in turn, glanced at Selena, who sat with her hands on her lap, staring at a patch of rustling ferns.

"You should ask Aidan yourself. He'll be here next week. Said he wanted to see you. Have more tea, Selena. Eat something, dear. You're too thin."

"I'm fine."

A new tat on the back of her wrist between thumb and forefinger looked like either a scorpion or a Buddha.

I could feel a current of tension flowing between us. At the time I was sure it was all about me.

"Suit yourself, dear."

She turned to me again:

"Andrew finally learned what happened to his family after his mother sent him away.

"Vera's business grew thanks partly to the network his brother developed in Siberia, where he'd been sent after Braunschweig. Aidan explained all this to me."

She sounded apologetic.

Was my father the traitor or the betrayed? To say he was both seemed glib. A further betrayal—this time, of my profession. Despite trends in the field, I remain committed to cause and effect.

Marian stared at me.

"You understand I'd never have backed his cruelty? But Aidan didn't talk to me about his work. It was only after he contacted Andrew that he told me I might be interested in one of his cases. *One of his cases.* You think life offers neat endings? It doesn't. Nineteen seventy-nine was the same year Sebastian was killed in Jerusalem."

"My father died for a cause," Selena spoke up.

"The cause was your brother's. Was it worth all those lives?"

"It was everyone's cause. Mine too."

Selena looked down. She was in a hard place.

"Aidan even flew Andrew to London for a meeting with the brother from Kyiv."

"You think Interpol really cares about the women?" Selena asked. "Since when does anybody give a fuck about people outside their clan?"

"Selena," Marian went on. "There are people who do."

"Makes it worse. Easier to hate widely."

After a period of silence, Marian continued:

"Aidan said they sold the girls everywhere: in Europe, the United States, the Middle East, Asia. All men hunger for blonds, it appears. What is it between you and them? One of the few aesthetic universals. But it isn't just sex. Your uncles sent us maids, laborers, gardeners. Who do you think cleans Europe's streets and scrubs our elders? Not our own, you may be sure.

"When one of Khoriv's competitors discovered he was working with the police, Aidan immediately told your father."

"How did Aidan find out?"

"Ask him. That's beyond me. He said it was bad news for your father.

"That's why he killed himself, I expect. When he realized he'd landed his brother in trouble again."

Her voice was disturbingly steady.

Our eyes met.

"I see I'm not telling you anything you don't already know."

I didn't respond.

"When you called . . . I can't tell you how astounded I was to hear your

voice, seemingly out of the blue. Only it wasn't out of the blue. It was because of what Aidan began. I didn't know a thing about you. Hadn't ever
imagined Andrew's life in America. I'm rather a narcissist, I'm afraid. Oh,
Selena, what *are* you thinking?"

A jackhammer sounded over the wall. It was Monday afternoon. Outside the garden, life rattled on.

I didn't mind letting Marian squirm.

Selena stared over Marian's shoulder. It came to me then who this mute
witness, with her high cheeks shining in the afternoon sun, her seething
eyes seeing every word Marian spoke, reminded me of: the oblique inward-
ness, the same ability to make her presence felt without saying a word. The
same undercurrent of rage. Who else but Father?

"Never imagined they'd drag you to Kyiv. Wouldn't have let you go if I
knew," Marian said.

"You could have stopped me?"

"I hoped Vera would tell you everything. I'd known about her for so
long. She's been a silent presence in my life since I was ten. I wondered
what she'd say. When we didn't hear from you after that first day, I grew
worried. Aidan himself called to calm me. He knew you'd be fine.

"But Aidan is another matter. I won't discuss him now."

Marian's voice trailed off as though she were on a boat slowly drifting from shore. Selena, meanwhile, appeared to stiffen at the mention of
Aidan's name.

A volley of laughter erupted down the street. A gassy, postindustrial
smog misted the air. In the heat the roses seemed to exhale puffs of scented
petrol.

"You should know," she said, "I never stopped loving your father. All
through my marriage with Hugh, the first person I thought of when I
opened my eyes in the morning was Andrew. It was Andrew I longed to
find lying beside me."

Wind flipped the leaves. A butterfly flitted among stalks of lavender
and bee balm.

I remembered arriving at Heathrow, sure I'd find all the answers in
England. England was the Source Book.

What might have happened had I never gone to see Vera, if I'd taken a
different turn? What was the good of knowing what I knew?

I still wonder.

Late August light bathed the garden, falling soft and sober on the ivy and flowers. The fruit on the plate stayed untouched. A bottle fly prospected an apple's red skin.

"Khoriv's version is a little different," I finally said.

Marian registered my words slowly, as though she'd had to translate them. She gave me a worried look.

"Oh?"

"Not about your side of it, Marian. I'm not saying that," I assured her. "But it's no surprise he saw things from another perspective. He was the one who was sent back. Until I showed him Father's letter, he had no idea Father had seen him in Braunschweig. He simply assumed he'd been repatriated along with everyone else. Which was true. How could he have known who was on the other side of the door? For that matter, he never knew about you and Father, or who Aidan was, beyond his affiliation with Interpol. When my father contacted him, Khoriv assumed it was because he had become a powerful man. He believed Father's intervention saved him from being arrested. As I suppose it did. Not only didn't he blame Father, he thanked him. Khoriv was grateful for everything.

"He has some trouble because of it now. Doesn't seem to bother him."

Marian's eyes widened until they reminded me of Vera's after she'd seen me with her nurse.

"People there take things differently. It's as if they feel they deserve to be punished."

The image of Khoriv sobbing in my room at the Widows would never fade.

"He even apologized to me. It was incredible. He said it was his fault Father killed himself. Out of shame. Khoriv wasn't the operator I'd been expecting."

This time there was no songbird to layer our mood.

"Shall we go in?" I suggested.

— 2 —

I decided to walk through town before the last light had faded.

Passing the grand homes on Banbury Road toward St. Giles, I wondered what it must have been like for my father to enter such a house. To become part of a family as vulnerable as any and yet, compared to the world from which he had fled, wasted by famine and revolution and already preparing again for war, where nothing was stable, from which his mother had rescued him at such a cost, to have been saved from all that, and to have come here . . . how must it have looked to a ten-year-old? The language, culture, and class—all new.

Class. Now there was a word.

I stopped on Magdalen Bridge. People were out for an evening's stroll. There were Indians and Arabs, Africans and Asians, couples with kids, and moody-looking young women my age ambling along the Cherwell. In the distance I could see someone punting. This was the island I'd longed to visit as far back as I could remember. And it had not disappointed.

I turned up Cornmarket and headed into the center of town.

Could my father have forgiven Marian for *her* father's behavior? It would not have been easy. Had they married, he would certainly have been rejected by some of her family. Yet at least they would have had a chance. Together they might have forged a life.

Instead, he gave up. Was it because the person he could not forgive, the person he held responsible above all others, was himself?

I stopped before the Sheldonian, that elegant domed jar of Wren's, its graceful arches and lacey stonework proving rock could soar, where the surest minds in the world had lectured.

A group of kids studied the poster advertising a fall Mozart series.

As I reflected on Marian's tale, a countervoice said I was being soft. Had Father forgiven the colonel, he'd have destroyed himself that much sooner. People smell weakness. They count on it. And once they find it, they move in. Father would have become a toady, Gordon's bitch. Damaged goods. He'd have ended up drinking himself to death at some petty bureaucratic post in some postimperial office job, some other Vienna, rehearsing in his mind the moment when he forgot who he was and gave up his brother.

Instead, he gave him up twice.

———•———

That night, I knocked on Selena's door just as Marian was walking by.

"She's out," Marian informed me.

"Say where?"

"No."

I told Marian I'd forgotten our appointment.

"Apologize at breakfast. She'll understand." Then she added: "She worried about you. A lot."

I slipped a guilty note under Selena's door before turning in.

The next morning, though, I lingered in bed, smoking under the watchful gaze of the gnu. One cigarette relayed another.

I stared at Selena's paintings, unfolding her tribal tale. I'd traveled far to gather the pieces of my own. Soon I'd start fitting them together. The only peace of mind I've ever known has come from the process of giving a shape to the past.

I spent the morning in my room making notes about the last weeks. I skipped breakfast, forgetting again my promise to Selena. I suppose I was avoiding her, unready to pick up where we left off. But so much had happened since our little tryst, she couldn't blame me if I seemed distracted. Later I took a walk to the library. Khoriv was right: the battle of the books was the only one for which I was suited. By the time I returned, it was mid-afternoon. The clouds had come in from the south and looked like they'd stay awhile. I settled down to read in the drawing room.

—•—

Aidan arrived an hour before teatime. I was alone reading about Byron when he entered.

I rose to greet him.

As I said before, Aidan was the runt of the litter. It looked as if someone had taken Bulwer's head and flattened it with a hammer to see how much give the bones had. His squat body and thick limbs reminded me of Sheba, the seal. He wore a plaid bow tie and three-piece suit. His thin lips were curtained with a mustache. His hair was jaundice colored. He kept dabbing his nose with a monogrammed handkerchief.

"I'm s-s-s-so-sorry, old fellow. Understand you had quite an adventure in the old cun-cun-country."

He sneezed.

"What did you mean?"

"What?" he played dumb.

"Before I left. You said I'd killed my father."

"Young ma-ma-man. You know exactly."

He stood his ground firmly, a dwarf Churchill puffing away. His lower lip thrust forward in a girlish pout.

I tried putting myself in his place. What drove him to say that? Why had he chosen to play such a starkly hostile role in my life?

TEN

Aidan the Spider, His View

What, you wonder, might drive a man to murder his own father?

Or, you might as well ask what keeps *everyone* from wanting a shot?

First you must imagine the father. A big man, bear sized. Bigger. Who roared clearing his throat, took no prisoners in an argument, nor any account of the wishes of others; someone who was self-absorbed, with a personality charring all in his range.

Not at first, mind you, but later, after he returned from Germany.

Is it uncharitable of me to speak so truthfully? It's probably not the image you have of him thus far. But, consider the source.

Besides, there are always things official reports can't say. So you do some digging around on your own. Because I know that Andrew, the younger Mr. Pak's father, was not a person of such delicate sensibilities that he would ever do something as scrupulous as kill himself out of regret.

How well I recall the deceased Mr. Pak!

Andrew's intrusion into our family circle was one of the watershed moments of my childhood—imagine the shock of another boy sprouting up in your house, as if the superabundance of siblings like Bulwer, Sebastian, and Marian weren't challenge enough for my four-year-old self. Parental caresses were already scarce. And one day, there he was. Large, gawky, ill-spoken.

Don't mistake me. It wasn't envy that drove me to punish the boy Father consented to raise, who in the end treated Daddy and Marian so cruelly.

It was a question of justice.

I knew from the start that the brigand with the long ears and the wide thick mouth was a different kind of animal, a cheater, the sort who shied from our rules because they weren't his. There is the famous story of his pretending not to know English—the charade of his version of charades, if you will. Marian thought she alone had seen through it, but though I was barely four, I had my eye on him from the moment he walked in.

We had servants, of course. However, Mother wanted us to learn self-reliance, to which I say bravo! At one point, Andrew's task was polishing the silver. It was an impressive and heavy set, neatly hidden in an ornate walnut side table, and on Friday morning Andrew took up a cloth and set to buffing. Although I was still confined to a cage in a corner of the living room, supposedly under the supervision of a nanny who took Mummy's absences as occasions to tuck into Mr. Spenser, the butler, I knew how to spring myself free. Many days, unknown to my keepers, I ranged through the house, regarding my fellows like inmates. Our gangly newcomer at work was an especially intriguing subject.

He began legitimately enough, daubing the polish onto the white cloth, covering an entire knife with it, then when it dried, buffing it off. One, two, maybe three pieces received the full treatment. Hard labor. And then he began skipping. Every other piece of silver, followed by every third, and so on. I won't say the boy used spit, but then I was not always there to see.

This trivial transgression would have remained filed away in the dusty back rooms of memory had it been the exception. Sadly, it was not. In game after game—of Conkers; Queenie, Queenie; Please Mr. Crocodile; why even in something simple as Oranges and Lemons—he took short-cuts, or tried to advance his position by questionable means. Cutting corners was a hallmark of our seductive guest's nature—and it augured ill.

Marian's attraction to him was evident from the start. Like Mummy, she was both blessed and cursed with a heightened empathy characteristic of the finest of her sex, which we mislabel "the maternal instinct." I say mislabel because the wish to help is sexless, genderless—I'd even venture, divine.

Until Andrew crossed our threshold, I was the primary recipient of the women's rapturous attention.

With horror I watched this Slavic spider spin his woozy web, draping it with glittering words, perfuming it with false smiles and flatteries, until a hereditary innocent like my sister stood not a chance. My darling was drawn in. And slowly, slowly he warped his web around her, but so gently she might have imagined herself at Liberty's being suited in silks—for a shroud. And even less innocent souls, like my father, who was indeed a hard man—in a good way, mind, a man who knew what needed to be done—even Father was stung by the lackadaisical poison secreted by this boy he rescued from the embrace of a mother who plied her trade as an entrepreneurial whore.

Well, Daddy and Marian were both chumps for uniforms, and Andrew's suited his tall, svelte physique exquisitely well, as I noticed when he returned from Germany where he'd gone to work for Father. A paramilitary Adonis, he was. But character—a quaint word, I'll grant—reveals itself in a slow dance through time.

After Germany, Andrew's gloves were definitely off. I'll never forget that mortifying, aborted picnic drive. I was trying to amuse with banter about Russian spies, when suddenly this heretofore perfect cod-English mannequin exploded, showing himself for what he was. He shouted at me. He railed at my sister, reducing her to tears. He'd never even noticed my smiles, my painful attempts to connect.

Unfortunately, his gloves were not all that came off that day—and here I am ashamed to say that I can offer an eyewitness account. My childhood habit of crawling around the house had grown into a need to see how people acted in what they believed was the dark. Would that I'd never watched half of what I've been forced—not merely by duty but by an inner calling, you might say—to observe. I shudder, recalling the scenes and tableaux played out before me. It seems that in the putative privacy of a closed set, people change. Startling how many take freedom for license. Were I only permitted to open my files, the stories I'd share. And so it was from an inborn sense of obligation, and by relying on nothing more than a keyhole, that I made myself watch every second of their vicious match, which none among you would describe as *making love*.

I knew soon enough what the consequences were for my sister. I was at the time her primary—her only—confidant. Bulwer was busy debating with God; Sebastian was on his own mission to Palestine to placate his guilt without a source, which I believe Andrew's presence encouraged. Andrew emanated—I don't say he did it consciously, but a man must take responsibility nevertheless—a resentment of our ways, our relative wealth, our manners, our success. His very existence was an indictment of, more, an attack on, our way of life, on our very being. We were the victims of a professional victim, though we'd done little or nothing to cause his plight, no matter what Daddy's relations with his whoremistress mother, Vera, might have been.

After his monstrous treatment of my Marian, I wanted only to shoot him.

Of course I was still a boy, and there was nothing much I could do. I delivered food to her seedy digs in Brixton. I was there when my niece, Vera, was born.

I was the one who sent Andrew the jar.

Even so, little Vera became my favorite. I visited her regularly—though Father and Mother condemned me for it. Marian had anticipated their response accurately. The consequences of her afternoon's fever cost her all. She saw Mummy and Daddy only years later, as they were dying, after I finally persuaded them to relent.

Marian's lot was a hard one until Sir Hugh entered her life, and for a short time, redeemed it.

My own career, on the other hand, proceeded apace. Years of studying keyholes proved just the sort of vocational testing I needed. I knew from the start that police work was what I wanted to pursue, at a level commensurate with the family's standing and expectations. When I finally took the position at Interpol, in the trafficking division, I knew I'd found a home.

The organization, founded in Germany after the First World War, was an emblem of cooperation desperately needed in our world.

I didn't begin with a vendetta in mind.

The destruction and privation of the war years had imprinted themselves deeply on my boyhood memories. Eternal vigilance seemed the price of peace, and I'd been raised in a vigilant clan. Public service hardly even seemed public. It was an extension of family management.

I was assigned to trafficking during a time when international commerce in humans was again on the rise. Not that it had ever died out. Its slow march extends back far as recorded time, and there has never been a period free of slavery.

I don't use the term loosely. The distinctions between slavery and servitude may seem fine points to some, but not to me. Oh, I recognize that a man can be a wage slave, but that modification means all. With proper motivation, some imagination, pluck, and will, a wage slave can *hope* to better his lot, whereas a true slave has no choice. Without choice, he is effectively dehumanized, his status lower than an animal's because he has no place in the natural order of things, which was what I saw, over and over again. In Marseille, in Srebrenica, in Odessa, even in Manchester, we uncovered places where girls—they were mostly girls—were kept against their wills, and it was enough to set your blood boiling and firm up your resolve to put an end to such evil. The girls were trafficked by "business-men" peddling sex and cheap labor. Not all the thugs wore leather—some favored military uniforms, others the hand-tailored Italian suits of govern-ment ministers. Big business needs big friends to flourish.

During a raid—this was in the late seventies—we found the six women huddled together in a room in a hotel only a few blocks from the Blue Mosque in Istanbul. In its day, which wasn't so long ago, the city rivaled London, Paris, Moscow. Nearby stood Hagia Sophia, now a mosque. Once it had been the largest church of its kind, after St. Peter's. (Eight other girls were later found installed at the plush Kempinski Palace on the Bosporus. No doubt more were scattered in hotels of all stripes around the city. They were, after all, importing a harem for the Shah.)

The call to prayer sounded while I waited for the pale-fleshed ducklings to gather their things.

The girls were variously half dressed.

I asked a redhead:

Where are you from?

Bucharest, she answered.

You understand English?

I do?

She'd not lost her insouciance.

How is that?

I used to work for an English family that settled there after the war.

Which war?

Hitler, she said.

Ah, I said, thinking immediately of Daddy in Belgrade, and Sebastian in Palestine. How could I not feel a pang at the dispersal, the scattering of so many? Yet there is no going back to a simpler way. We fare forward, or we fall.

The girls were extraordinarily pretty: though blonds dominated, there were also brunettes and redheads. One girl had shaved her hair completely.

We were tipped off to them by a rival house. Madame Claude, of Paris, guarded her territory jealously, and Madame Vera had violated her turf. We had friends in Paris. Madame Claude had more than once shown us her client list. We don't, you see, try to engineer human nature. We aim to understand it. And it has always struck me as remarkable how precisely criminal businesses mirror legitimate ones, from organizational structures to rivalries for market share. In any case, Madame Claude herself contacted one of our agents directly to alert him to Istanbul, saying, in her near-perfect English, that it would be well worth the agency's while.

The rubber-muscled, sniveling tough with the oil-black eyes guarding the girls collapsed under questioning in minutes. It took no time at all to get the address in Vienna. And so it was that, in the late 1970s, Vera's House of Widows fell under my gaze.

Simply closing the place down would have had no lasting effect on our primary goal, which was to stop the girls from getting netted in the first place.

Many arrived on their own—escaping the boredom of poverty, small-town life, dull husbands, brutish fathers—but the others . . .

In any case, it can take years to gather enough evidence to make a successful case.

Once I stumbled on the link between the House of Widows and Andrew, that spoiler of my youth, however, a process began that lasted more than a decade.

It happened because of a letter. I don't know—or care—how he himself traced his mother. There's a vast and complex subculture among our myriad immigrant groups, with networks as sophisticated in their own ways as ours. They carry news between worlds: sometimes it's the whisper of a glimpse in the village of someone presumed dead; or word of a wedding; or a tap on the shoulder at a funeral. *Did you hear so-and-so had a boy,* and so forth.

Nothing changes who your mother is to you. He began writing to her. He was under the impression she was poor. We monitored all their exchanges. And once I understood that his mother ran Widows, and Andrew was the man raised from boyhood by Father . . .

I didn't make the connection right away, though.

Find out what you can about this Andrew Pak, I said to George Grozny, my Russian-born assistant at the time.

Pak. I didn't recognize the last name. In truth, I don't recall ever hearing it growing up.

But George was thorough and before long I had a dossier—a history of Andrew's peregrinations across the West, along with a photograph. The picture told all. An old passport photo. When I finally met with Andrew a year later—it took us that long to think our way into a plan—I was shocked by how little he'd changed. Gray, yes, but still svelte, still the seducer.

The plan was not mine.

Colonel Winnington-Ingram said it came to him over breakfast the day after I explained the curious and fateful coincidence—that I had known one of Madame Vera's sons. Rather well.

We should use this, Gordon, he said to me.

We must, sir.

And I know just the way.

I leaned in. Reluctantly, because Winnington-Ingram smelled. As always. Of cheese. It was his peccadillo, his secret vice—he carried crumbly Stiltons wrapped in white cloth napkins in his jacket pocket the way others stash sweets or cigarettes.

We'll get the brother to work with us. You say he already did once before. It will be to his advantage, to everyone's. A place like Widows has decades of contacts: local gangs, suppliers. The political class. Not just in Austria, Iran, or Ukraine. The cover is powerful, but we know a thing or two about their supporters, eh?

He was referring to the cabinet member we knew (never mind where) who profited from the House, and who would have killed his own granny before letting word of his complicity become public.

He won't give us any trouble.

Agreed.

Go to the States. Put this to your man directly. Then we'll fly him to London to meet with his brother. This could work out rather well.

Much depends on what is meant by "well."

It was a shock seeing Andrew these decades later even though, as I said, in many ways, he'd changed very little. He wore a plaid shirt and blue jeans. Gone were the days when he slicked down his hair and put on a tie before dinner. Yet his features were still strong and clean, and he held himself straight as ever. The military had left its mark. Only his pretty blue eyes showed the effects of years of the bottle—they were all surface, like stone. The shock was caused by the confrontation with time. We grow so used to ourselves, we need others to mirror who we've become.

Then there was his peculiar way of speaking about himself in the second person. Had he done that from boyhood? I didn't recall.

He repeated my name several times as if it were a hook for fishing up memories.

Aidan, Aidan, Aidan.

When I told him why I had gotten in touch with him, he took the news hard.

You're sure of it?

Nevertheless he gradually recognized that what we were offering was an opportunity to help his brothers and mother. He owed them. Khoriv especially.

We never mentioned the scale of their business. I merely said they were involved in trafficking.

You're certain? he asked again.

We were sitting in a coffee shop in the neighboring town of Gloucester.

Gulls patrolled the skies above the boats in the harbor.

I thought of Alfred Hitchcock's *The Birds*. Something similarly ominous hung in the air.

As sure as I am that's the sea, and the tide's coming in, I said, pushing back my half-finished Sam Adams (the traitor!), dabbing my lips.

A girl on a boat held up some bread. The birds attacked.

Flying home, I brooded. On the one hand I was smug about my success at recruiting Andrew. He would help us in our negotiations with the House of Widows. He would meet with his brother. When he finally accepted what his brothers were doing (Vera was out of the business by then), he saw it was in his interest to work with us. I promised we'd leave Khoriv alone—so long as he supplied us with information about the other traffickers. When he asked why we didn't go to his brother ourselves, I paused.

Because he'll trust you, Andrew. He'll know you're trying to help. And you are. We could arrest them any time. But if he agrees to cooperate, send information to you . . .

You want it sent here?

This was Winnington-Ingram's idea—it kept Interpol at a further remove. If Khoriv's competitors ever discovered he was feeding information to someone, it would be better for him if they thought the recipient a private individual. Andrew might simply be Khoriv's man in America. They have nothing to connect him with us.

We hope, I said, to find out where and how they get their girls. And their guns. The guns more than the girls, when it comes down to it. It might take awhile, I warned him. These things are slow. People in this line of work are inclined to paranoia; they change tactics regularly. It's never easy to build cases when there are borders and languages no one speaks.

Well, hardly anyone.

No, the trip *had* gone well. Andrew grasped all the angles. At the same time I did, once or twice, try imagining how it might have looked to him—the spot I'd put him in could not have been comfortable. But such was my duty.

Thus Andrew became Her Majesty's translator once more.

———•·•———

I had of course never expected Andrew's story to end quite this way.

For nearly a decade Khoriv provided information about shipments of weapons and women. He was by now working quite high up in the Ukrainian government. Occasionally we arrested someone based on his news. But we had our priorities, and our eye was on Big Red—the name we gave Khoriv's leading competitor. And we were very close. We could see the short hairs on the backs of their thick necks. And then someone on their side got wind of it.

It nearly broke me when I gleaned from our monitoring of a rival gang that Big Red had learned Khoriv was feeding someone in the States dates and times. This wouldn't reflect well on Khoriv. Still, thanks to our precautions, because we hadn't been in touch with him directly, Big Red had no reason to think he was in touch with the police.

I gave Andrew the news by fax. I left it to him to warn his brother.

It was a bad moment, yes. Very bad, even. Still, it was no cause for topping. Not in my book. Or even, for that matter, stopping. I had hoped for a surge of spirit: we can turn this around, that sort of thing. Tough it out, oh my brother. For the cause. But, whose? The girls? Foolish of me to expect it from him, I see that now.

At the time, I was caught up in the game. The little game. When I heard what happened—that instead of telling his brother he'd been exposed, he killed himself—I was disappointed. We were so close. Years of work gone in a pulse of gun smoke.

The son had never been a factor in my plans. I hardly knew he existed—we're trained to focus, and the rest is what Americans call "collateral damage."

I pondered what my men had discovered when they poked around Devon, Massachusetts (New England hardly sounds new). Andrew was a screamer, his temper noted by neighbors and coworkers alike. My men spoke with his wife, who was stunned yet not grief stricken. I think she must have assumed they were simply part of an investigation team looking into the suicide—she spoke quite freely. Andrew had left her after decades of marriage. She told them about his drinking, his rages, his DWIs.

My men did not, however, speak to the son. On my instructions. It was a hunch—because, as it happens, only a week before Andrew's death, my beloved Marian called to say she'd heard from him. James.

James Pak, it turned out, was coming to England.

My people told me they'd learned James had fought with his father.

This gave me an idea—it was mad, of course, but you'd be surprised how often madness pays off in this world.

I knew there was something more to Andrew's suicide than just our business. I felt it in my bones.

James may not have pulled the trigger, but I had a hunch he too had a hand in his old man's death. As the poet said, we do not die of death, we die of disappointment. I felt certain enough something was up to accuse him—though I confess I hadn't really planned to say it; it just came out.

But how would I use what I suspected? That was the question I put to myself on my way to Oxford after James returned from his jaunt across Europe. I even wondered whether we might not turn him, get the son to pick up where the father left off. Let him connect with the brothers, then take it from there.

And suddenly I, who thought myself ancient history, felt reborn. I had a vocation again. One final play.

At the same time I was distracted. After all, I was not coming to Oxford to see him but rather to see Selena.

Oh my Selena. This was not what I had planned for you, believe me.

If I say *my* Selena, don't misunderstand. I mean she was *mine.* Every inch. Every crevice. Each rainbow tattoo. Many of which I paid for, watched them burned into her skin by a young Turk in Bayridge. We had been lovers for over a year. She was young only by our standards—in her culture she was practically an old maid. She was my sweet, my sweetest girl, my sable slut. And I was her Boy. That's what she called me. Boy. As Mummy and Marian had. Before Andrew arrived.

I thought I might accomplish both missions at once.

I had James in my sights when the door to Marian's study flew open and Marian herself stumbled in, her left foot all but buckling under her as though she'd flubbed a curtsy. Her hair looked windblown. She'd forgotten her glasses. Her eyes darted wildly around the room.

"It's Selena," she said sharply.

"What?" I asked, looking at James, who'd gone white.

"She's hysterical. Locked herself in her room. She's asking for you, Aidan."

How unfair it is we cannot pause life like television. Marian's timing was all wrong. Here was the boy, confused, perfectly vulnerable, and here was my sister, pulling me back. I was angry. But she would not relent.

"Go," she said.

I turned and hurried off to confront my own private storm—and no one could have been more amazed that I was involved in this tempest than I was myself.

ELEVEN

Fathers and Sons

. . . all the old ladies I ever knew wanted to teach me something . . .
SYLVIA PLATH

Marian watched Aidan hurry out.

"I'm sorry. Haven't had a minute to tell you."

"About?"

"Aidan, my awful brother . . ."

"Awful?"

"Dreadful . . ."

"Why?"

". . . about Aidan and Selena."

And just when I thought I'd figured out all the angles, I was surprised.

"What can you possibly mean?"

"Yes, who would imagine?"

"Imagine what?"

"That he'd do such a thing. In my house. I don't blame *her*, of course. She's just a child. No sense of future, poor thing. She came to me with it only a few days ago."

Again I found myself lost.

"I don't know what you'll think of us now."

"Marian."

"Selena's pregnant. By Aidan. Do you see? He's taking her to London tomorrow. He wants the child. She doesn't. I've told him to honor her wish."

I knew then that I wouldn't be staying in Marian's house much longer.

Bulwer wandered in: "What were you saying, dear?"

The high windows flaunted a gloomy patch of gray.

Over the last month I'd dug up enough history to make me long for a

229

new world of my own. My mistake lay in thinking I alone was trapped
in the floatsam's fierce rush. Small wonder that people left home seeking
fresh starts.

"Nothing, Bully. Nothing. We'll be out in a minute, dear."

Aidan and Selena disappeared together the next day without saying a word.

I was devastated. I'd never suspected she too had been lying.

Or maybe she was simply trying to protect me.

The following days dissolved in a cloud of vague images and snatches
of overheard conversation. In my heightened state I felt anything that was
said somehow reflected back on me. Girls whispering in British accents
were surely sneering. The sleepy river grew cold. The days grew shorter.
The dark deepend.

I took long walks, but I may as well have been strolling the desert. I saw
nothing, felt less.

Back on Drummond Street, Marian paced, out of her mind with rage
and worry, while Bulwer and I both steered clear.

A few days after the unhappy couple disappeared, I was breakfasting
with Bulwer when Marian burst into the room; her cheeks were rubbed
raw from crying.

She'd just had a phone call from London. Selena wasn't coming back.
She was staying with the family of an old school friend. She wasn't sure how
long she'd be away. She'd asked Marian to send up some of her things.

"Can I take them?" I offered.

"She specifically asked that it not be you."

What?

The next day a letter Selena sent from London arrived in the mail:

Dear James,

*I am so very sorry. I hadn't expected you, you see. I hadn't planned you.
Forgive me. Overnight I made you my one hope. It was terribly unfair
of me. Then I discovered what I should have known before, that hope is
not something to look for outside yourself. I should have dealt with Aidan
before you arrived. That was another reason it was so hard to talk to you.
I had this other matter to settle. The only thing that worries me is whether
I'll stay eighteen forever after I'm dead. Eighteen isn't easy, in case you've
forgotten. I don't know why I feel something is going to happen, but I do*

feel it. You are very sweet. Stay that way. Remember the truth of the room. It's all that matters. Maybe I'll see you again. How does that song I hate so much go? Don't know where, don't know when.

Love,
S

She must have written the letter before the abortion, in a moment of panic when she worried she might not make it through. Perhaps she regretted sending it, which was why she asked that I not be the one to bring her things up to the city.

The note shook me. I heard her voice, with its edge and its tenderness, reminding me of our youthful conviction that the truth as it reveals itself to two people in love is the foundation of what matters most.

I wasn't sure what to believe. Selena must have known she was pregnant the night she came into my room. She may have been fond of me—it's not impossible. And maybe she wanted to break it off with Aidan and a part of her rage was about him.

The next week a steady drizzle drove us inward. We spent too much time surrounded by the trompe l'oeil wallpaper whose grapes and roses had begun to rot: yet one more illusion to penetrate.

I told myself I hadn't turned from Selena in malice or deceit. I'd been temporarily overwhelmed by the world.

But no one had accused me of anything. Besides, in the end, you have to pay attention, no matter what.

I turned to my work. I visited the Bodleian, where I held actual letters Byron had written. There was something moving in his scorn for all norms. George Gordon bowed before no man, and all women. His brazenness inspired me. I almost forgot our domestic drama. He believed; he fought for his beliefs; he died young—though not before finding time to versify his regrets.

So I prepared for the start of the term.

Our little menagerie was irreparably shattered. When I told Marian I was moving, she didn't try talking me out of it. I took a room closer to the college. Bulwer walked over with me. We shook hands at the door to my new home like old, if somewhat formal, friends.

In my new digs, I made it a point to keep my distance from my hosts.

This led to a fruitful and even happy year. I hunkered down in the library and the lecture hall—both places where I knew how to lose myself without endangering others.

Near the holidays, as November gave way to the first winter frosts and the ground along the riverbank and the greens whitened as though someone had lathered the grass for a shave, I dragged out the winter clothes I'd lugged with me only to find that I had forgotten to bring a coat. This gave me an excuse to spend a day in London, where I finally visited Harrods. On the evening train back, the first snowflakes melted against the window and I was struck by how quickly the days were passing. My first term was nearly over.

That evening, I had a call from Marian. She'd been on my mind as I composed an excuse to offer my mother about why I wouldn't be returning to the States for Christmas.

"Selena's in town. She'd like to see you."

I was surprised by how pleased I was to hear her voice—something I managed to hide nevertheless by saying:

"Why didn't she call me herself?"

After a familiar silence, she whispered:

"I wanted to invite you for tea. It would be nice to see you."

Confronted directly, could I refuse?

The next day I found myself once more in the hallways with the William Morris grapes gone to raisins and Disraeli's clock.

The house reeked of tobacco.

Marian, still sober in black, looked more composed than when I'd last seen her. The color had returned to her cheeks.

"Bulwer's newest passion: the pipe," she said, explaining the smoke. "Now the rest of the world's gone off tobacco, he finds it a virtue to foul my air."

After she lead me into the study, the pipe-master himself shuffled in, handsomely swathed in a true green-worsted *le smoking,* warming a meer-schaum. His free hand gripped mine firmly:

"Find any Christians in your part of town? Thought not. Keep looking. But be careful. And let me know if you do."

He chuckled to himself and shuffled out.

Marian then appeared with the tea tray, heaped with a plate of crustless finger sandwiches. She poured two cups. I thought she was about to sit down when she said:

"That's all right then. I'll leave you. Don't be a stranger. Remember us. Do drop by."

And she too was gone.

I sat there a minute wondering why I'd returned, but then the room cast its old spell, and I began to reflect on my earliest encounters with the English, when the steeples still evoked wizard hats, and the enchantment of literature was most of what I knew. I hadn't realized how readily I'd adapted. By now I felt accepted and as at home in Oxford as ever in Boston. I'd made friends, visited London on errands, hiked in the Lake District. I'd also written a letter to Vera, but hadn't heard anything back. In the library stacks one day I happened to see an article in a paper from 1906 about "the White Slave trade." An epidemic was plaguing Europe, and a conference was convened in Paris to articulate outrage and develop a strategy for ending it once and for all. At that moment I saw how right Tariq had been—it was a story whose narrative thread continued unbroken across ages. Same causes, too: war, corruption, etc.

Inside this room with its high windows—even on a day gray as this one—such realities seemed as distant as the waters of Mars.

I hadn't heard the door open. I was so startled to hear my name whispered, I shot up.

"James."

I turned.

Selena was wearing black—in this house of perpetual mourning—her skin pale as a scallop.

She stepped forward and extended her hand. Very formal. I noticed she wasn't wearing any studs that I could see.

"Thanks for coming," she said, walking around the table and sitting down before the other cup Marian had poured.

"How's London?" I asked quickly, unwilling to let awkward silence claim the floor.

"Oh, I always love London."

"You're working?"

"Virgin Records. Isn't that funny?"

"Living alone?"

"No, I'm staying with the family of a friend I went to school with. They're Palestinian. Very rich. Very nice. And you? How's Byron?"

"Byronic," I said stupidly, compounding it by adding: "Galling, really. He's a hard man for any man to spend time with because he so quickly makes you feel . . . unmanly. His women, his revolutions . . ."

She smiled.

"You've had your women. All you need's a revolution."

"And there's no shortage of those around. The problem is knowing which to settle on."

"Have a sandwich." I pushed the plate toward her.

She shook her head.

"Look, I know this is uncomfortable. But it's good to see you. And I'm sorry, but there are things I wanted. . . . If I could, I'd have planned this all very differently."

Involuntarily skeptical, I angled my head:

"What do you mean?"

"This whole last year. It's lucky you came. We were locked into something here, and we needed an outsider to kick it loose. If you hadn't come, who knows what I'd have done?"

"Like what?"

"Killed Aidan. I thought of it. Or myself. Thought of that, too."

"Not something to joke about with me, Selena."

She frowned and leaned forward. Her hand was about to touch the back of mine, but then she withdrew it and sat up.

"Sorry. But I'm not joking. Before you came, I felt trapped. It was a nightmare. I didn't know how to tell Marian about Aidan. And then Aidan wanted to have the child, can you believe it?—I didn't see any other way out.

"Then you arrived. And we had that talk . . ."

"Ah, the talk."

"Don't be like that. You reminded me of something I'd known and forgotten. You made me feel I had choices. I wasn't locked in or defined by what had already happened—never mind by what happened before I was born. That helped me. Really."

I sat back and took in her face, the sharp grade of her cheeks, the dark eyes in which I knew other worlds had bred a gaze of such depth I could hardly sustain looking into them. I noticed a cut under her chin—and I had to wonder if that was an accident or a sign of maturity and restraint.

"Sounds like you're going back to what we call your roots."

"Because I'm living with a Palestinian family? But you're right. It's deeper than that. I'm thinking now I'll go to school back home. I know things that would only make sense to others who do too—I need a context that recognizes me for what I am. There's a new university called Al-Quds being set up in Jerusalem. They say it will be world class. We'll see. Might take a year or two to sort things out."

I wasn't sure what she expected me to say—that I'd wait for her?

"That's great. I'm glad."

"Thanks. And for coming over. I was afraid you'd be so pissed you'd say no. That's why I asked Marian to call."

"You look good," I said, thinking she was thinner than ever.

"Liar. I appreciate the spirit."

Then we fell silent. All the passionate declarations I'd rehearsed—of love and regret—had frozen or dissolved in the moment's bewilderment. Yet sitting together felt fine. At that age, one expects things not to last though the shock of it is both greater than what you remember and not as overwhelming as you feared. Besides, time is infinite, and you feel the promise of adventures without end around the corner. The exquisite edge is one definition of beauty.

Finally, we both rose. She walked me to the threshold.

"I'll say good-bye. I'd like to sit here awhile. Good luck with your thesis and all."

The pull to lean over and kiss her was strong. Her dark eyes sent signals I no longer trusted myself to translate.

"Thanks. You too."

We kissed on the cheek, then I hurried out. It was the last time I saw her.

By the end of the following term, my month at Marian's had begun to fade into a dream.

In May, my ex-girlfriend Charlotte, who'd broken up with the boyfriend she'd ditched me for, came over to visit. We traveled to Paris together, seeing the sites, riding a *Bateau-Mouche* down the Seine, where I threw up over the side because I'd drunk too much wine. When the time came for me to return to the States, where Charlotte was waiting to spring wedding plans on me, I was too harried to stop and say good-bye to Bulwer and Marian. I settled instead on a note. Letters had brought me to England; it seemed right that letters should be my passport home.

Once I was back in Boston, I thought of mailing Aidan the jar, but decided against it.

TWELVE

19 Berggasse

Wien, Wien, nur du allein,
sollst stets die Stadt meiner Träume sein.
FROM A POPULAR SONG

— 1 —

Vienna, 1 May 2006: Evening

The minute Silvia walks into the apartment, I ask: "Why so bitchy?" I'm still smarting from the morning's snub. Besides, she's over an hour late. Forlorn and cold, the chicken and cabbage nap on their plates, tucked in fat.

I glower over my wineglass. It's been a wet afternoon.

She lifts the easel that's blocking the hall and rests it against the bookcase. In the last year I've taken up digi-oils, mainly historical scenes: a way to relax, mixing pleasure with vocation. History's a long mural of meetings anyway, I've decided, an infinite scroll of portraits and panels of men too long chained to chairs—in offices, libraries, studies—ideas like cataracts glazing their eyes. That's why I paint them with animals. Sometimes I leave the men out completely. Animals look at what's there. Moreover, painting helps me appreciate the company I keep in this city of painters—at the Secession Museum down the block I study the eros and rage Klimt heard in Beethoven's music. Plus, painting helps with the vertigo.

All embodied by Silvia—eros, rage, vertigo—who perches on the rattan chair long enough to peel off her boots.

"That's supposed to be Trotsky?" Her mother's a painter; I'm not up to her standards. Pointless to argue that Photoshop is its own art.

"With cat," I point out.

She doesn't even look at the food on the table.

"Did you eat?" I ask.

"Stopped for sushi with Katrin," she answers, no hint of sorry. Katrin's a college pal I met once in passing.

She massages her feet—a sight worth paying for, though if I told her, even joking, she'd start to charge. Young women today are different. They cost-benefit handshakes and offer discounts only on smiles bought in bulk—and who can blame them, when they're forced to pay cash for earth, water, and air? Today, nothing is promised. It takes a special kind of courage to stand for nothing.

She rises from the chair and shakes her head. The thick, black coils bounce around her face. She knows I need comforting, a mother's arms more than a lover's.

Mother died six years ago. After the suicide, her life narrowed. For decades she'd lived under siege, but when she was liberated, all the fight left her. There had been joy and meaning in battle.

"You don't want anyone to suspect, do you? Darling." Silvia finally replies to my protest over how she cuts me in public. Lot of data to process in that pretty head, and upgrades cost money. Her south-Austrian accent turns crisp Anglo-Saxon gothic. Despite everything, I smile. Suspect? I'd love them to know. Eat their hearts out. Is there a law against fucking that I missed? With so many new ones back home, could well be.

She goes to the kitchen and puts on the kettle for tea. Then she marches straight for the bedroom. I follow. I cough and sigh onto the bed. Soft mattresses are favorites among embassy staffers unpropped by trust funds. I'm not complaining—my salary's fine, even if my apartment was starting to resemble Father's last dive. Then Silvia arrived. She may not have values, but she certainly has taste, and Lord knows I both need and love her. Every visit she brought something lovely: a Venetian vase, an orange silk pillow, a hooked rug from Turkey I've managed to stain. The immediate neighborhood isn't glamorous, yet there's the Naschmarkt, the dense open-air market across the street where before dawn the farmers start shouting above the truck engines while unpacking crates of tomatoes, and florists trade randy tales from the night before as they unbundle their tulips and roses. The porn shop on the corner's just closing as their day begins. One Sunday I observed a man leap onto a truck bed and start hurling armfuls of peonies into the air before the vendors grappled him down. The rest of the day cars ground petals into the street. Occasionally one would drift by the window like a moth. Moreover, I'm mere blocks from the Opera and the Hofburg. Some mornings I step out around five to take in the smells and the noises. Everyone's happy. At that hour, men still have hope. Who knows what's promised? Women, wealth, wisdom . . .

Silvia watches me watching her peel off her pants.

The day's memories undo me, and I broach the subject I should never have raised to begin with.

"So I should ignore them?"

"Is it your business?" she asks, pulling on the blue sweats she stashes here. "They paying you to embarrass your government? And if you do? Press for a day. Maybe. Flamed on the Web—certainly."

"But look at this."

I hadn't planned to involve her. There's always leakage.

It's not that I want to do good. I'm not that kind of American. Only . . . something. Because it's on my desk, like underwear on the table. If someone saw Silvia's thong coiled on my files, would they ignore it? If they couldn't, could I? And this isn't underwear, it's people. Photos, too.

We all know more than we want to know: the question is what form our denial will take.

This afternoon, returning from the Children's Hospital, I made one final detour. I entered Freud's house, which he quit at the last possible moment in 1938, and from which most of the familiar pieces, like the couch, have been stripped. Instead, there's a gift shop peddling T-shirts and mouse pads. Anna's room displays modern art. But I did see his study, his homburg, a pen; a pair of shiny black shoes under glass; page proofs from Deuticke with his notes in the margins. All underwhelming, except for the films. Seeing the bearded man as beardless youth disturbed me. Time shouldn't stay this accessible. I remembered a line from a poem: *In his eyes, dream,* the German for which sounds like *trauma.*

"I'll be a hero to some," I venture.

"Name one hero from the last twenty years? Just one."

Each name I think of died decades ago. Then I say:

"Father Daniel Berrigan."

"Who?"

Yet not even Silvia's mocking yanks me from the parallel world I inhabit more deeply each day—of memories, mine and those of the others from my "oral history." Then she adds: "On the other hand."

And I'm all ears, listening. Silvia has never before shown me her other hand, though I always suspected she had one.

It's you, I think, not believing it myself, and yet subscribing to it completely. Isn't it? Silvia.

The kettle is boiling.

She gives me a look and walks out.

Now I'm sure of it. It's Silvia and her friend Katrin. They gathered the files. Didn't Silvia say she'd belonged to some Green group in college? Not radicals. Kids with faith. Believers. My God. Should I pursue it? Force a confession . . .

I am not a political man. The great names of history interest me only for the spells they cast over people. We're at the mercy of how our leaders sleep: an epidemic of nightmares can make daylight a trauma.

I drum my fingers on the desk. Unfortunately I don't keep cigarettes in the apartment.

Outside, an accordion rips a melody from the darkness, followed by the tremolo voice of old Wien.

Oh Silvia, thank you, I want to say when she brings in the tea. Thank you. For all tender mercies in untender times. A sweetness floods me, making me long to wrap my arms around her with all the green force of spring, shield her from the cold, this fearsome frigidity overspreading our world.

The odor of jasmine fills me. I pick up the runny strudel, which falls apart in my hand. I wipe my fingers on the blanket.

She puts down her tea and sniffs under her arms.

"I need a shower."

Steam billows from the blue cup.

Silvia goes to the bathroom, runs the water, slips in, pulls the curtain. The door, however, is open. Pipes sing. Why did she bother with the sweats?

The bedroom's packed with canvases layered three deep. I review the faces: young Napoleon's first pony; Tolstoy's dog, a spaniel-poodle; the three dukes of Yalta as ducks. The Web's a trove for a man of my parts.

The soldiers I read about in the files also have faces and family. Their victims had pets—birds, children, friends. Our task is to give faces back to the dead.

Now my mind's scattered, my thoughts flit from one thing to another. For some reason I think of Elizabeth Shoumatoff, the society portrait painter FDR called Shoumie. On April 12, 1945, she entered the small room in the Little White House in Warm Springs, Georgia, just a few minutes before the president himself, to lay out her palette. Accustomed to deadlines, she sensed she'd have to move double-fast. Feddy—as she called him—hadn't looked well all week. Too thin, too pale, too limp. Chatting, she simultaneously painted for him an image of her native realm. Like other émigrés, she helped to shape Roosevelt's vision—as the Iraqi exiles did for G. W. B. That's how it works.

Years ago I took courses using live models. They unnerved me. I lost myself staring at wrinkles and veins; I could hear blood winding through them. Photos are better. They let me imagine the bodies wherever I'd like.

Silvia, towel on head, tubed in white cotton, pads in and turns on CNN.

She looks at me and smiles for the first time today.

"Good shower."

I nod, taking the credit.

The secret history of fifty years ago is still being written. It may take as long to crawl out of what's swallowed us: when we finally emerge we'll be old. Maybe dead.

The last war I watched on television with Selena's spirit peering over my shoulder. This time, although the statistics in the paper spell disaster, CNN features a behind-the-scenes look at the life of Tom Cruise—not, I assume, named for the missile.

"I can't just ignore them."

"Everyone else has."

She sits beside me.

I lower my chin and press my forehead to hers. Her breath smells like she's been chewing grass. But I know she's a meat eater.

She pulls away. She's worried for me. I feel it. It's touching. For the first time since we've been together I suspect she might actually care, a feeling I've not had since my last S.

"Because of Selena?"

My Silvia spooks me.

I say nothing. I grope for my smokes before remembering again I tossed them last week. May be one buried somewhere, though.

Silvia thwacks my chest with the back of her hand, at least half in earnest, and bolts to her feet.

"That was fifteen years ago. Stop it!" Her eyes set fire to the bed. "You want to destroy your life too?"

It's a question. *The* question, really. I'm not a kid anymore. A conscience isn't an Xbox. I can't afford to play Zorro. Where would I go?

Back to the university to fulminate with my colleagues over crimes in high places while waiting for June, when all the clear consciences summer abroad.

Am I wrong? Maybe it's not her at all.

I look up. Fifteen years ago, Silvia was in grade school learning to count.

Is it just my need to believe she's more than what she appears to be, a smart, beautiful woman?

My mind's racing now. Whose agent am I? Whom do I serve?

Her towel drops, and she doesn't retrieve it. Her breasts look my way. Her generation doesn't register the difference between secrecy and privacy. Everything's out there and means the same thing, the same nothing.

She unwraps the turban while talking:

"Look, Jimmy: today people get traded in blocks by the millions. Saves money that way. Saves time."

I kneel on the bed, sinking in quicksand. I can't think with her towel off, so I lean toward her, brushing a wet strand from her forehead.

"Well, I won't make any decision tonight."

I never expected tracking Father's past to end as it did. Hell, it's not over yet.

When I returned from Kyiv to Oxford, I had no idea what I'd been through or done, not a clue what turns the turns I'd taken would later force me to take. Only in light of this moment can I look back and see.

But I have to move quickly. Memory is a cracked Etch A Sketch tablet on which the heart draws figures. When the tablet wobbles, all's wiped away.

Silvia lets me circle her with my arms. She sinks back down with me. I turn off the light.

Then she cries:

"Ow!"

She bolts up.

"Something stabbed me."

I turn the switch.

She fumbles amid the blue cotton sheets and pulls out my Old Holland Kolinsky Sable brush.

"Oh, Jimmy," she sighs.

The moment is gone, the mood lies soiled in moonlight on vinyl. She rolls out of bed and pulls on her sweatpants.

"I'm still hungry," she says and heads to the kitchen. "Want anything?"

But I don't answer.

So much for seizing the moment.

Shoumie assaulted the canvas, but when she looked up at her subject, Roosevelt was dead.

– 2 –

Vienna, 2 May 2006: 4:00 a.m.

The children of suicides do not necessarily repeat their fathers' mistakes. Sometimes they let others do it for them.

Silvia's sleeping at last. The smell of her clings to my mustache. Ammonia to quicken the dead and keep the dying from dreaming of anything but its source. I sit in the alcove next to the bedroom where my desk faces the window and turn on the computer. Again Al Jazeera. In 1999, if you'd asked me, I'd have said Al Jazeera was a stand-up comedian of Italian American ancestry.

I'm scanning for stories about the deserters, our own soldiers who refuse to return to Iraq, knowingly risking court martial, maybe decades in jail.

The Web streams its data—clips of firefights, midnight raids, a veiled mother's clenched plea.

I have to run my fingers along the edge of this simple pine desk to remind myself where I am. A quiet place amid peace-loving people.

Plugging the memory stick into the USB port, I open the files I digitized on the scanner this afternoon. One by one, I study the photos and read the soldiers' tales.

Reading, I imagine the bodies of the dead laid side by side, mapping the borders of the wholly new world in which we now live.

I click back and forth on the Web to search for a context for what I'm reading. But the postings are mainly from amateurs, and who do you trust when *nobody's* lying?

Katrin, I think. That's who approached me and Akash outside the Hawelka—Silvia's friend Katrin. I'm almost certain.

Later today, I say to the girl in my head, I'll either send or bury them, these documents showing what men will do when conditions allow—as my father found out when he took Sir Anthony Eden's creed *(mustn't be sentimental!)* for his own.

I was reminded of Sir Anthony while visiting Venice last winter. Someone pointed out the walled garden on the Giudecca his grand-uncle designed in the mid-nineteenth century, which the family still owns. At four acres, Eden's garden is the largest privately held space in the city—not bad for the second home of a man from a small island nation.

When I returned, I was inspired to create a digi-portrait of the late prime minister clutching a cuttlefish—the significance of which I can't exactly explain. Hanging in my office, it wins the praise of my colleagues, who must have cut the State Department's classes on irony. Their small, earnest faces fatigue me. Had the ambassador not hired Silvia, I'd have quit long ago.

A confirmed ironist himself, Sir Anthony fought in the Battle of the Somme. His brother was killed in World War I. He had reason to mistrust the heart because it was so often broken. Eton, where he studied, rhymes with "beaten." Churchill was his mentor. When Iran nationalized the Anglo-Iranian Oil Company, Minister Eden ordered MI6 to take down the government. So they did, with our help. And the consequences continue playing out to this day.

But isn't every revolution sentimentality's child?

I read online the other day that on the east coast of Turkey fifteen hundred sheep ran off a cliff. No warning, no prompt. Whole families—not just the sheep, but also their owners—ruined. Before I left for Europe that first time, friends and teachers offered all kinds of advice. I was told to be watchful in Naples, to cold-shoulder the French before they did it to me, and never to leave my bags unattended. Useless counsel. Nothing was as I'd expected it. If simple sheep can still shock their shepherds, surely humans are even less predictable.

History's neither searchlight nor camera: it's a flickering candle we use to read the marks on the wall as we crawl from that cave where only the shadows of images play. Often it's of no use at all. When it deserts us, where do we turn?

To desert: to leave one's post; to abandon; to quit.

My father's brother deserted his army. My father deserted his brother, Marian, and my mother. Eventually he deserted the world. Now I'm working with the files of American deserters. Such operatic exits leave the rest of us with much work to do. Betrayal's a self-service affair.

I turn from the screen and listen to a cat wailing outside my window. It's a dear sound: the desire so pure, the need so local. Who, on bad days, doesn't wish to quit this so-called civilization? Freud showed its price: from priestly abuses to wars, the toll repression exacts in return for power. If you take the long view, history is the nightmare during which it is impossible to stay awake.

Will I be able to help even one of the thousands of my countrymen or their victims?

Returning to Boston in August of 2004 for Uncle Bill's funeral, I sat beside a marine on the Lufthansa flight out of Frankfurt. No more than twenty, he was soft spoken, shy, insecure. This was before the desertions started in earnest. Did my father at the same age, flying from Braunschweig to London, secretly long to confess what he'd seen? I didn't press the young man leaning his forehead against the window. When we landed, I wished him safe passage. Yet I wondered where he was from, about his family, and who he became once he put on his gear.

Uncle Bill stayed Father's friend to the end. We buried Father while the Democratic Convention unfolded at what was once called the Boston Garden. It's been rechristened several times since. How would Europeans feel about renaming their landmarks: the Sony Colosseum; the Mitsubishi Sistine Chapel; Toyota Big Ben?

The day was hot. Sweat mixed with tears yet laughter abounded—our fine Irish flair at the finish. Years had passed since I'd lived among them. I felt surrounded by amiable strangers—a curious culture of hip flasks and Boston College MBAs talking Red Sox. My mother's sister, the nun, hugged me close, her breath brandy sweet.

In the middle of the reception at the Beacon Hill town house Mother so loved, I ducked out for air. Below me, the city seemed deserted. The Swan Boats in the Public Garden sat empty. I was startled by the number of cops milling about. Not milling, no—rather, frozen, stiff as Saint-Gaudens's black soldiers in that sculpture crowning the Common. I wandered toward Faneuil Hall, where the colonists rallied to foment revolution. That building too was circled by helmeted troopers in wraparound sunglasses, leather boots, and black gloves in the August heat. Totally gay. There were hardly any other civilians out on the street.

I fled for the harbor. A hot wind frothed the water, and light blinded the panes of the rose-brick buildings swelling up at land's end. Across the bay, on Deer Island, prisoners fitfully hammered the bars. Seals barked in the Aquarium pool, delighting the children. The whale-watch boat was returning, its passengers from Ohio, Texas, and New Jersey damp and faintly angry with themselves for expecting that the mere sight of whales might free them. A plane flying into Logan seemed to hover while I imagined how this might have looked to the voyagers ripe with hope for new beginnings who sailed in over three hundred years before. What cures had they brought to counter the plagues that had wasted their homes? The plane descended. I walked back up the hill.

I was glad to return to Vienna.

Freud's house, I thought, is no Freudian symbol. It's a page mark in history, a clue to one of several climactic moments in the European drama whose cost is still being paid. And it's rude to remind us of this.

Silvia dear, I envy your obliviousness—if that's what it is—but I can't live it, I think, looking out at the street. Soon the farmers will arrive and the day will begin all over again. How can that be?

– 3 –

Only one question remains:

Did I murder my father?

Often over the years he pushed me to the breaking point with his fits. Booze over time frayed his temper. He mainly took it out on Mother, whose toughness was no match for his bellowing or the cold lapis light of his eyes. At some point he began wearing the hair shirt of the past like it was the only one he owned—or as if he alone owned one. What our neighbors made of the screams echoing from our windows at all hours I can't guess.

After one of his tantrums, I tried to set the uniform in his closet on fire, as though I knew instinctively it was to blame, but Mother came in just as I'd brought my bright red Bic to the fraying black threads of its sleeve. She seemed to know just where I'd be.

As I grew older I learned to stand up to him, though in our show-downs I was the one who blinked first.

Until I discovered Vera. Every man has the same Achilles' heel, the same tendon: Mother. And those who don't aren't human. Once I had hold of his mother, I had him. He broke faster and harder than I'd ever imagined. That had never been my design.

But to return to the question: Did I murder my father?

The answer is, indirectly, in a way, maybe.

I didn't drive north with that in mind, I promise.

Because I knew he'd be out hunting first thing, I left Devon early. I'd been staying with Mother, trying to console her, without success. She regretted everything—everything, that is, but the presence of yours truly. For that, she said, she'd endure all of it over again. It killed me to hear it—and suddenly I grew tired of dying. Why should I die so that he could live and continue dispensing misery wherever he turned?

I've already described the drive up. He was standing on the porch when I got out of the car. He had on his uniform. He looked strange. But he'd looked stranger. More than one wild-eyed moon watched him race down the night to his boat, half-crocked, heading for water having laid waste to Mother and me with his shouting.

His eyes scrunched in surprise. His face was clean shaven, the shirt freshly ironed. Even now, standing tall in his uniform he was an impressive figure.

"James," he whispered in that guttural drunk's voice of his.

I could smell the whiskey six feet away. I drew closer. A pistol bulged under his belt.

Around us, the leaves flickered brightly, light took the tree in its yellow embrace. The late spring air bristled with the promise of endings.

He reached into the pocket of the drab calf-colored coat and dragged out a cigarette.

He flicked the filter with the nail of his index finger.

"You've decided to come hunting after all," he said.

We looked at each other.

His eyes were flat, fathomless.

Leaves crackling, twigs breaking, men's voices.

I whirled around. For a moment I was sure someone else was there.

Then he said:

"Me. You're hunting for me."

His lips arced in a half-smile. He took a long drag on his cigarette. Then he flicked it away and pulled out the gun. Clutching it in his right hand, he ran the fingers of his left hand along the barrel. He released the safety.

He waved the pistol at me.

"Take it."

I came closer. He thrust out his arm.

Obedience is a habit not easily broken.

"Take it. Don't think." His voice regained its old authority, suddenly steady. "Get close. Drop to one knee. Aim at my head . . .

"I'll even eat it."

He brought the gun back to his mouth, lipping the barrel like a crooner.

Removing it, he said:

"Think I've liked it? What I had to do."

His voice trailed off. He pushed the gun at me. My fingers curled around the steel.

At that moment I had no idea what he was saying. It was only after Khoriv and Marian filled in the blanks that I understood.

"Mustn't be sentimental," he smiled. "Don't think. Remember the letter."

Sweat blurred my vision. In a surreal moment, his features seemed to swim loose. My heart pounded. My fingers felt ancient, arthritic, unable to move.

Then he barked:

"Shoot."

In the long silence who knows what rushed through my head? Sheba the seal barking from the porch in the morning, trekking Plum Island's dunes amid hordes of monarchs, fist to bone.

I dropped the gun in disgust and turned, muttering: "You're crazy."

So he picked it up and did it himself.

Mother was right to suspect me. And nothing I learned in Europe relieved my guilt or brought peace, except for my work.

In the end, I don't even condemn Aidan. Ever since taking up with Silvia, I've felt a new generosity toward my fellow man. From my little alcove I see her sleeping in the next room. She tosses her arm over a pillow. She whimpers.

Youth is a desert. We enter singing, but we crawl out hoarse.

What had all this been for? I didn't know my father any better now than when I set out to find him. I knew more of what happened to him, of what he did, of what some people thought of him. But the man remained elusive. All my research brought me no closer than had I kept dreaming.

That year in Europe I satisfied many dreams of dubious pedigree: I saw the ceilings of the Vatican, visited Barcelona, the Louvre, and the Père-Lachaise cemetery, where I found the graves of Wilde, Balzac, and Jim Morrison. I stayed up late drinking in Madrid and watched a live sex show in Amsterdam. In Oslo I visited the Munch museum. In place after place I observed the fierce division between country and city life, the rhythms decreed by trees and the pace of life set by the microchip, and wondered what this meant for the world.

If youth is a desert, then what's middle age? An afterlife of a kind. What to look forward to next?

What will I tell my child?

It's what Silvia and I fought over the other evening.

For the second month she's missed her period.

Doesn't mean anything, she assured me. Happens sometimes. But we played it out a bit. *What if?* That old game.

To my surprise, she wants to keep it.

What she may not want is me.

Hearing that, I shouted—just like my father.

Her response was to cut me all day. She knew I regretted it. She knows I love her. If I hide behind irony, can she blame me? She's read the book of betrayals I'm trying to close.

Tonight things were different. Tonight I curled up at her side and wept. Startled, she stroked my head, kissed my eyes.

What? She asked. What's wrong?

Things don't change. Things continue. Selena told me her mother's songs defined her long before she ever met me. What music made you?

When I said this, she looked down. She put her hand on my forehead and ran it down my cheek. There's the mother's song, she said. But there's also the song of the wife. Or the lover.

You're saying that to me? I asked.

I am.

Then I do, I said.

We lay there together until she fell asleep. Slowly pulling my arm out from under her head, I rose, unsure of what, if anything, we'd agreed to, and went to my desk.

Now I gaze out at the Naschmarkt. The first vendors have started arriving. Nearing dawn. Why stop with *Der Standard*? I have friends at the BBC, AP, other places. The world is neither watching nor waiting, but so what?

There's a noise from the bedroom. Footsteps. I focus on the screen. The toilet flushing. Silence again.

I enter my e-mail, open my address book, and select all—nearly a thousand names. A man who maintains his contacts. I attach the file, which I've titled *Gone Fishing*. For Mustafa, Selena, Silvia, Mother, Vera, her nurse.

Clicking *send,* I sigh and sit back, face to the window.

Too late for bed. Only the dead could sleep in the glare of this light.

22 July 2007

Acknowledgments

All books have roots in the places where they were written, among the people and the other books that helped carry them forward. My gratitude for the wise counsel of Tom Bahr, Sven Birkerts, Martha Cooley, Maureen McLane, Edward Melnyczuk, Tom Sleigh, Jason Shinder, and Lloyd Schwartz. A bow too to Martina Schmidt for her help with the Viennese passages. My thanks to Jen Beagin and Erica Mena for assistance in preparing the manuscript.

Thanks to the community of the Kurukulla Center, whose support is invisible yet everywhere.

As always, thanks to the editors of the journals who published chapters and excerpts: Don Lee and Rosanna Warren from *Ploughshares;* Christine Thompson from the *Harvard Review;* and Willard Spiegelman of the *Southwest Review.*

Among the books I consulted several proved invaluable, in particular: Peter Ackroyd's *London: The Biography;* Tom Segev's *One Palestine, Complete: Jews and Arabs under the British Mandate;* Wilfred Scawen Blunt's *Secret History of the English Occupation of Egypt: Being a Personal Narrative of Events;* Carl E. Schorske's *Fin-de-Siècle Vienna: Politics and Culture;* Frederic Morton's *A Nervous Splendor: Vienna 1888–1889;* and *At the Crossroads* by Yuri Luckyj.

Readers are reminded that history in fiction follows the needs of its host.

My agent Lane Zachary has my abiding gratitude for believing in the book when it was just coming to light. Thanks too to my once and future editor Fiona McCrae, whose queries and insights helped the book to grow. The team at Graywolf has been a good dream. Hats off to Katie Dublinski, Anne Czarniecki, and Rolph Blythe for their patience and devotion to the details.

Finally, and again, Alex Johnson gave me more than I had any right to hope for.

ASKOLD MELNYCZUK's novel *Ambassador of the Dead* was one of the *Los Angeles Times* Best Books of 2002; his first novel, *What Is Told,* was a *New York Times* Notable Book. He has also published a novella, *Blind Angel,* about the life of Rimbaud. He has received a Lila Wallace Writer's Award and the McGinnis Prize in fiction. His work has appeared in the *New York Times,* the *Gettysburg Review,* the *Los Angeles Times, Ploughshares,* the *Antioch Review,* and the *Nation.* He has taught at Harvard University and currently teaches at the University of Massachusetts, Boston, and in the Bennington Graduate Writing Seminars.

The text of *The House of Widows* has been set in Adobe Garamond Pro, drawn by Robert Slimbach and based on type cut by Claude Garamond in the sixteenth century. Book design by Wendy Holdman. Composition by BookMobile Design and Publishing Services, Minneapolis, Minnesota. Manufactured by Versa Press on acid-free paper.